BUILDING A FUTURE

AN AMISH LEGACY NOVEL

BUILDING A FUTURE

AMY CLIPSTON

THORNDIKE PRESS
A part of Gale, a Cengage Company

LIBRARY OF CONGRESS CIP DATA ON FILE.
CATALOGUING IN PUBLICATION FOR THIS BOOK
IS AVAILABLE FROM THE LIBRARY OF CONGRESS.

ISBN-13: 979-8-8857-8100-8 (hardcover alk. paper)

Published in 2022 by arrangement with The Zondervan Corporation LLC, a subsidiary of HarperCollins Christian Publishing, Inc.

Printed in Mexico
Print Number : 1   Print Year : 2023

With love and hugs for Maggie,
the bravest person I know.
Your friendship is a blessing to me.

GLOSSARY

ach: oh
aenti: aunt
appeditlich: delicious
Ausbund: Amish hymnal
bedauerlich: sad
boppli: baby
bopplin: babies
brot: bread
bruder: brother
daadi: granddad
daadihaus: small house provided for retired parents
daed: father
danki: thank you
dat: dad
Dietsch: Pennsylvania Dutch, the Amish language (a German dialect)
dochder: daughter
dochdern: daughters
dummkopp: moron
Englisher: a non-Amish person

fraa: wife
Frehlicher Grischtdaag!: Merry Christmas!
freind: friend
freinden: friends
froh: happy
gegisch: silly
gern gschehne: you're welcome
Gude mariye: Good morning
gut: good
Gut nacht: Good night
haus: house
Ich liebe dich: I love you
kaffi: coffee
kapp: prayer covering or cap
kichli: cookie
kichlin: cookies
kinner: children
krank: sick
kuche: cake
liewe: love, a term of endearment
maed: young women, girls
maedel: young woman
mamm: mom
mammi: grandma
mei: my
naerfich: nervous
narrisch: crazy
Ordnung: the oral tradition of practices required and forbidden in the Amish faith
schee: pretty

8

schmaert: smart
schtupp: family room
schweschder: sister
schweschdere: sisters
sohn: son
Was iss letz?: What's wrong?
Wie geht's: How do you do? or Good day!
wunderbaar: wonderful
ya: yes

THE AMISH LEGACY SERIES FAMILY TREES

Crystal m. Duane Bontrager
|
Tyler (mother—Connie—deceased)
Korey (mother—Connie—deceased)
Jayden (mother—Connie—deceased)

Elaine m. Simon Lantz
|
Lainey m. Noah
Michelle
Jorie

Lainey m. Noah Dienner
|
Jana Beth

NOTE TO THE READER

While this novel is set against the real backdrop of Lancaster County, Pennsylvania, the characters are fictional. There is no intended resemblance between the characters in this book and any real members of the Amish and Mennonite communities. As with any work of fiction, I've taken license in some areas of research as a means of creating the necessary circumstances for my characters. My research was thorough; however, it would be impossible to be completely accurate in details and description since each and every community differs. Therefore, any inaccuracies in the Amish and Mennonite lifestyles portrayed in this book are completely due to fictional license.

CHAPTER 1

Michelle Lantz placed a fresh pitcher of lemonade on the folding table near the three makeshift volleyball courts where members of her youth group played. Her friends laughed and hooted while the volleyballs floated up through the air over the nets. Other members of the youth group sat on the grass nearby and clapped, while the warm, early-September afternoon sun smiled down from the clear cerulean sky.

Today was Michelle's turn to host the youth gathering, and since it was an off-Sunday without a church service, her friends had arrived in the early afternoon to play volleyball, eat supper, and sing hymns.

"Here are more *kichlin.*" Her younger sister, Jorie, set down a platter of chocolate chip cookies they had baked yesterday.

Michelle smiled down at the cookies. She had insisted that they bake chocolate chip since they were her boyfriend's favorite. She scanned the volleyball teams until her eyes found Korey Bontrager. He pushed his hand through his dark-brown hair and laughed at something his best friend, Dwight Smoker, said before serving the ball to the opposing team.

Tyler, his older brother, bumped, and Korey jumped up and effortlessly sent the ball back over the net. She grinned as she admired his tall, muscular physique and his handsome face. His milk-chocolate eyes were hidden by the mirrored sunglasses he always wore on sunny days.

Korey had been her boyfriend now for thirteen months, and since they were both approaching twenty-five, she had a feeling he might propose to her soon. Her heart lifted as she imagined the day he asked her father's permission to marry her.

She could almost see their wedding in her mind's eye. They would stand at the front of her father's largest dairy barn. Michelle would have her younger sister at her side, both of them clad in the rose-colored dresses she'd made, and Korey and his older brother, Tyler, would stand across from them as their bishop —

"Michelle? You okay?"

"Huh?" Michelle spun to face her younger sister, who studied her with the bright blue eyes she had inherited from their mother. "Sorry. I was lost in thought."

Jorie folded her arms over her black apron and scanned the table, which included two pitchers of lemonade, two bowls of chips, a bowl of pretzels, and a tray of cookies, along with cups, napkins, and plates. "I think we're all set here."

"*Ya*, I do too. I'll make some iced tea."

"Michelle! Come join the game!"

She faced the volleyball court where her best friend, Charity Swarey, waved her over.

Korey stood beside her, also waving. "Come on, Michelle! You need to play."

"Go on." Jorie gave her a gentle nudge. "I'll make the iced tea."

Michelle touched her sister's arm. *"Danki."* Then she trotted over toward the volleyball court.

"Yay!" Charity jumped up and down as Michelle approached them.

Korey pointed toward the opposing team. "They need you."

Michelle moved around the net and nodded at Tyler as she joined him on the back row.

He flashed a wide grin. "Welcome to the best team."

"We'll see about that, Ty," Korey called from across the net as he prepared to serve

15

the ball.

Michelle pushed the ribbons from her prayer covering behind her shoulders as she stood to Tyler's left. "I'm ready." And then she met Tyler's smile. "Let's show Korey and Charity how it's done."

"I like your spirit." Tyler laughed.

Korey served the ball, and Michelle held up her hands, ready to bump it back. As the ball curved to her right, she moved in the direction it was headed.

Just as she prepared to bump it back, she slammed into Tyler's side as he tripped over her feet. They stumbled toward each other, bumping their heads together before falling onto the grass in a heap.

Michelle groaned and rubbed a throbbing spot on her forehead as she looked over at Tyler, who also groaned.

Tyler gave her a sheepish expression. "Are you okay?"

Michelle opened her mouth to respond, and a laugh burst from her lips instead.

Tyler hesitated and then joined in. Soon they were hooting and gasping for air.

Their friends gathered around them with concerned looks.

"Michelle!" Korey jogged over. "Are you hurt?"

She shook her head as she tried to catch

16

her breath. "I'm fine."

Korey frowned at his older brother. "Did you really have to knock my girlfriend to the ground?"

Tyler sniffed and wiped his eyes. "It wasn't intentional, Kore."

"Michelle!" Charity exclaimed, appearing at her side. "Are you injured? Do you need a doctor? Should I call 911?"

"I'm really okay. Just a little sore."

Tyler climbed to his feet. His expression became embarrassed once again as he reached out his hand to her and then cleared his throat. "Let me help you."

"I've got her." Korey blocked him and held out his hands. "Are you okay?" he asked her again.

Michelle latched on to his hand and allowed Korey to lift her to her feet. "Yeah." She brushed her hands down her black apron and blue dress, checking for grass stains. Then she looked over at Tyler, who was dusting off his dark trousers and blue shirt. "I'm so sorry."

Tyler met her gaze and looked apologetic. "It's my fault. Really."

"Maybe you should sit this game out." Charity touched Michelle's arm.

Michelle blinked at her. "Are you kidding?" She smiled over at Tyler. "We're going to win."

"As long as we don't wind up injuring each other," he said.

Michelle's smile brightened as she peered over at Tyler. "Challenge accepted."

"I think you should sit down before my clumsy brother really hurts you," Korey snipped.

Michelle squared her shoulders. "I'm not made of glass. I can take care of myself." She pointed to the other side of the net. "Why don't you go serve the ball?"

While the opposing team took their spots, Michelle glanced over at Tyler. "I'll try not to run into you."

"I'll be more careful too."

Then Michelle turned her attention to the ball as Korey served it again.

Later that evening, Michelle gathered up a tray full of the desserts the other young women had deposited in her kitchen before the youth gathering started, and moved toward the back door.

"Wait," Jorie called after her. "I'll get the door for you." She hustled through the mudroom and pushed open the back door.

"Danki." Michelle stepped out onto the porch just as Charity climbed the steps.

Her best friend held out her arms. "Let

18

me get that for you."

"Great. I'll go get more." Michelle reentered the kitchen, where *Mamm* and Jorie were loading up more trays with desserts. "*Mamm,* you don't need to help. Jorie and I can handle this. You can go rest with *Dat* in the *schtupp.*"

Mamm craned her neck over her shoulder. "I like helping."

Michelle was so grateful for her mother. With her near-constant bright smile, *Mamm* resembled a ray of sunshine, and she also was Michelle's and her two sisters' confidante, offering her sage advice whenever they needed her to listen to their problems.

Mamm held out a tray containing a pound cake, oatmeal raisin cookies, and brownies. "You can take this out, Michelle."

"I've got it." Jorie balanced a tray with more cakes and cookies and reached for the one *Mamm* held.

Mamm shook her head. "Jorie Lynn, you're carrying enough."

"We're fine." Michelle took the tray from her mother and followed Jorie out the back door to the table, where Charity stood arranging the variety of desserts on serving plates. "We definitely have enough food."

Michelle and Jorie added their desserts to the table, and then Michelle gathered up

19

the trays.

Charity sucked in a breath as she stared behind Michelle's shoulder. "Here comes Tyler." She rubbed her hands down her black apron and green dress that complemented her gorgeous green eyes. Then she touched her prayer *kapp,* which covered her shiny blond hair.

Michelle and Jorie shared a look. When had her best friend developed a crush on Korey's older brother?

Charity took a step toward him as he approached the table. "Would you like some *kichlin* or *kuche*?"

"Actually, I was wondering if I could use the restroom." He jammed his thumb toward the porch as he divided a look between Charity and Michelle.

Michelle folded her arms over her apron and lifted her chin. "No, you can't."

"Why?" Charity spun toward Michelle, her blond eyebrows forming a *V.*

Tyler cleared his throat as his cheeks flushed bright red. "Um . . ."

"I'm kidding." Michelle beckoned him to follow her as she started toward the porch. "Come on." As she climbed the stairs, she looked over her shoulder to where Tyler and Charity were close behind her. "How long have I known you?"

20

"Our moms were *freinden,* so my whole life?" He shook his head. "No, your whole life since I'm a year older than you and Korey."

"And how long have you been coming here for church and youth group?"

He gave a palms-up. "Forever?"

"So why are you asking permission to use the bathroom?"

"Because I have manners?" he countered.

She laughed and opened the storm door, which squeaked in protest. "Go on." She motioned for him to enter. "Shoo."

"Thanks." Tyler's grin was embarrassed as he rushed into the house.

Charity rested her hand on Michelle's shoulder. "He's *so* handsome," she gushed, her voice low.

"When did you suddenly start liking Tyler?" Michelle questioned as they walked into the kitchen, which was now empty.

"I don't know. Last week I was watching him during church, and I suddenly realized how gorgeous he is with those bright hazel eyes, that dark hair, and that smile." Charity pressed her hand to her chest and gave a dramatic sigh. "If only he'd notice me . . ."

"Of course he notices you. You're so *schee* and sweet."

"Just think about it, Michelle. You're dat-

21

ing Korey, and if I dated Tyler, then we could possibly get married and start families at the same time. Our *kinner* would grow up together. Wouldn't that be great?"

"*Ya,* it would." Michelle snapped her fingers. "I could help you with Tyler."

"Shhh," Charity warned. She glanced toward the doorway that led to the family room and bathroom, and then she turned back to Michelle. "What do you mean?" Her green eyes sparkled in the sunlight pouring in through the kitchen windows.

"I could put in a *gut* word for you with him."

Charity rubbed her hands together. "Really?"

"*Ya.* The next time I have an opportunity to talk to him, I'll suggest that he ask you out."

Charity opened her mouth to speak and then stopped when Tyler's muffled voice sounded from the family room. Michelle's parents both responded before Tyler appeared in the kitchen.

He stopped in the doorway, and his dark eyebrows lifted as he held up his hands. "Did I do something wrong?"

Charity's smile was nervous. "No, you just startled us."

"Have you knocked any more *maed*

down?" Michelle leaned back against the counter and grinned at him.

Tyler rubbed his clean-shaven jaw as he walked over to her. "I am so sorry about that."

"I'm just teasing you again." Michelle chuckled.

He pointed to her black shoes. "I stepped on your feet pretty hard. Are you sure you're okay?"

"I promise you I am."

Tyler seemed unconvinced. "Well, if Kore comes home and threatens to beat me up for injuring you, then I'll know you're lying."

"I'm not lying." Michelle waved him off.

Charity looked stunned. "Do you and Korey really fistfight?"

"No." Tyler laughed. "But we do argue pretty often. See you later." He headed out the back door.

Charity sighed. "Do you think you could convince him to ask me out?"

"I can try."

"You're the best *freind* ever."

Michelle touched Charity's shoulder. "You're not so bad yourself."

CHAPTER 2

"You ready to go, Ty?" Jayden, Tyler's youngest brother, asked later that evening.

Tyler nodded as they switched on the little flashlights they each kept in their pockets and followed their friends out of the barn after singing hymns. "*Ya,* we have to get up early for that job over in Lititz."

He looked up at the dark sky and breathed in the scent of wet grass mixed with animals while a chorus of frogs croaked nearby. He nodded at friends who said good night on their way to their buggies.

When Tyler felt a hand on his shoulder, he pivoted to where Jonah Chupp, his best friend since first grade, grinned at him. "Are you heading home?"

"Yup." Jonah shook his hand. "Have a *gut* week."

"You too. See you at church."

Jayden waved at him. "Bye, Jonah."

"I'll beat you two at volleyball next Sunday," Jonah quipped.

Tyler laughed. "We'll see about that."

"Well, at least I won't trample Korey's girlfriend." Jonah winked at them before walking backward. Then he laughed as he turned and continued on toward the line of buggies.

Tyler groaned.

Jayden smirked at him. "You do realize you're never going to live that down, right?"

"It's becoming apparent." Tyler shook his head, and heat crawled up his neck as he recalled the disaster. If only he'd been paying better attention, he wouldn't have stepped on Michelle's feet, banged his head against hers, and knocked her down. He couldn't recall an instance when he'd been more embarrassed. At least Michelle had a sense of humor about it. Clearing his throat, he tried to shake off his humiliation and remorse.

Jayden pointed toward the house, where their middle brother climbed the back steps, carrying a folding table. "I guess Kore is going to stay and visit with Michelle."

"I suppose we should check with him before we head out."

Tyler and Jayden weaved through the crowd until they reached the back porch. They climbed the steps and entered the kitchen, where Charity washed serving trays and Michelle dried them. Jorie dried and then dropped clean utensils into a drawer.

Charity's eyes met Tyler's, and she beamed, her pretty green eyes sparkling in the light of the lantern hanging above her. "Tyler. Hi."

He nodded at her and then focused on Michelle. "We were wondering if Kore was planning to stay and visit with you."

"I think so." Michelle pointed to the doorway behind her. "He was just storing the folding tables in the utility room for me."

"Do you need more help?"

Michelle shook her head. "No, but thanks."

"We have it under control." Jorie looked at them over her shoulder as she set empty plastic pitchers in a nearby cabinet.

Charity's smile became hopeful as she studied Tyler. "But you're welcome to visit if you want."

"We really need to get home. We have an early day tomorrow." Tyler shifted his weight on his feet.

Korey emerged from the utility room. His brow puckered as he walked toward his brothers. "What's going on?"

"We were wondering if you were going to

walk home with us or if you were staying to visit for a while," Tyler said.

Michelle dried two serving platters and handed them to Jorie. "I told them that I thought you were going to visit, but I wasn't sure."

"I was planning to stay." Korey leaned on the counter beside Michelle.

Jayden took a step toward the doorway that led to the mudroom. "We'll tell *Dat.*" Then he waved to the women. *"Gut nacht."*

"Are you sure I didn't sprain your ankle or anything?" Tyler asked Michelle.

She dropped the dish towel on the counter and jammed her hands on her hips. "Tyler Bontrager, if you ask me if I'm okay one more time, I'm going to scream."

"Please don't make her scream," Jorie whined. "She's super loud and gives me a headache."

Tyler laughed as Michelle grinned at him. "Okay. I won't ask again. *Gut nacht."*

He followed his youngest brother out through the back door and down the porch steps, where they flipped on their flashlights and waved as friends passed by in their buggies, guiding their horses home. Tyler and Jayden descended the rock driveway and continued down the road toward their nearby house.

Cicadas sang their nightly chorus, lightning bugs flickered past, and the stars shimmered in the sky above them. Their flashlights bounced on the pavement in front of them while they traipsed down the road toward the house where Tyler and his brothers had been born and raised.

Tyler lost himself in thoughts of the upcoming week and the jobs their roofing company had scheduled. He had poured himself into the business during the past two years, undertaking a business plan not only to grow their customer base and profits but also to prove to his father that he would be prepared to inherit the company when his father was ready to retire.

"I think Charity likes you." Jayden's declaration broke through Tyler's thoughts.

Tyler's focus snapped to his brother. "What makes you say that?"

"Please." Jayden snorted. "Tell me you didn't see how her face lit up when you walked into the kitchen. Surely you noticed she wanted you to stay and visit with her."

"I did."

"Why didn't you?"

"Why didn't I what?"

Jayden rolled his hazel eyes. "Why didn't you stay and visit with her? She's *schee* and she likes you."

"I don't have time to date."

"That's what you always say, but you're twenty-five now. Don't you want to have a family?"

Tyler stopped walking and shot him a hard look. "You sound like *Dat.*"

"He isn't wrong." Jayden shrugged.

Shaking his head, Tyler continued toward home. "You're not dating, so why are you hassling me?"

"I'm not hassling you. I'm just wondering why you aren't interested in Charity when she's so obviously interested in you. Besides, I'm only twenty, and I haven't seen any *maed* who pay any attention to me, which is fine."

"I'm too focused on keeping the business running. I'm going to ask *Dat* if I can run a second crew."

"Really?"

Tyler nodded as their house came into view. When he spotted a lantern glowing in the kitchen, he quickened his stride. Since his father was still awake, he might bring up the subject now. "*Ya.* We could take on more work. I could run a crew, and *Dat* could run the other."

"That's a great idea, Ty."

"And that's more important to me than dating right now."

Tyler and Jayden hustled up the rock driveway that led to their two-story brick home with a small front porch. A red barn where they housed their horses and buggies sat behind it, along with the long cinder-block supply building for their tools and supplies for their roofing business.

They entered the mudroom and hung their straw hats on pegs before removing their shoes and moving to the kitchen, where *Dat* sat at the table, thumbing through a catalog.

"Hey, *Dat.*" Jayden waved as he continued toward the stairs that led to their bedrooms. "I get the shower first. *Gut nacht!*"

Dat grinned after him, the skin crinkling around his brown eyes. "Nice talking with you, Jayden." He rubbed his salt-and-pepper beard as he looked up at Tyler. "Did you have a *gut* day?"

"Ya." Tyler sat down across from him. "Korey is staying to visit with Michelle for a while."

"I assumed he would."

"Did Crystal go to bed?" he asked about his stepmother. Tyler's mother had passed away nearly three years ago after a battle with cancer, and his father had remarried a year ago. While Tyler liked his sweet stepmother, he still missed his mother every day.

Dat closed the catalog. "*Ya.* She was tired."

"Is there a reason why you're still up?"

"No. I believe that second cup of *kaffi* after supper was a bad idea. Too much caffeine keeps me awake for hours. I figured I'd wait out here to see how you three enjoyed your day."

Tyler nodded and studied the tabletop as his discussion with Jayden about the business echoed through his mind.

"Did you talk to any *maed* today?"

Tyler folded his hands and swallowed back his frustration. "No, *Dat.*"

"Not one all day long?" *Dat* raised a dark eyebrow.

"How about we talk about something besides my lack of a love life, *Dat*?" Tyler took a deep breath. "I've been thinking. We could double our profits and expand our customer base if we ran two crews instead of one." When his father frowned and opened his mouth, Tyler held up a hand. "Please let me finish."

Dat nodded. "All right."

"You trust me to write estimates by myself, so why won't you trust me to run my own crew?"

"It's not that I don't trust you. I just don't know if the fall is the time to do this. It

31

would be *schmaert* if we waited until spring when business picks up after the winter."

"But it could still be warm here into October."

Dat paused and smiled. "Tyler, I admire how hard you've been working, and I'm proud of how you've started taking on more responsibility. And to be honest, I've already thought about giving you your own crew to run. I just think that we should wait until the spring to expand. Trust me on this, all right?"

"Of course." Tyler stood and covered his mouth as he yawned. *"Gut nacht, Dat."*

"See you in the morning."

As Tyler headed toward the stairs, he considered his father's reasoning for waiting until spring to add a crew. Still, deep in his gut he felt the urge to convince his father to allow him to expand the business now. Somehow he'd find a way to persuade him.

Michelle pushed the porch swing into motion and rested her cheek on Korey's shoulder while they sat on the porch later that evening. She gazed out over her father's vast pasture shrouded in darkness and took in the bright stars above them. The frogs and cicadas serenaded them as fireflies provided their own personal fireworks display. "It's the perfect night."

"It is." Korey nodded.

The warm yellow glow from the lantern at their feet illuminated his handsome face. Reaching up, she ran her finger over the stubble on his chin and silently admired his angular jaw.

Korey Bontrager was one of the handsomest men in their youth group, and she'd been so grateful when he'd asked her to be his girlfriend last year. Since their mothers had been best friends, she'd always felt a connection to the Bontrager sons — especially Korey. After all, she and Korey were the same age, and they were both middle children. While he had older and younger brothers, Michelle had older and younger sisters.

She sat up straight and shifted her body toward his on the swing. "Did you have fun today?"

"Ya." He shrugged. "Didn't you?"

She laughed as she recalled her run-in with his older brother. "Tyler is so funny. He felt so bad that we collided, but it was as much my fault as his. I had to threaten him to get him to stop apologizing."

Korey gave a derisive snort.

"Did you know Charity has a crush on him?"

"No." He leaned back, extending his arm across the back of the swing behind her shoulders.

"*Ya.* She was flirting with him. I told her that I'd put in a *gut* word for her with him the next time I'm at your *haus.*"

"You'd be wasting your time. Ty is more focused on working than dating."

Michelle felt her brow pinch. "Why?"

"That's how he's been ever since . . ." His voice trailed off.

Michelle's heart ached for Korey and his family. They'd lost their *mamm* nearly three years ago. She gave Korey's hand a gentle squeeze, hoping it would give him the courage to continue. "I'm sorry," she whispered.

"Anyway," he began, moving his hand out of her grip, "*mei dat* has been on him to think about more than just growing the business, but Ty doesn't want to discuss dating or having a family. *Dat* insists it's how Ty handles his grief, but I think he's just determined to make sure he inherits the business and I don't."

"Korey, you can't possibly believe your *bruder* would take the business away from you." She clucked her tongue.

"You know he and I butt heads often. We're always in competition."

"But he's your *bruder.*"

34

Korey shook his head as his milk-chocolate-colored eyes focused out toward the far pasture.

Silence fell between them, and she lost herself in thoughts of planning a future with Korey. She tried to imagine a little house that he might build for her on his father's land or her father's farm. Perhaps they'd have a few bedrooms, which if God saw fit, they might fill with children. If only he'd ask her to marry him . . .

He shifted on the swing, and she covered his hand with hers.

"I can't believe we'll have been together for thirteen months in a couple of weeks," she began. "The year just flew by, didn't it?"

He nodded, keeping his attention directed toward the pasture.

"Are you okay, Korey?"

"*Ya.*" He turned toward her. "I'd better get going. Our driver is going to pick us up early tomorrow for a job over in Lititz."

He trailed his fingers across her cheek, and she held her breath. Maybe tonight would be the night that he kissed her lips. It seemed as if it had been months since their lips had touched.

Korey leaned down and brushed his lips over her cheek. "Have a *gut* week. I'll call you." He stood and jogged down the porch steps, pulling his small flashlight from his pocket and switching it on.

"Gut nacht," Michelle called after him. She stood on the porch until the beam of his flashlight disappeared into the dark, and then she carried the lantern into the house.

After locking the back door, she ascended the stairs to the second floor, where her bedroom, Jorie's bedroom, and the sewing room, which had once been her older sister, Lainey's, bedroom, were located.

A warm yellow light glowed under Jorie's door, indicating that her younger sister had at least attempted to stay awake to talk to Michelle, which she often did after youth gatherings. Jorie enjoyed discussing the latest gossip about the friends they shared, despite their three-year age difference. At times, however, she fell asleep with her lantern glowing, and Michelle would sneak into her room and flip off the light for her.

After padding into her bedroom, Michelle changed into her plain pink nightgown and brushed her waist-length, light-brown hair. Piles of notepads full of her pencil drawings were strewn about on her dresser and desk, evidence of her favorite hobby — drawing landscapes and nature scenes. Michelle had started drawing the moment her mother had put a pencil in her hand, and it seemed as if she'd never stopped. It was her favorite way to relax after a day of chores around her father's dairy farm.

A soft knock sounded on her door, followed by her younger sister whispering, "Michelle? Are you awake?"

Michelle smiled. "Come in."

The door opened, and Jorie rushed in clad in a blue nightgown. Her thick light-brown hair cascaded down her back in waves as she sank down on the end of Michelle's double bed. "How was your visit with Korey?"

"Gut." Michelle sat down on the chair across from her.

Jorie's pretty smile was wide. "Maybe he'll propose soon."

"I hope so." Excitement bubbled up in Michelle's chest. Oh, she couldn't wait to be married and start a family! It was her heart's greatest desire to be a wife and a mother.

"I think he will." Her sister's smile dimmed. "I'll miss you when you move out, but I'll visit you all the time."

Michelle reached over and touched her sister's hand. "I'd love that. In fact, we need to go see Lainey soon. It's been too long."

"I'm sure Jana Beth has gotten even bigger." Jorie turned and gasped before popping up and scrambling toward Michelle's desk, where she picked up a painting of a farm scene. "Michelle! When did you start painting landscapes?"

Michelle sidled up to her younger sister. "I told you that I picked up some paints when we were at the store last week. Why?"

"It's spectacular." Jorie ran her fingers over the painted landscape featuring the patchwork of farmland dotted with cows, houses, barns, and split-rail fencing. She swiveled toward Michelle. "The colors really bring the scene to life. When did you paint this?"

Michelle shrugged. "Friday night."

"You painted this in one night?"

"Why are you making such a big deal about this, Jorie? You know I like to draw for fun."

"But the paintings really highlight your talent more than the pencil drawings. You should ask *Dat* if you can sell your art. The tourist shops always feature things made by the Amish. They would love this."

"I doubt it. My paintings aren't any different than the ones you see in the gift shops in Bird-in-Hand."

"But what if you painted the scenes and framed them? Tourists would buy your artwork and hang it in their homes."

Michelle folded her arms over her chest and considered that. "Maybe." Then she took the painting from her sister and placed it on the desk. "I'll think about it."

"Could I have that?"

"What are you going to do with it?"

"Hang it in my room." Jorie lifted her chin. "It would look so *schee* above my bed."

Michelle laughed as she gave her sister a gentle shove. "You're a mess, Jorie."

"I'm serious. I'm proud of your talent."

"*Danki. Ya,* you can have it." Michelle's heart swelled with love for her sister. "You're the best."

"No, you are. *Gut nacht.*" Jorie picked up the painting and hurried out of her room.

Michelle smiled as she climbed into bed.

CHAPTER 3

The following morning, Michelle clipped a pair of *Dat*'s trousers to the clothesline that stretched from the back porch to an oak tree by her father's pasture. The midmorning sky was bright blue and brushed with white, fluffy clouds. Birds sang in nearby trees while the colorful flowers in her mother's garden danced in the warm breeze. Two squirrels raced by, chattering on their way toward a large oak tree. The air smelled of moist earth mixed with animals.

Michelle turned to her mother and took another pair of trousers from her. "You can go inside if you want to do something else."

"I don't mind helping you." *Mamm* smiled as she lifted two more pairs of *Dat*'s trousers from the large basket. "It seems like everyone had a lot of fun yesterday."

Michelle pulled two clothespins from the pocket of her apron and began hanging a pair on the line. "*Ya,* we all had a great time,

40

and Korey stayed to visit for a little while last night."

She moved the line out toward the tree as thoughts of her boyfriend tumbled through her mind. She'd kept replaying their conversation from last night while she'd washed her family's clothes. Korey had seemed distracted, and her nerve endings jangled as she wondered if he had been considering asking her father's permission for her hand in marriage. "I was thinking of doing something special for Korey. Maybe I could bring a meal over to his *haus* for him sometime?"

"That's a lovely idea. I'm sure he'd appreciate that very much."

Michelle smiled as she hung the second pair of trousers on the line. "How long did you and *Dat* date before he proposed?"

"Well, you know that your *dat* and I had grown up together and been *freinden* in school and youth group."

"Like Korey and me." Michelle pinned one of *Dat*'s shirts on the line and then pushed it out.

"That's right. One day at youth group he asked if he could give me a ride home, and soon after, he asked *mei dat*'s permission to date me. We dated almost a year before he proposed. Then we were married that fall."

Excitement whipped over Michelle. "Do

41

you think Korey might ask me soon?"

"He might." *Mamm* handed her two more shirts. "You just have to be patient. Some men are more *naerfich* than others, but it will happen in God's time."

"Right." While they finished hanging out the laundry, Michelle made small talk with her mother about the chores they planned to complete during the rest of the day.

Mamm picked up the empty laundry basket. "Why don't you go check the messages, and I'll start sweeping the downstairs."

"Okay." Michelle loped down the porch steps. Her black shoes crunched along the rock path as she headed toward the stable, where the phone sat on a small desk. She dialed the voice mail and began writing down messages for her parents and Jorie, hoping to hear Korey's voice as he left a message for her, but he hadn't.

She shook her head and silently scolded herself as she wrote down the last message, which was from one of her mother's friends, inviting her to join them for a quilting bee. Since Michelle had seen Korey last night, it would be preposterous for him to have called her already today. She sent up a quick prayer for Korey, his father, and his brothers, asking God to bless them with a good,

42

productive day.

Michelle pocketed the messages and then turned toward the door. When she spotted a tall stack of old milk cans, she picked up one of them and took off toward the house as an idea engulfed her mind.

Tyler sat back on his heels, lifted his straw hat, and swiped his forearm over his sweaty forehead later that afternoon. He scanned the large roof of the motel in Lititz where they had been working all day. His brothers were crouched at the far end of the roof, hammering shingles, while *Dat* continued to work across from him.

His mind replayed his conversation with his father from the night before, and disappointment clung to him. He'd stayed awake most of the night puzzling over how to convince his father that he was ready to run his own crew. If only he could find the right words.

Tyler pursed his lips. *"Dat."*

"Ya?" *Dat* sat on his heels and blew out a deep breath. "It's hot up here today."

Tyler fidgeted with his hammer and cleared his throat. "It is. Listen, I wanted to talk to you about my idea. I know you think it's too late in the season, but what if we just tried it out? Maybe we could move up

43

some of our jobs that are scheduled for October, and Kore and I could run a small crew while you and Jay continue with the other jobs. We could see if any of our *freinden* want to try working as roofers and get them to help us. We can give it the month of October, and if it doesn't work out, then we'll go back to just running one crew in the winter."

"Tyler . . ." *Dat* shook his head.

He held up his hands. "Just listen, okay? You remember that business plan I put together last year, right?"

"Of course I do. It was a great plan."

"*Danki.* That's why I need you to trust me on this."

"I do trust you, Tyler. I've already told you that's not an issue. I just don't want to overextend us financially."

"But it won't overextend us. I told you that I've planned for this, and I think now is the time to do it."

Dat breathed in through his nose. "I'll consider it."

"*Danki.*" The tense muscles in Tyler's shoulders relaxed slightly.

"What are you two discussing so intently?"

Tyler peered up to where Korey looked down at him from behind his mirrored sunglasses, and Jayden stood behind him.

"Work."

"Because that's all you talk about," Korey muttered.

Tyler glared at him but decided to let the comment go instead of snapping back at his middle brother as he normally would. He was determined to prove to *Dat* that he was professional enough to run his own roofing crew.

"*Dat,* I forgot to tell you that I need to leave early today. I have to call Drew to come and get me around four," Korey said, referring to their driver, Drew Cooper.

Tyler stood as annoyance nipped at him. "Why do you have to leave early at the last minute?"

"Why is it any of your concern?" Korey demanded.

Tyler took a step toward him, his anger flaring. "Because we're not supposed to leave early unless it's an emergency."

"Whoa, whoa, whoa." *Dat* appeared between them, placing a hand on each of their chests. "What have I told you about being professional at a jobsite?"

Korey pointed at Tyler. "He started it."

"Good grief," Jayden mumbled, rolling his eyes. "Why can't you two just get along for once?" He lifted his hat and pushed his hand through his thick, sandy-brown hair as he traipsed back toward the far side of the roof.

"What's the emergency? Are you going to see Michelle?" Tyler asked him.

Korey shook his head. "No, I'm going to help Dwight."

"Help Dwight with what?"

"Since when is it your business?"

Dat gritted his teeth. "Are you two done *yet*?"

Tyler blew out an embarrassed sigh. So much for being professional. If only his middle brother didn't get under his skin with his snarky comments! He had to find a way to keep his temper in check. "Sorry, *Dat*."

Korey's lips twisted, and he remained silent.

"Why do you need to leave early, Korey?" *Dat* asked.

"Dwight is working on his parents' *daadihaus* so it's ready for when he and Kendra get married in December. He asked me and a few of the other guys if we'd help. He's adding on a couple of bedrooms and another bathroom."

Dat nodded and pulled his cell phone from his pocket. "Fine. Here, you can call Drew."

"Thanks," Korey muttered as he took the

phone and walked toward the far side of the roof.

Dat turned to Tyler once Korey was gone. "You're going to have to prove to me that you and Korey can maintain a mature working relationship before I can trust you two to run a crew without me."

"I will, *Dat*."

Tyler's posture sank as *Dat* returned to hammering shingles on the roof. He'd blown his chance at earning his father's blessing for his business proposal today, but he wasn't going to give up. He'd convince him he was ready to run his own crew before the cold weather descended upon Lancaster County. He was determined to make that dream a reality.

"Michelle?" Jorie called the following evening. "Are you in here?"

"I'm in *Dat*'s old woodworking shop. Come join me!" Michelle called to her sister while she sat at the large table surrounded by paint, brushes, and old milk cans. A row of lanterns on the surrounding toolboxes illuminated the room at the back of one of her father's barns. The fragrance of paint, animals, and wet hay filled her nostrils.

Jorie appeared in the doorway. "*Mamm* said you were working on a project. What are you doing in here?"

"You inspired me to try something. Come over here and tell me what you think."

"What did I inspire you to do?" Jorie sidled up to Michelle and gasped when she looked down at the milk can painted with a farm scene. "Michelle, this is amazing."

Michelle scrunched her nose as she looked up at her sister. "You really think so?" She pointed at the painting. "The cows are too big, and the barn is kind of lopsided."

"You're always your own worst critic. This is fabulous. You need to find a gift shop that will sell this, because the tourists are going to buy all of these up. Trust me, Shell."

Michelle touched her sister's arm. "Thanks. I asked *Dat* if I could have the old milk cans for a project, and he said yes. He also said I could make his old woodworking shop my studio since he doesn't work with wood much anymore. Now I just need to paint a few and then ask his permission to sell them."

"He'll say yes, for sure." Jorie sat on a stool beside her.

"Did you check the messages?"

"*Ya,* there were a few for *Mamm* and *Dat.*"

"Did Korey call for me?"

Jorie looked apologetic as she shook her

48

head. "No. He's probably really busy at work."

"I'm sure he is." Michelle forced her lips into a smile and tried to ignore the disappointment that filled her. She climbed down from the stool. "It's getting late. I'll clean up my brushes and then come inside to get ready for bed."

"I'll help you."

Michelle smiled, and she and Jorie began cleaning up the table. She was so grateful for her younger sister.

CHAPTER 4

"What's the latest news?" Michelle asked as she and Jorie joined their group of friends talking outside the Yoder family's barn Sunday morning before the service.

"I was just talking about my wedding." Kendra Beiler lifted her chin, and her dark eyes glittered. "*Mei schweschder* and I picked out the material for our dresses yesterday. It's perfect, isn't it, Lisa?" She turned to her younger sister.

Lisa brightened. "Oh yes! The green is just perfect to go with our strawberry-blond hair. I can't wait to see the finished dresses!"

Charity moved to stand beside Michelle.

"Dwight is working on the *daadihaus* on his parents' farm to get it ready for us. He's adding on two bedrooms and a bathroom. That means we'll have three bedrooms and two bathrooms! Hopefully the Lord will see fit to send us *kinner* to fill the *haus* with laughter and love," Kendra gushed. "December will be here before we know it, so Dwight and his *freinden* have been working so hard to get the *haus* ready." She pointed at Michelle. "Korey has been kind enough to help him."

Michelle beamed. "Oh, how nice." She glanced at Charity and noticed her best friend's smile seemed forced.

"Soon I'll sit with the married women during the service and I won't be able to sit with all of you. I'll certainly miss you all." Kendra's pretty faced contorted with a feigned frown. "But that's just what happens when you get married. Oh, I can't wait to change my last name to his!"

While Kendra continued on about her wedding and bright future, Michelle turned as a line of young men began filing into the barn for the service. Her heart warmed when Korey smiled and nodded as he and Dwight moved past. Tyler and Jonah followed behind them, and Tyler grinned and lifted his hand in greeting. Michelle couldn't stop her smile as she nodded in reply.

Charity placed her hand on Michelle's forearm and steered her away from their group of friends. "Oh, Michelle, I've been meaning to ask you something really important," she said, her voice sounding a little too bright.

"What's that?" Michelle asked.

"Nothing. I just had to get away from Kendra," her best friend mumbled. "I'm so tired of her bragging about her wedding. I'm *froh* for her, but it's all she talks about. It just gets to be too much, you know?"

Michelle nodded, but excitement swirled in her chest as a thought suddenly hit her. If Korey was helping Dwight work on his house, perhaps he'd be inspired to propose to Michelle! She gave a happy sigh at the idea of planning her own wedding soon.

Charity's green eyes studied her. "What are you pondering so intently?"

"Nothing." Michelle shook her head. "I was thinking of bringing supper over to Korey's *haus* this week, and I'm working on something special to give him as a gift."

Charity's smile wobbled and then recovered. "That's fantastic."

"Why are you upset?"

"I'm sure you're the next one to get married. I'm so *froh* for you, but I'll miss sitting with you in church."

Michelle touched Charity's shoulder. "I promise you that we'll always be close."

"I hope so." Charity's eyes focused on something behind Michelle. "It's time to find our seats."

Michelle and Charity followed the other

unmarried women into the barn and settled onto the benches in their section. Her eyes quickly found Korey over in the unmarried men's section between Tyler and Dwight. Korey whispered something to Dwight.

"If only I could get Tyler's attention," Charity whispered in a dreamy voice.

As if hearing her words, Tyler peered over at them, and he smiled and nodded. Charity responded with a sigh under her breath.

Michelle turned toward her best friend. "You should talk to him today."

"Maybe I will."

Just then the song leader began singing the opening line to the first hymn, and the congregation joined in.

"How are things at the bulk foods store?" Tyler asked Jonah while they sat across from each other and ate lunch after the service.

The congregation ate in shifts, and after the benches were converted into tables, the women served the men first before they took their turn to eat.

Jonah shrugged and picked up a pretzel. "The same. The days sort of blend together at the store. How about the roofing business?"

"It's fine. We're booked into October." Tyler studied the lunch meat and two pieces of bread on his plate as his conversation with his father trickled through his mind. He stacked the lunch meat on the bread and tried to wipe away the embarrassment that took hold of him when he recalled how he'd allowed Korey to get under his skin once again.

"That's *gut* that you're staying busy. That business plan you wrote last year has really taken shape."

"Thanks. I'm working on improving it. I have some ideas, and I've been trying to convince *mei dat* —"

"*Kaffi?*"

Tyler peeked over his shoulder to where Charity stood holding up a carafe. A bright smile turned up her pink lips. "*Ya*. Please." He handed her his cup.

"How was your week?" she asked.

Tyler peered over at Jonah and then back at her. "My week?"

"*Ya*, your week, Tyler." She filled his cup and then handed it back to him.

"*Gut*," Tyler said. "Yours?"

Charity reached for Jonah's cup. "*Gut*." She filled it and then handed it back to him. "See you later." She moved down the table, stopping to offer coffee and fill more cups.

Jonah smirked and then sipped his coffee. "You look like you're bursting at the seams to say something witty." Tyler lifted his sandwich and took a bite.

"She likes you."

Tyler chewed and then swallowed. "Jayden said the same thing last Sunday when we walked home from Michelle's *haus.*"

"Jayden is right."

Tyler took another bite of his sandwich and gazed over to where Charity stood near the end of the table and filled Jayden's cup. He tried to imagine dating Charity, but the image just wouldn't appear in his mind.

He turned his attention back to his best friend. "Is your *dat* still talking about expanding his store?"

"*Ya,* he is," Jonah began.

Tyler and Jonah fell into an easy conversation about work for the remainder of the meal.

After lunch, Tyler stood and climbed over the bench. When he turned to go, he bumped into Michelle. She gasped, and he grabbed her tray full of cups before it spilled onto the barn floor.

"We need to stop running into each other like this," he teased as his neck flushed.

Michelle laughed. "You know, Tyler, I'm starting to think it's your life's goal to knock me to the floor."

"Well, you've figured me out." He blew

out a dramatic sigh.

She grinned as she took the tray out of his hand. "*Danki* for not completely knocking me over this time."

"The pleasure was all mine." He bowed with a flourish, and she laughed again.

Jonah appeared beside Tyler as Michelle walked away. "Real slick, Ty," he said, patting Tyler's shoulder. "The women love when you step on them."

"Ha, ha," Tyler deadpanned.

"I was thinking I could bring you supper sometime this week," Michelle told Korey as she settled into the seat beside him in his buggy while they traveled toward the youth gathering after the women had eaten lunch. "I thought I'd make your favorite — sausage and cheese lasagna casserole and a chocolate chip cheesecake for dessert."

Korey nodded while studying the road again. "Okay."

"I'm also making you a special gift as a surprise." She forced a shaky smile and held her breath, hoping he'd look over at her, but he kept his milk-chocolate-colored eyes trained at the intersection as he halted the horse at a red light. Perhaps he was deep in thought about something important — such as his father's business — or maybe something was wrong at home.

"Korey . . ." She drew out his name.

His eyes snapped to hers. "What?"

"Is anything wrong?" She tried to chuckle, but it sounded more like a squeak.

He blinked and then his brow furrowed. "No. Why?"

"You didn't answer me." She stroked the hem of her black apron.

His handsome smile turned up his lips. "I'm sorry. I was deep in thought about something."

"What?" She leaned toward him. He was finally talking to her! When he hesitated, she said, "You know you can tell me anything."

"It's nothing you need to worry about."

"Why don't you let me be the judge of that?"

"It's just work."

A horn tooted behind them, and he guided the horse through the intersection as her shoulders sagged. So much for getting him to bare his soul to her.

She shook off her disappointment as the *clip-clop* of hooves, the whirl of the buggy wheels, and the sound of passing cars filled the buggy once again while Korey stared out the windshield.

"Anyway, I thought I could bring you a

meal and a special surprise on Thursday. Does that sound okay?" She studied his handsome profile.

He remained silent, and frustration churned through her.

"Korey? Do you want to talk about what's bothering you?"

"Not really."

"Maybe it will make you feel better?"

He snorted. "I doubt that."

"When I get something that's upsetting me off my chest, I always feel better."

Korey remained silent.

Look at me! She sighed and settled back on the seat. Perhaps he was just too tired to talk — even to his girlfriend of more than a year.

But if that was true, then he seemed to be tired all the time lately. After all, she'd felt as if she were pulling information from him for at least the past month. She always did all the talking while he just nodded or graced her with one-word responses.

Silence stretched between them as Korey continued to guide the horse without even a glance toward her. Michelle racked her mind for something to say, but she came up short. She was grateful when they turned onto the road that led to Suzanna Mast's farm.

As teams of volleyball players and clusters of young people talking and laughing came into view, she gripped the plate of chocolate chip cookies she had baked yesterday.

When Korey halted the horse near the barn, Michelle turned toward him. Doubt and worry hit her as she considered her future with him. Perhaps she had been kidding herself when she imagined his proposal and their marriage. After all, he'd seemed to be pulling away from her. Maybe he didn't see her as a part of his future but was too afraid to tell her. Worry settled heavily on her shoulders as she imagined losing him and trying to start over in a relationship with someone new.

His dark eyebrows rose. "Why are you looking at me like that?"

"Korey," she began, her hands trembling. "Is everything okay between us?"

He gripped the reins and gave a nervous laugh. "Sure. Why not?"

"You never seem to talk to me anymore." She held her breath and hesitated.

Then Korey reached over and touched her hand. "I'm sorry. I've just had a lot on my mind lately. Just be patient with me, okay?"

"Of course," she said. "I'll always be patient with you."

They climbed out of the buggy, and while

Korey cared for his horse, Michelle made her way to the house, where she found her group of friends in the kitchen. She set her plate of cookies on the counter beside a variety of cakes, pies, cookies, and brownies.

Kendra stood in the center of the group. "Dwight's favorite dessert is red velvet cake, so my aunts and cousins are going to make red velvet cakes for the wedding."

Michelle leaned against the counter, and when her gaze met Charity's, her best friend rolled her eyes. Michelle clamped her hand over her mouth to stop her laugh.

"Oh, Kendra," Suzanna gushed, "I can't wait for your wedding! It's going to be so *wunderbaar.*"

Suzanna's younger sister, Mary, nodded, and the ribbons on her prayer *kapp* bounced off her shoulders. "Oh *ya.* The desserts will be out of this world."

"And what about the main dish?" Willa, another friend, asked.

Kendra brightened. "We're talking about baked chicken."

"When Korey and I get married, I think we'll have lasagna," Michelle said.

All of the eyes in the kitchen focused on Michelle as her friends all gasped at the same time.

"You're engaged?" Suzanna blurted out.

Mary grinned. "Congratulations!"

"When did Korey ask you?" Kendra inquired. "And why didn't you tell us?"

"Have you set a date?" Willa asked.

"I hope it's not the same day as Kendra's wedding," Lisa said.

Michelle stood up straight, and her cheeks felt like they might spontaneously combust. "No, he hasn't asked yet. I-I-I just meant when he does, I'd like to have lasagna," she stammered as she shot Charity a sideways glance. *Save me, Charity!*

"Hey, Michelle!" Charity said, her voice a little too loud. "How about we go play some volleyball?"

Michelle nodded and cleared her throat. "Great idea." Her face continued to burn as she and Charity rushed out the back door and started toward the volleyball nets. "*Danki* for saving me."

"That's what best *freinden* are for." Charity looped her arm around Michelle's shoulders and gave her a side hug.

Later that afternoon, Tyler dropped down onto the grass beside Jonah and swiped his arm over his sweaty forehead. "That was a *gut* game."

"At least you didn't trample anyone,"

61

Jonah teased.

Tyler shook his head and sipped some water from his cup. "That was so funny I forgot to laugh," he deadpanned.

"That will never get old." Jonah gave Tyler's shoulder a playful shove.

Looking out toward the makeshift volleyball courts, Tyler snorted as Korey served the ball and then Jayden, on the opposing team, bumped it. He turned toward the sidelines, where Michelle and Charity stood, seemingly engrossed in an intense conversation.

Tyler turned to Jonah and picked up his empty cup of water. "I'll go get us a refill."

"Thanks."

Tyler sauntered over to the folding tables with the snacks and drinks and began refilling their cups with water.

"Hi, Tyler."

He looked up as Charity approached the table. "Hi."

"Are you having fun this afternoon?" She fiddled with the tablecloth.

"*Ya.* How about you?"

She nodded. *"Ya."*

They studied each other, and he picked up a small plate and began to fill it with cookies just to give his eyes something to focus on.

"Are you going to play more volleyball?" she asked.

"*Ya*. Are you?"

She shrugged. "Maybe."

"Why not?"

"I'm not that *gut.*"

Tyler smiled. "It's not about talent. It's about having fun — so you need to play."

"Okay."

Silence fell between them, and he searched for something to say as they stared at each other.

Finally, he balanced the plate on top of the two cups and then lifted them. "Well, maybe we can play on the same team."

"*Ya,* maybe."

Tyler rejoined Jonah on the grassy hill and handed him a cup of water.

"I saw you talking with Charity. What was that all about?" Jonah nodded toward the refreshment table.

"She was trying to make conversation with me." He held up the plate of cookies, and Jonah picked a macaroon. "It was mostly awkward."

"You should ask her out."

Tyler lifted an eyebrow. "We're just acquaintances."

"That's why you should date her and get to know her."

"I don't know . . . I'm so busy with work and —"

"Tyler," Jonah interrupted him. "You can't plan a future with work. You can't marry work or start a family with work. Do you get what I'm saying?"

A burst of laughter exploded from Tyler's lips as he looked at his best friend. "That was a bit of a stretch."

"Well, you know what I mean, okay? You're going to wind up alone if all you care about is your job."

Tyler allowed Jonah's words to soak through him while he gazed over to where Michelle and Charity spoke by the refreshment table. He picked up a chocolate chip cookie as an idea formed in his head.

The next time he had a chance to talk to Michelle alone, he'd ask her if Charity really liked him and if Michelle thought it was a good idea for him to ask her out.

Surely Michelle would tell him the truth, and because she would probably be his future sister-in-law, he valued her opinion.

CHAPTER 5

Later that evening, Michelle peered over at Korey and took in his handsome face, illuminated by the lantern on the floor of his buggy as he guided the horse toward her house. "So I'll bring the meal over Thursday at six, okay?"

"Sure." He kept his eyes focused on the dark road.

"I can't wait. I have a surprise for you."

He nodded.

"I'm making you a present."

Korey nodded again.

Michelle sighed, but she held on to a shred of hope. Maybe when he saw what she had done for him, he'd realize he really wanted to marry her and then ask her father's permission. She smiled as an image of their wedding filled her mind once again.

Korey guided the horse into her driveway, and she angled her body toward his. "Have a *gut* week," he said.

"You too." She retrieved her flashlight from her pocket, pushed open her buggy door, and ambled up the back porch steps. When she reached the porch, she turned to wave, but Korey's buggy was already gone.

Michelle tiptoed into the house and up the stairs to her room. After changing for bed, she peeked out her bedroom window toward the Bontragers' farm down the road but found only darkness staring back at her.

As she climbed into bed, she smiled. She couldn't wait until Thursday night. Perhaps Korey would finally tell her that he was ready to plan a life with her. The idea sent excitement pouring through her.

Thursday evening Michelle stood in the kitchen and faced her mother and sister. "How do I look?" She glanced down at her favorite pink dress and black apron and then up at her mother and sister.

"You look *schee, mei liewe.*" *Mamm* touched her shoulder.

Jorie nodded. "Everything is perfect, Michelle. The casserole smells amazing, and your cheesecake came out perfectly." She pointed to the tote bag that held the surprise gift. "And he's going to love what you made him."

Michelle bit her lip. She'd spent nearly all

day preparing for this special night. She hoped everything would be perfect, just like Jorie said.

Mamm picked up the portable casserole dish and cake plate. "Go have fun."

"Do you need help carrying everything down the road?" Jorie asked.

"No, *danki*. Just get the door, please." Michelle hefted the tote bag onto her shoulder and balanced the casserole and cake containers in her arms. She had wrapped a couple of dish towels around the casserole dish after baking the casserole in the oven.

After saying goodbye to her mother and sister, Michelle began her trek down the road. Excitement and anxiety spun within her as she imagined presenting her meal and surprise to Korey. She'd planned to call him yesterday to remind him about their supper date, but time had gotten away from her. She was so busy finishing her chores and preparing everything for today that she forgot until she was climbing into bed.

But surely Korey had written a reminder on his stepmother's calendar that she kept in the kitchen. And surely he was just as excited as she was to spend time together.

Michelle glanced around at the rolling green pastures. Birds sang in the nearby trees, and a couple of chipmunks scuttled by as she breathed in the scent of rain. Above her, puffy gray clouds clogged the sky. She felt a flurry in her chest when she reached the Bontrager family's rock driveway that led to their two-story brick home with the small front porch.

She readjusted the warm portable casserole container in her hands and the cake container and tried to ignore how the handles on her tote bag bit into her aching shoulder. She climbed the few steps, and then balancing the portable containers in one hand, she knocked on the door.

After a moment, footfalls sounded from inside the house. Her lips lifted in a smile as she imagined Korey coming to greet her. Perhaps he had a special gift for her since she told him she had spent all week creating something for him.

The door opened with a squeak, revealing Tyler clad in dark trousers and a blue shirt. His dark hair was damp as if he had recently stepped out of the shower.

He grinned and then pushed the storm door open wide.

"Wie geht's?" His bright hazel eyes moved to her arms. "Oh! Let me help you." He took the two portable containers from her. "Oh my! This smells heavenly."

"*Danki.* I made Korey's favorites."

"How nice," he said as a strange expression flickered across his face. He shifted backward and propped the door open with his foot. "Come in."

She followed him through the large family room, which contained a sofa, two wing chairs, and a recliner, along with a coffee table, two end tables, and two propane lamps, before they entered the kitchen.

She set her tote bag on a kitchen chair while Tyler placed her containers on the counter. A pile of journals, an accordion file, and a pen sat on the table. It was then that she realized that the house was quiet.

"Where is everyone?"

Tyler turned to face her and pushed his hand through his damp hair, causing it to stand up at odd angles, making him look younger than twenty-five. "I'm actually the only one home." He leaned a hip against the counter.

"Oh." Michelle blinked. "Where's the rest of your family?"

"*Mei dat,* Crystal, and Jayden went to supper at Crystal's *bruder*'s *haus.*"

"And Korey?"

"He went to help Dwight work on the *daadihaus.* Apparently he's adding on to it before he and Kendra get married in December."

"Oh. So maybe he'll be back soon?"

"Ah." He rubbed at a spot on his cheek. "I don't know about that. He normally gets home late after helping Dwight and then is a complete grouch the next morning due to lack of sleep." He hesitated for a moment. "Did he know you were coming tonight?"

Michelle opened her mouth and then closed it before turning toward Crystal's calendar and searching for today's date. She read, "Supper at Kane's," in Crystal's beautiful handwriting, but nothing else was written in the box.

When she faced Tyler again, she latched on to a fiber of hope. "So Korey never mentioned that I was bringing him supper tonight?"

"No," he said before holding up his hands. "But maybe he told *Dat* and Crystal when I wasn't around."

She nodded as disappointment wrapped around her lungs and squeezed. She glanced down at her black shoes and then up at Tyler, who watched her with a warm expression. "I suppose it's my fault for not calling and reminding him that I was coming tonight."

"When did you and Korey talk about having supper together?"

70

"Sunday." She recalled how Korey had seemed lost in thought. Perhaps he hadn't been listening to her at all. Her heart began to crumble at the thought, and she pointed to the counter. "Well, I'll leave the food for him. Just tell him I was here."

She glanced at the tote bag on the chair, and frustration spiked through her along with her anger. If he had truly forgotten her or ignored her offer of supper, then he didn't deserve the gift she'd spent all week creating for him.

She hefted the tote bag onto her shoulder and started toward the door. "Have a *gut* evening."

"Wait."

Michelle stopped moving and pivoted toward him.

"You're welcome to stay." Tyler smiled. "After all, you made this amazing meal. You deserve to enjoy it."

She fingered the handle of her tote bag and silently debated if she wanted to spend the evening with Korey's older brother. Even though she'd known Tyler her whole life, she didn't think they'd ever had a one-on-one conversation before. It could be awkward. Well, it still beat stomping back home, basking in her disappointment, and feeling sorry for herself.

71

He gave her a palms-up. "Maybe Korey is on his way. He could've been planning to be here by six but was delayed."

"I hadn't considered that." Michelle felt her irritation and frustration subside a fraction.

Tyler opened the refrigerator. "I just made some iced tea. Would you like some?"

"Yes, please." She set the tote bag back on the chair while Tyler poured two glasses and then carried them over to the table.

He placed a glass in front of her and then moved around the table before putting his glass down beside the pile of books. "Have a seat."

"Danki." She sank down into the chair. Then she took a sip of iced tea before moving her fingers through the condensation while trying to shake the feeling that her boyfriend had forgotten her.

"Do you want to talk about it?"

Her gaze flittered to his, and she found him watching her with a sympathetic expression that calmed her. For a split second, she found herself longing to unload all of her burdens on Tyler's ears. She wanted to ask him if he thought Korey truly loved her and if he wanted to marry her. She craved Tyler's advice on how to get Korey to open up to her.

But Tyler was Korey's older brother. Surely he wanted to stay out of his brother's relationships.

Tyler leaned toward her. "You okay?"

"*Ya,* of course." She sat up straight in the chair. "Why didn't you go to Kane's *haus* for supper?"

He blew out a breath through his nose. "I told *mei dat* I wanted to get caught up on the books, but I haven't made much headway." He touched one of the journals.

"Couldn't you work on that after supper?"

"*Ya,* I could have."

"So why did you *really* not go to supper with your family?"

He took a sip of iced tea.

"I'm sorry, Tyler. That's none of my business."

He placed the glass on the table and smiled at her. "You're very perceptive." He folded his hands on the table and looked as if he was working through a puzzle in his mind. "The truth is that I've been trying to convince *mei dat* to allow me to . . ."

He looked down at the tabletop and then back up at her. "I have ideas of ways we can expand our business and make more money. I almost had him convinced, and then I messed up and caused him to lose confidence in me."

"I find that hard to believe."

Tyler's brow crinkled for a split second. "What do you mean by that?"

"I've seen how you and your *dat* interact. It's obvious he respects you very much." When he continued to look unconvinced, she fingered her glass. "I've been here many times when you and your *dat* were discussing work, and your *dat* always asks for your opinion."

He leaned back in his seat. "Name one time when he asked for my opinion."

"Okay." She tapped her chin, considering the challenge, and then snapped her fingers. "I've got it. One time you and your *dat* were talking about a big job over in Millersville."

He smiled. "Right! That was a restaurant."

"Exactly. And your *dat* asked you if you thought he was charging the customer enough. You suggested an amount, and he agreed to that. If he didn't respect your opinion, then he wouldn't have asked you for it."

Tyler pursed his lips and rubbed his chin. "That's true."

"What could you have possibly done to ruin that?"

Tyler looked down at the edge of the table and then met her gaze. He grinned and pointed to the tote bag. "So, what's in the bag?"

"Tyler Bontrager," she began with a smirk, "you're not going to change the subject on me that easily." She tapped the table with her finger. "I want to know what happened, and you're going to tell me."

"But I really want to know what's in the bag."

She laughed, and his grin widened. "Fine. I'll make you a deal. You tell me why you think you've lost your *dat*'s respect, and I'll share what's in the bag."

He took another drink of iced tea.

"I feel this is a fair deal."

"It is, but I'm too embarrassed to tell you the story."

"Why? I've known you my whole life."

"That's true, but it involves your boyfriend, which makes it awkward."

Michelle glanced up at the clock and then back at Tyler. "Well, your *bruder* is almost thirty minutes late for a supper I spent all day planning for him, which means I won't be offended if you tell me something negative about him." She sighed. "Besides, I know you and Korey don't always agree."

"That's exactly the problem."

"What do you mean?"

"Korey and I bicker a lot, which isn't news

75

to you. You've witnessed our arguments often."

She nodded.

He explained how he had almost convinced his father to allow him to run a second crew, but then a disagreement with Korey derailed his father's agreement. "So now I have to prove to *mei dat* that I'm mature enough to be in charge of another crew."

"That shouldn't be difficult, right?" She shrugged.

"It's a little difficult for me to convince him when Korey just —" He stopped and shook his head. "It's really not appropriate for me to share this with you." He leaned forward and reached for her bag, his lips twitching.

She smacked his hand. "Hey!"

"Ow. That stings." He rubbed his hand and then started laughing.

She joined in, and the sound of their laughter floated around the kitchen. "I'm so sorry. It was a knee-jerk reaction. Do you need some ice?"

"No. I suppose that was payback for trampling you on the volleyball court."

"You seriously need to let that go. Now, what's the issue with Korey? Maybe I can help." She snorted. "Right. As if I could ever help. I can't even get him to show up for a supper I made." She looked up at the clock and more irritation flowed through her. Then Michelle turned back to Tyler. "Are you hungry?"

"Very."

"How does sausage and cheese lasagna casserole sound?"

"Much better than the ham and cheese sandwich I was going to make."

Michelle stood. "Let me see if I need to warm it up." She tried to smile. While she had planned this meal for Korey and was disappointed he wasn't there, she was thankful she had a friend in his older brother.

CHAPTER 6

"Are you sure the casserole is warm enough?" Michelle asked Tyler as they sat across from each other at the table.

Tyler smiled. "I would tell you if I thought we needed to warm it up in the oven. Is your piece warm enough?"

She nodded as she chewed.

"I agree." He pointed his fork at his serving of casserole. "It's positively *appeditlich*. Korey is missing out."

Michelle stopped chewing and looked up at the clock again, finding it was almost seven.

"I'm sorry."

She turned back to Tyler, who frowned. "It's okay." Worry coursed through her. "Do you think Korey was in an accident?"

Tyler shook his head as he chewed. "To be honest, I think he forgot."

"Or he never heard me," she quipped.

"What do you mean by that?"

"Lately he's been sort of in his own world. It's as if he changed after our one-year anniversary last month. I keep wondering if he still cares for me." She wagged her empty fork again. "Wait a minute. You did it again. You changed the subject on me."

Tyler gave a sheepish expression. "I would never do that to you. You know me better than that."

She laughed again and then wiped her mouth. She studied him as she contemplated why she and Tyler had never really talked like this before.

"Why are you looking at me as if you just met me?"

"I was just thinking that we've never really talked before."

"We've talked plenty, but apparently it hasn't been very memorable."

"We've never talked like this." She motioned between them. "Now, what is it about Korey that is interfering with your relationship with your *dat*?"

Tyler released a heavy sigh as he set his fork down beside his plate. "Korey and I argue because we rub each other the wrong way. He just gets under my skin, and I can't keep my mouth shut. I need to figure out a way to let the snide things he says go or handle them with more maturity." He paused. "And to be clear, he's *mei bruder.* He's important to me, and I need to figure out a way that we can work together and treat each other respectfully. So, that's it." He pointed to the bag. "Now, it's my turn. What's in there?"

"It's a gift for Korey."

"Let me see it."

"If you laugh, you'll hurt my feelings."

He drew an *X* on his chest as if to cross his heart. "I promise I won't hurt your feelings."

"I'm trusting you, Tyler." She opened the bag and pulled out the milk can she had painted and set it on the table between them. "Well, here it is." Then she held her breath, awaiting his reaction.

Tyler grinned and turned it around slowly, examining the farm scene. "Oh wow. This is neat. Where did you buy it?"

"Buy it?" She chuckled. "I painted it."

Tyler's eyes widened. "You painted *this*?"

"*Ya.*" She shrugged as heat infused her cheeks.

"Wow! This is amazing, Michelle!"

"*Danki,* but you're just saying that to be nice." She took another bite of the casserole.

"No, I'm not." He pointed to the landscape. "This is professional. These cows are so realistic, and just look at the detail in the barn and the pasture. You're truly talented."

She shrugged as she chewed, certain her cheeks might spontaneously combust. She swallowed and then said, *"Danki."*

"How long have you been painting?"

"I've always liked to draw, and I've started dabbling in painting a little bit lately." She explained how she had painted a farm scene, and her sister told her that it would sell. "I saw the old milk cans, and the idea was born."

Tyler touched the can again. "I hope you're going to make more and sell them."

"I'm going to ask *mei dat* if I can since *mei mamm* and Jorie make quilts to sell." She took a sip of iced tea. "Do you really think people would buy them?"

"*Ya,* for sure. These are unique, and tourists will love them."

"Danki." She slipped the milk can back into the bag.

They ate in comfortable silence for a few minutes.

"Do you remember the time our *mamms* took us to that playground when I was five, and you and Korey were four?"

Michelle snorted and then covered her face with her hands as she laughed.

"I've never heard you snort before!" Tyler declared as he chuckled.

Michelle continued to laugh as her eyes watered. She picked up a paper napkin from the holder in the center of the table and wiped her eyes. "Stop making me laugh," she managed to say while trying to catch her breath.

"I'm sorry, but I didn't do that deliberately."

"Don't make me laugh again, Tyler. And yes, I do remember that trip to the park. You were frustrated with me because I said I wanted to go down the slide, but when I got to the top of the ladder, I hesitated. Then you gave me a shove and I went down on my stomach. I loved it so much, I spent the next hour sliding down on my belly."

"Yes!" He shook his head. "I was thinking about that the other day. I was convinced *mei mamm* was going to spank me, but our *mamms* just laughed and laughed — after you made it down the slide safely, of course."

"We had some great times with our *mamms.*" When she realized what she'd said, she sucked in a breath and looked over at him, waiting for him to shut down the way Korey did when someone mentioned his mother. "I'm so sorry."

"For what?"

"For mentioning your *mamm.* I know it

upsets Korey."

Tyler studied his plate and the small amount of casserole remaining. "Sometimes it helps to talk about her." He tilted his head as he looked at her. "Korey won't talk about her?"

"He used to, but ever since your *dat* remarried, it's rare." She began folding her napkin.

"I miss her." His voice was a hoarse whisper.

"I miss her too."

Their eyes locked and something unfamiliar passed between them. For a moment, the atmosphere felt charged around them.

She tore her eyes away and picked up their dishes. "Would you like a piece of cheesecake?"

"Oh, I shouldn't eat more of the meal you made for Korey."

She eyed him. "Are you insulting my cheesecake?"

"No, your cheesecake is amazing, but you didn't make it for me."

"I'm going to cut you a piece and put on *kaffi* for us."

"Let me help."

Tyler popped up from his seat and got the percolator going while Michelle washed their dishes and forks and set them in the drainboard. Soon the percolator was sputtering to life. Tyler filled two mugs and brought them to the table, and Michelle retrieved the cream and sugar. Then Tyler flipped on a few lanterns, casting a warm yellow glow over the kitchen.

Michelle cut two pieces of cake and joined him at the table. The delicious fragrance of coffee and chocolate chip cheesecake filled the kitchen.

"This is fantastic," Tyler said after swallowing a bite. "So moist."

She smiled. *"Danki."*

She glanced at the clock, finding it was seven thirty. Her heart felt heavy. Korey had most likely forgotten about her. In fact, he had chosen helping his friend over spending time with her.

And a man who made his friends a priority over his girlfriend would never want to marry her. Her throat dried as sadness welled up in her chest.

"Do you remember that time we were at the park with our *mamms,* and Lainey stepped on a bee?"

Michelle turned her focus back to Tyler. His expression was warm and open as he smiled at her.

"*Ya,* I do. I think I was maybe five, so Lainey was nine. I still remember how she sobbed as *mei mamm* pulled the stinger out." She shivered at the recollection. "I felt so sorry for her that I held her hand and cried along with her."

He lifted his mug of coffee. "How is Lainey doing?"

"Really well. She's expecting her second child soon."

"That's exciting."

They ate in silence, and Michelle felt herself relax slightly, despite the anguish expanding in her chest.

"I have a question," Tyler began. "Does Charity like me?"

"I think she's kind of made it obvious."

Tyler nodded, and they both laughed. "So I'm right she does like me. I mean, she wants to date me."

"Okay." Michelle set her fork on her plate. "I'm going to tell you the truth."

"I hope you'll always tell me the truth, Michelle."

She took a deep breath. "Charity likes you a lot. In fact, I promised her that I would talk to you about dating her." She shook her head. "She talks about how if I married Korey and she married you, then we both might start families at the same time and raise our *kinner* together."

Tyler swallowed, and something that

resembled shock flickered over his face.

"Oh no," she groaned. "I shouldn't have told you that. Please don't tell her I said that."

"Don't worry, I won't."

"Tyler, Charity is super sweet and she's so *schee*. You know I've been close with her since we were *kinner*. I think you two would make such a cute couple."

He took another sip of coffee and looked as if he were pondering something.

"What's on your mind, Ty?" she asked before finishing the last morsel of the cheesecake.

Tyler held on to his hot mug. "Everyone is pressuring me to start dating."

"Who's everyone?"

He began counting off on his fingers. "*Mei dat,* Jay, Jonah."

"And you don't want to date?"

"It's not that I don't want to." He tapped one of the journals beside his plate. "I'm just so focused on work and proving to *mei dat* that I can run my own crew that I don't need the distraction of trying to be a *gut* boyfriend too. *Mei dat*'s company is my future, and I need that future in order to provide for a family someday. I don't think I'll be able to focus on being a *gut* boyfriend or future husband until I'm settled in my career."

She nodded slowly as his words saturated her mind.

"Now you're staring at me like I'm *narrisch.*"

"No, I don't think you're crazy, but maybe you're a bit of a control freak." She held up her thumb and forefinger. "Just a *teensy* bit."

He laughed. "I appreciate your honesty."

"I can't help it." She shrugged.

"Do you think Charity would go out with me?"

Michelle tilted her head. "Are you teasing me now?"

"No." His expression was serious. "Rejection is a serious fear for men."

She guffawed. "Please, Tyler. She nearly trips over herself when she sees you. She would be delighted if you asked her out."

"I'll consider it." He grimaced. "Please keep this between us, okay?"

"You have my word." Michelle's focus drifted to the clock again, and her stomach tightened. "It's almost eight. I should clean this up and get going."

"I'll help with the cleanup. It's the least I can do after that *appeditlich* meal."

She piled up their dishes and forks and

carried them to the sink, where she began filling up one side with soapy water.

Tyler sidled up to her and set the mugs in. "How about you wash and I dry?"

"Sure." She tried to smile, but more disappointment flooded her.

She had spent nearly all week preparing for this special night, and Korey had let her down. Perhaps this meant that their relationship would soon dissolve like the morning dew. Her chest heaved and she swallowed back her threatening tears. She had to be strong. She would not allow her heartache to break free in front of Tyler.

Out of the corner of her eye, she spotted Tyler watching her, and she busied herself with scrubbing a dish to avoid his gaze.

"I hope you're planning to paint more milk cans," Tyler said. "I'm sure you'd sell a ton at a store."

Michelle rinsed a dish and handed it to him, careful not to make eye contact. *"Danki."*

While he dried and stored the dish in the cabinet, she washed and rinsed the second dish and then began scrubbing the utensils. Silence filled the room while they worked.

"Do you remember that time we went sledding with the youth group, and Korey and I ran our sled into yours and Jorie's?"

he asked.

Michelle couldn't stop her laugh as she turned toward him. "I do!" She rested a hand on her hip. "You also ran into me when we went ice-skating. I'm starting to see a pattern. You just like to run into me!"

"Now, wait a minute. *You* ran into *me* when we were ice-skating. I remember that distinctly." His grin was wide.

"Oh no, no, no. I'm an expert ice-skater. It was clearly your fault."

"Expert!" he challenged. "So, that's why you put your skates on and promptly fell down into the snow. I remember you sprawled out and laughing because you couldn't get up."

"That's right!" She hooted, and they both started laughing. Michelle couldn't stop, and she bent at the waist and wiped her eyes.

"What's going on here?"

Michelle spun and found Korey in the doorway. She stilled and then scowled as her hands fisted. "I was just leaving."

CHAPTER 7

Michelle pivoted toward Tyler, whose expression had clouded with a frown. "Keep the leftover casserole and cake here, and I'll pick up my dishes later."

Tyler nodded.

She picked up her tote bag from the chair. When her eyes flitted to the painted milk can sitting in the center of the table, she contemplated the hours she had spent painting that can for Korey and imagining his excitement and appreciation for the gift. For a brief moment, she considered slipping it into her bag and carrying it home.

Instead, however, she shouldered her empty bag. She would leave it for him, and perhaps it would be a parting gift in case he broke up with her. After all, it seemed that he had stood her up on purpose. A lump began swelling in her throat as she turned toward the doorway.

Korey divided a look between her and

Tyler as suspicion filled his handsome face. Then his eyes widened, and his mouth opened and closed. "Oh no. Was tonight the night we were supposed to have supper together?"

She glowered and pointed to the counter. "I brought your favorite casserole and cheesecake."

"Michelle, I'm so sorry." Korey cupped a hand to his forehead. "I completely forgot. Dwight needed help and —"

"It's fine. No big deal." Her voice quaked, and she cleared her throat. "I put leftovers in the fridge. I'm going home now. *Gut nacht.*" She took a step toward the doorway, and he moved to block her. "Excuse me."

Korey held up his hands. "Michelle, forgive me. It's all my fault."

Michelle lifted her chin and tried to stop her hands from trembling. "Korey, please let me by."

"Let's talk about this, okay?" Korey's dark eyes pleaded with her. "I messed up."

She breathed in through her nose. "I have to get up early tomorrow to do my chores, which means I need to go home." She reached into her apron pocket and swallowed a groan when she realized she'd forgotten her flashlight. Then she craned her neck over her shoulder to where Tyler remained by the sink, his expression hesitant. "Could I please use your flashlight, Tyler? I left mine at home."

"Sure," Tyler said. "It's in the mudroom."

Korey held his hand out to her. "Michelle, please let me walk you home so we can talk. I'll make it up to you."

She hesitated as she took in the contrition she found in the lines of his face. "Fine," she mumbled.

"Just let me run to the restroom, and then we'll head to your *haus,* okay?"

She nodded and then peered down at the toes of her shoes as her eyes started to sting. She sniffed. *Don't cry! Keep it together, Michelle!*

After Korey left the room, she felt a hand on her arm, and her gaze flickered to Tyler's sympathetic face.

"I'm sorry he hurt you," he whispered.

She sniffed and shrugged. "Like I said, it's not a big deal." Her voice came out in a quiet rasp.

His expression became incredulous. "It *is* a big deal." He handed her a tissue, and she wiped her eyes and nose.

"You want to know what makes it worse?" She tossed the used tissue in the trash can. "I thought maybe he might propose tonight since we've been together more than a year now." She faced Tyler and found pity in his eyes.

Oh no. I said too much!

"I'm sorry," she said, shaking her head as if it would chase away the humiliation swelling in her chest. "Forget I said anything."

Tyler opened his mouth and then closed it as he focused on something behind her.

She spun toward Korey, standing in the doorway, looking humble. "I'm ready."

"I made you a gift. It took me all week." Michelle pointed to the milk can on the table.

Korey nodded. "Oh. That's cool. Thanks." He held up his flashlight. "We should go." Then he stepped out the doorway.

"Gut nacht," Tyler said softly.

Michelle nodded and then scurried toward the front door.

"I'm so sorry," Korey repeated as they walked down the road together, their shoes crunching on the pavement.

The stars sparkling above them seemed to mock Michelle's foul mood. The scent of rain she'd smelled earlier was replaced by the familiar aroma of animals and wet grass while the cicadas sang their usual song.

Michelle kept her eyes trained on her dark house at the end of the road. If only she

93

had brought her own flashlight! Then she could have trotted ahead alone, locked herself in her bedroom, and allowed her tears to break free privately.

"I know I messed up. Our date completely slipped my mind, and when Dwight called me asking for help, I just —"

"Do you even love me?" she demanded, spinning to face him and interrupting his words.

Korey nodded. "Of course I do."

"Then why don't you ever tell me that you do? You used to tell me all the time. Why did you stop saying it?"

"I-I don't know. It's just not easy for me to express my feelings."

"We've been together for thirteen months, Korey." Her voice quavered. "That's more than a year. By now I would have imagined you were open to expressing how you feel to me. You'd think it would be second nature."

He swallowed, and when he remained silent, the truth besieged her.

"Do you want to break up?" Her words came out in a rough whisper.

"No." He shook his head. "No, I don't, Michelle. I just messed up tonight. Please give me another chance, okay? I'll make it up to you. I'll make supper for you one night, okay?"

Michelle hesitated, wanting to believe him, but she could already feel the foundation of their relationship crumbling. She turned and barreled forward toward her house, longing for privacy.

Korey jogged after her. "Wait for me. Will you let me make you supper one night? I can make anything you'd like. Just tell me what you want."

"It's not necessary, Korey."

"You love spaghetti and meatballs. I could ask Jay to help me make it for you. He's a really *gut* cook."

"I'll think about it." Michelle kept walking, grateful they had reached her driveway. She quickened her pace, and relief rushed through her when she spotted a lantern glowing in the kitchen. Hopefully *Mamm* was still awake!

Just as she reached the porch steps, Korey gently took her arm and spun her to face him.

"Please look at me." His voice creaked. "I know you're angry with me, and you have every reason to be." He threaded his fingers with hers. "I need you to give me another chance. I don't want to break up. I promise I will do a better job of being your boyfriend if you give me a chance."

She looked up at him and couldn't bring herself to say no. After all, she could envision a wedding, a home, and a family in her mind's eye when she thought of their future. She couldn't give up on that dream. "Okay."

He released her hands, and she started up the stairs.

"Michelle."

She turned toward him once more, and he hopped up two steps before leaning down and kissing her cheek.

"Gut nacht," he said.

Michelle nodded and then slipped into the house. When she reached the kitchen, *Mamm* looked up from a cookbook and set her reading glasses on the table.

"How was supper?" *Mamm* smiled.

Michelle slipped into the chair across from *Mamm* and let her tote bag drop to the floor by her feet. "Tyler enjoyed it."

"Tyler? What about Korey?"

"He wasn't there." Michelle fingered the tan place mat and tried to stop her emotions from spilling from her eyes.

Mamm closed the cookbook. *"Ach* no, *mei liewe.* What happened?"

Michelle managed to keep her heartache and frustration at bay as she explained how she spent the evening with Tyler since Korey had forgotten about their date and

96

helped his best friend, Dwight, instead. She also detailed Korey's apology during their walk to her house.

"He begged me to forgive him, and he promised he'd do better." Michelle folded her arms on the place mat.

"And how do you feel about his apology?"

"I can't shake the feeling that he doesn't really love me. In fact, now I'm wondering if he ever has loved me."

"Do you want to break up?"

Michelle shook her head. *I want to get married!* "No."

"So then why don't you give him some grace? We all have made mistakes."

"You're right." Michelle nodded, but doubt still plagued her.

"What's on your mind?"

Michelle rested her chin on her palm. "Did *Dat* ever stand you up or hurt your feelings when you were dating?"

"Hmm." *Mamm* got a faraway look in her eyes as if contemplating the question. "We actually did have an argument before we were married, and we almost broke up."

Michelle sat up straight. "You never told me that."

"Looking back, it was petty, but at the time we both thought we were right. We were both stubborn."

"What did you argue about?"

Mamm gave a wistful smile. "We had been dating for about six months or so, and we were invited on a camping trip with our closest friends. We had planned to go, but at the last minute, your *dat* backed out to help his *bruder* with a project on his farm. I was angry because we had made these plans, and we were going with other couples. Of course, we had chaperones too. I didn't want to go alone and be the odd one out, you know?"

"So what happened?"

"Well, we had this ridiculous argument. Lots of yelling and cross words, and we broke up."

"No!" Michelle leaned forward.

Mamm nodded. "We did. I went on the trip without him, and my closest *freinden* told me that it would work out. I was certain it was over. A couple of days after I got back, your *dat* came to the house with a bouquet of flowers. We both apologized, and we agreed to give it another try. Then he told me that he had spoken to *mei dat* while I was gone on the trip, and he got permission to propose. We were married that following fall."

"Wow." Michelle heaved a deep breath.

"Do you think I'm being petty and stubborn?"

"No, *mei liewe.* I didn't mean that at all. He definitely hurt your feelings, and you have a right to be disappointed. But if you truly love him and would like the possibility of a future with him, I think it would be best if you give him some grace and allow him the chance to right his wrongs. Let him show you how much you mean to him and then see how you feel about planning a future with him."

Michelle nodded. "You're probably right."

Mamm reached over and took Michelle's hand in hers. "You're a sweet, kind, and thoughtful *maedel,* and I know you'll make the right choice. Maybe you got Korey's attention tonight and he realized how much he hurt you. Give him a chance to make it up to you. And if you're still doubting your relationship with him after that, then maybe it will be time to cut your ties. But don't give up on him so soon. God doesn't give up on us, right?"

"Right." Michelle nodded. *"Danki."*

Mamm pushed back her chair and stood. *"Gern gschehne.* Now get some sleep."

"Gut nacht." Michelle picked up a small flashlight and headed upstairs to her room.

As she changed into her nightgown and

brushed her hair, she allowed her mother's words to roll through her mind while she replayed the events of the evening. She couldn't stop herself from wondering if Korey's heart was still in their relationship.

By the time she climbed into bed, she found one question still haunting her — Would Korey ever propose, or would he eventually give up on her?

Tyler sat on the porch swing, his eyes trained on the driveway while he waited for Korey to return from walking Michelle home. The lantern at his feet illuminated his impatient foot as it tapped the floor.

He folded his arms over his chest and sucked in a deep breath as he tried to imagine what he would say to Korey. He'd promised himself to stop letting Korey get under his skin, to be more patient and more understanding, to respect his middle brother. But how could he possibly respect Korey when he clearly took Michelle for granted?

Tyler had been stunned when Michelle had arrived at the door with the meal and gift for Korey. The disappointment and hurt on her face were clear when he told her that Korey wasn't there, and he'd invited her to stay, hoping that Korey would arrive home soon to enjoy what she had brought to share.

As the evening wore on, Tyler had enjoyed talking with her, and he'd found himself opening up to her without a second thought. He leaned back on the swing and raked his hand through his thick hair. He recalled the tears shimmering in her blue eyes when she admitted that she had believed Korey might propose to her tonight. He had been so surprised by her confession that he'd found himself speechless. She was funny, honest, intelligent, and sweet. And he couldn't understand why his brother would risk losing her.

A beam of a flashlight bumped along the driveway, and Tyler sat forward, resting his elbows on his thighs. He tried to tamp down his anger and frustration with his brother as the flashlight drew closer and Korey's silhouette came into view.

Korey reached the bottom step and then stilled, his face twisting into a simmering stare. "Let me guess. You waited out here to lecture me about what a lousy boyfriend I am. Well, don't waste your breath. I know I messed up, and I'm going to make things right."

"I don't want to argue, Kore." Tyler held his hand up. "I just want to talk."

"About what?"

"About Michelle."

Korey started up the steps. "Ty, it's none of your business." He yanked open the back door.

"It's my business when she cries to me," Tyler called over his shoulder.

Korey stopped and faced him. "What's that supposed to mean?"

"It means she was upset that you weren't here. And she was near tears when you came home and admitted you had forgotten about her. She had prepared your favorite meal and painted that gorgeous milk can for you, but you had forgotten her."

The *clip-clop* of horse hooves and the whir of buggy wheels drew Tyler's attention to the driveway, where a horse and buggy approached the barn.

"*Dat*'s home," Korey muttered and then pulled the door open again.

Tyler stood. "Wait."

With a dramatic sigh, Korey let the storm door click shut and then turned toward Tyler again. "Look. I don't need advice from someone who hasn't been in a relationship in years."

"Just give me the benefit of the doubt. I mean it when I say that I don't want to argue with you. In fact, I'm tired of always arguing with you."

"Then keep your nose out of my business," Korey seethed.

Tyler's jaw worked as he felt himself losing his temper.

"Hello," Crystal, their stepmother, said as she climbed the porch steps and stood between them.

Tyler nodded. "How was supper?"

"It was very nice. The *kinner* missed you both." She looked at Korey and then at Tyler, her brow wrinkling. "Is everything okay here?"

"*Ya,* of course. We were just talking." Tyler fastened a bright smile on his lips and hoped it was convincing.

Korey was taciturn, but he pulled the door open for Crystal.

"*Danki,*" she said. "Well, *gut nacht.*"

"Good night, Crystal," Tyler said.

He and Korey remained silent for a few moments, and then Korey's frown returned.

"I don't need you butting into my relationship with Michelle."

"I realize that, but I still don't understand why you take her for granted." Tyler stopped and bit back more accusing words. "Look, Korey, all I wanted to say was that she really cares for you, and you should be more aware of how you treat her. That's all. It's just a little bit of brotherly advice."

Korey snorted. "Right. Because you really care about me. Tyler, the only person you care about is yourself."

"What do you mean by that?"

"Just think about it." Korey nearly spat the words at him before disappearing into the house.

Tyler rubbed his face, trying to scrub away his misery. *Great job! We wound up arguing again!*

"Everything okay?"

Tyler turned and leaned against the side of the house as *Dat* and Jayden came up the steps. "Yeah."

"I'm heading upstairs to shower," Jayden said and continued into the house.

Dat remained on the porch, studying Tyler. "Did you and Korey have another argument?"

"Sort of, but I had just tried to give him advice. He took it the wrong way." Then Tyler explained how Michelle had come by to bring Korey a meal and a gift, but Korey had forgotten they had made plans. He shared how he and Michelle had talked all evening and that she was upset when Korey finally got home. "I just tried to tell him that he needed to not take her for granted or he was going to lose her."

Dat pursed his lips. "I know you mean well, but you need to let Korey live his life and figure out his mistakes on his own."

"If you'd only seen how upset she was, you'd understand why I want to try to help them."

"That's kind of you, but some lessons you just have to learn through experience." *Dat* gave Tyler's shoulder a gentle pat. "It's getting late. We need to be up early in the morning."

Tyler walked into the kitchen and said good night to *Dat* and Crystal before heading up to the second floor.

As Tyler moved down the hallway to his room, he smiled as he recalled his conversation with Michelle. He considered her thoughts about Charity, and he felt excitement build in his chest. He just might take her advice and ask Charity out. Maybe it was time for him to start dating.

Chapter 8

"I'm so sorry, Michelle. I can't believe he forgot about your date," Charity said Saturday afternoon.

The delectable scent of oatmeal butterscotch cookies baking in the oven filled the kitchen while Michelle sat across from her best friend at the table. Charity had invited her over to bake cookies for the youth gathering Sunday afternoon, and since Charity's parents had gone out shopping for supplies, Michelle took the opportunity to fill her in on what happened Thursday night.

Michelle shrugged as if Korey's standing her up hadn't shattered her hopes and dreams for their future. "It's okay. *Mei mamm* told me to give him some grace, and he's apologized numerous times."

"Have you talked to him since Thursday?"

Michelle picked up her glass of iced tea. "*Ya.* He called and asked if he could pick

106

me up for the youth gathering tomorrow. He insists he'll make it up to me, so I'm giving him a chance." She took a long drink.

"Wow." Charity shook her head. "I'm so surprised at him." She hesitated, and then pink infused her cheeks. "So, you said you ate with Tyler, right?"

"We did talk about you if that's what you want to ask me." Michelle smiled.

Charity reached across the table. "Tell me everything."

"I encouraged him to ask you out. I told him that you're sweet and *schee.*"

"And you told him I liked him?"

Michelle nodded.

"What did he say, Michelle?" Charity demanded.

"I think he's going to talk to you."

"Oh, *danki*! You're the best."

"You don't have to thank me. Tyler and I had a really *gut* talk. He's sweet and a very *gut* listener. I'm sure he'll be a wonderful boyfriend to you."

"I can't wait," Charity said. Then she smiled. "And I'm sure Korey will treat you better now. I'm glad you're giving him another chance."

"I'm praying it works out."

The timer buzzed, and Michelle popped up. "Let's check these *kichlin.*"

107

As Michelle turned her attention to the cookies, she hoped her best friend was right and Korey would become the boyfriend and eventually the husband she hoped he'd be.

"So, you all are headed to Paradise for that combined youth gathering today?" *Dat* asked Sunday during breakfast.

"*Ya.*" Tyler nodded and glanced around the table at his brothers. "I think we should take our own buggies today."

"I was already planning to take mine to pick up Michelle." Korey scooped more scrambled eggs onto his plate.

Crystal smiled as she added cream and sugar to her coffee mug. "That's nice. I just love that milk can she painted for you. I never knew she was so artistic. I remember the day I first met Michelle. She told me that she enjoyed working in the garden, but I never knew she could paint too."

Korey said nothing as he studied his plate.

Tyler bit his lip. While he'd had misgivings when his father had decided to marry Crystal a year ago, he had worked to be respectful to his stepmother. Korey, however, still gave Crystal the silent treatment, often not responding to her when she spoke. Tyler held his breath, fighting back the urge to tell his brother to answer Crystal.

108

Then he reminded himself that he would do his best to be more patient and prove to his father he was professional and mature enough to run his own crew. So, instead of verbally attacking his middle brother, he took a bite of his bacon.

"I didn't know Michelle could paint either," *Dat* said. "That milk can is lovely. I like where you put it in the *schtupp* so that we can all enjoy it."

Jayden nodded. "I agree. She's talented."

"I suggested she sell them at a gift shop." Tyler picked up another piece of bacon. "She said she was going to ask her *dat* for permission. I told her that she'll have trouble keeping those milk cans stocked in the store."

Crystal held her fork up in agreement. "Oh *ya*! I agree. The tourists will love them."

"Don't you think so, Korey?" Tyler asked.

Korey nodded but kept eating.

Tyler eyed him as irritation threaded through him. He couldn't remember the last time Korey had actively participated in a family discussion since their father remarried. "Aren't you proud of your girlfriend's talent, Korey?"

Korey blinked at him. "*Ya,* of course I am."

"Have you spoken to her since Thursday?" Tyler asked.

"I already mentioned I'm picking her up today, so *ya,* if it's any of your business, I called her."

"Gut." Tyler lifted his mug of *kaffi* and took a sip.

Korey eyed him. "You know, Ty, I've been dating Michelle for more than a year, so I think I can handle this. You need to back off and worry about the fact that you're still single."

"All right," *Dat* said. "That's enough, you two."

"Korey, I think it's wonderful that you and Michelle are working things out. I'm proud of you for apologizing and making things right. Everyone makes mistakes," Crystal told him with a smile.

Korey set his utensils on his plate and stood. "Excuse me. I'm going to finish getting ready to leave." Then he carried his plate and mug to the counter before disappearing through the doorway that led toward the stairs.

A hush fell over the kitchen as everyone continued eating.

After several moments, Tyler looked up. "I'm so tired of his attitude, and if Kore doesn't treat Michelle right, he's going to

110

lose her."

"Tyler, I know you feel compelled to give your *bruder* advice," *Dat* began, "but I've told you that Korey needs to figure out his relationships on his own."

Jayden smirked over at Tyler and changed the subject. "Are you taking your own buggy today because you're planning to ask a *maedel* if you can give her a ride home?"

"Possibly." Tyler shrugged.

Crystal clapped. "Who is she?"

"I'm so grateful, Tyler. You finally are taking my advice. You should be planning to settle down soon. After all, you're twenty-five," *Dat* said.

"Calm down." Tyler held up his hands. "There's no need to plan a wedding just yet. I'm only thinking about asking to give her a ride home. That's all."

Jayden grinned. "But it's a start."

"That's right," *Dat* agreed.

They finished their breakfast, and Jayden and Tyler helped gather up the plates and utensils and carried them to the counter while Crystal began filling one side of the sink with hot, soapy water.

"*Danki* for your help," Crystal told them. "You two run along and get ready to go."

Jayden padded out of the kitchen.

When Tyler followed him, *Dat* called him back.

"*Ya?*" Tyler asked *Dat*.

"Who is the *maedel* you're going to ask to give a ride home?" *Dat* stood by the counter.

Tyler hesitated. "Charity Swarey."

"Oh, she's sweet," Crystal said while scrubbing a dish.

"Now remember — I'm just giving her a ride. Don't start making plans for us, okay?" Tyler cautioned.

Crystal chuckled and rinsed the dish.

"I won't start making plans, but it is about time, *sohn,*" *Dat* said.

"We'll see what happens, *Dat.*"

"*Gude mariye,*" Michelle said as she climbed into Korey's buggy.

Birds sang in nearby trees as if celebrating the bright blue sky and the warm mid-September day.

Korey handed her a small bag. "I have something for you."

"Oh." Her lips lifted in a smile as she picked up the bag. "What a surprise." She opened it and pulled out a small bag of her favorite caramel-flavored popcorn. "Oh wow. How nice. *Danki.*" She leaned over and kissed his cheek.

He took her hands in his. "*Gern gschehne.*

I just wanted to do something for you to show you how sorry I am. I won't take you for granted anymore. *Danki* for giving me another chance."

"You can stop apologizing now."

"I feel like I need to keep apologizing." He scowled. "Tyler has given me so much grief about it this week. He keeps bringing it up."

"Really?" Michelle felt her eyebrows lift.

Korey's frown deepened. "*Ya,* really. I don't need my bossy older *bruder* giving me dating advice, especially when he's not even dating anyone." He leaned back against the door. "Anyway, I'd like to have you over for supper one night."

"I'll bring a meal then."

"No, I'll cook for you."

"Korey, you work long hours doing hard, physical labor. I don't expect you to cook for me, and I don't want Crystal to have to cook for me."

He cupped his hand to her cheek. "I want to do something for you. Let me make you supper, okay?"

She nodded and felt the pieces of her heart coming back together. Yet, at the same time, deep in her stomach, she felt a strange pit forming. As much as she wanted Korey to propose to her, she couldn't stop the feeling that he wasn't in a rush to get married, and she wasn't sure how long she could wait for him.

Michelle found her friends standing together near the volleyball nets. She said hello just as Charity took her arm and led her away from the group.

"Excuse us," Charity said over her shoulder to their friends before steering Michelle to a nearby tree. "How are things with Korey?" she asked once they were out of earshot from the groups of young people chatting and the folks playing volleyball over by the four nets.

"Fine." Michelle shrugged.

Charity lifted a blond eyebrow. "Just fine?"

"It's *gut.* He apologized and gave me a bag of my favorite popcorn. He says he wants to have me over for supper, and he'll cook."

Charity gave her hand a gentle squeeze. "That's great news! Maybe he'll even ask your *dat* permission to propose soon."

"We'll see." Michelle turned just as Tyler walked by with Jonah and a few of their friends. "There's Tyler."

When he met her gaze, he waved, and she returned the gesture.

Charity waved, too, as she whispered, "He

looks so *gut* today in that dark-blue shirt."

Michelle smiled at her. "He might offer to give you a ride home today."

"Oh goodness!" Charity smoothed her hands down her purple dress and black apron. "Do I look okay?"

"Charity, you always look beautiful, but most importantly, you're a kind and thoughtful person. He'd be blessed to call you his girlfriend."

Her best friend hugged her and whispered in her ear, "I'm blessed to have you as *mei freind.*"

"It's mutual," Michelle said, smiling.

Later that afternoon, Michelle descended the Zook family's porch steps and strolled toward the barn, where the youth group had gathered for lunch. The murmur of conversations floated out of the barn as she drew closer.

"Michelle!"

She turned to where Tyler walked toward her from the stable. She folded her arms and gave him a feigned pointed look. "What are you doing lurking out here?"

"Lurking?" He laughed. "Not exactly. It's my turn to check on the horses."

"Oh. Have you tried the desserts yet?" she

asked as he closed the distance between them.

"Why? Do you have any recommendations?"

She looked up at him, and for the first time, she noticed how handsome he was with those hazel eyes, dark hair, and angular jaw. "Charity and I tried a new *kichli* recipe, and I was wondering how everyone liked them."

He adjusted his straw hat on his thick, dark hair. "What kind did you bake?"

"Oatmeal butterscotch."

"Oh." He rested his hands on his flat abdomen. "They sound divine."

"Well, I hope they are."

"I'll let you know." He slipped his hands into his pockets and looked down at the toes of his shoes, suddenly seeming self-conscious. "I'm going to ask Charity if I can give her a ride home today."

"Oh, that's fantastic. She's going to be thrilled."

He kicked a pebble with his shoe and then rubbed his chin. "You think so?"

"Don't be *gegisch,* Tyler. She likes you a lot."

"We'll see." He folded his arms over his wide chest. "How are things with you and Kore?"

"Better. *Danki* for talking to him. He's apologized numerous times, and he brought a little gift this morning. He insists he's going to make supper for me one night."

Tyler scowled, shaking his head.

"Was iss letz?"

"My hot-headed *bruder* should do more than that."

Michelle opened her mouth to ask him what he thought Korey should do, but then she closed it.

"*Mei dat,* Crystal, and Jay were so impressed by your milk can painting. Crystal suggested putting it in the *schtupp* so everyone can enjoy it."

"*Danki.* That means a lot."

"I'm just telling the truth." He shrugged. "Are you working on any other milk cans?"

"*Ya,* I started on a couple of others. I've been trying to make each one unique."

"I'd love to see them." Tyler's attention moved to something behind Michelle, and he nodded. *"Wie geht's?"*

Michelle craned her neck over her shoulder and smiled at Korey. "Hi, Korey."

Korey's gaze bounced from Michelle to Tyler and then back to Michelle once again, and he looked curious or possibly confused. *"Wie geht's?"*

"We were just talking." Michelle shrugged.

117

"What are you doing?"

Tyler rubbed his hands together. "Well, I'll see you both later." He sauntered toward the barn.

"Hey, Tyler," she called.

He spun and faced her while walking backward. *"Ya?"*

"You'll do great later when you ask."

"I'll let you know how it goes." He continued toward the barn.

"What was that about?" Korey asked.

"Tyler is planning to ask Charity to ride home with him today. I was just encouraging him."

"You sure?" Korey ran his tongue over his teeth. "It looked like more than that."

"We were just talking."

"So, you're not punishing me for forgetting our date on Thursday?"

"Why would you accuse me of doing that?"

Korey gestured widely. "Because you haven't ever spoken to *mei bruder* except in passing. But ever since Thursday night, you act like he's your new best *freind.*"

"That's ridiculous," she told him. "I've known you and your *bruders* my whole life, and I've always been friendly with them."

"This is different. It seems like it's something else."

"Are you joking?" She laughed, brushing her hands down her black apron and green dress. When he continued to frown, she gaped at him. "You're serious?"

"You two looked awfully comfortable together."

"Korey, are you jealous?"

He looked down at the toes of his shoes. "No."

"Korey, look at me." She placed her finger under his chin and gently moved his face so that his eyes focused on her. "My heart belongs to you and only you."

"You sure?" he whispered.

She smiled. "*Ya,* I'm positive."

"Okay." His shoulders visibly relaxed.

She threaded her fingers with his. "Let's go finish our lunch."

Michelle steered Korey toward the barn as she contemplated his newfound jealousy. Perhaps he'd finally start being the boyfriend she'd always hoped he'd be and consider what their future might look like.

CHAPTER 9

Later that evening, Tyler's throat dried as he walked over to where Charity stood by her friends on the Zooks' back porch. Stars sparkled in the dark sky, and four lamps illuminated the porch with their happy, yellow glow.

He swiped his sweaty hands over his trousers and sucked in a ragged breath and then approached her. Now was the time to ask her to ride home with him. But what if she rejected him in front of her group of a half-dozen friends? He'd never live down the humiliation! In fact, it would be much worse than the day when he ran over Michelle during the volleyball game.

Michelle caught his eyes before she blessed him with a warm smile and an encouraging nod.

He felt his nerve endings ease as he smiled back, and a sudden surge of confidence propelled him forward. "Charity?" he asked.

Charity stopped speaking to Kendra and then turned toward him. Her pretty green eyes widened. "Yes?"

"Would you like to ride home with me?"

She nodded, the ties to her prayer covering bouncing off her slight shoulder. "I'd like that very much."

"Great." Tyler blew out a sigh of relief. When he peeked over at Michelle, she gave him a thumbs-up. He bit his lip to stop himself from chuckling. She was adorable!

Charity and Tyler said good night to her friends and then walked over to his waiting horse and buggy.

"Did you have fun today?" he asked as he opened the passenger door for her.

She climbed in. "*Ya*, I did."

"*Gut.*" He jogged around to the driver's side and hopped in. "It's a *schee* night."

"*Ya*, it is."

Tyler guided the horse toward the road, following a line of horses and buggies also starting their journey toward home. Silence filled the empty space between them, and he racked his brain for something to say to her. "So," he finally began, "how's your family?"

"*Gut.*"

He stared at the red taillights blinking back at them as the horses and buggies moved down the road. The hum of wheels and the *clip-clop* of hooves filled the buggy.

"How's your family?" she asked.

"Gut." He smiled over at her. "I imagine *mei haus* is much more chaotic than yours since you're an only child."

Charity laughed. *"Ya,* I imagine so.

Silence stretched between them again, and Tyler shifted in the seat. Were all first dates this awkward? Or was he just really bad at this?

"So . . ." he began. "Do you have any hobbies?"

"I like to sew, quilt, and bake."

"Oh, right. You and Michelle made those *appeditlich kichlin.* "

Charity angled her body toward him on the seat. "Did you like them?"

"Very much. Where did you find that recipe?"

"It was in one of my favorite cookbooks."

"How nice."

They both were quiet, and he once again felt at a loss for words. His mind wandered, and he contemplated Michelle. He imagined she and Korey were having a more riveting conversation during their ride home. Korey's curious expression filled Tyler's mind as he recalled their conversation outside the barn during lunch. He hoped Korey wasn't angry with Michelle and him for becoming friends. After all, they might be family someday if Korey married her. He swallowed a snort. That would happen only if his brother got his act together and started treating Michelle better.

"Tyler?"

"Ya?" He gave Charity a sideways glance and found her watching him. "I'm sorry. Did you say something?"

"I asked you if you have any hobbies."

He shrugged. "I work with wood sometimes."

"Really?" she asked as if he was the most fascinating man in Lancaster County. "What do you like to make?"

"Mei dat likes to make wooden trains and donate them to Christmas toy drives, and I help him in the fall."

"You'll have to show me one sometime."

"They're very basic, but I enjoyed the one he made for me when I was a kid."

"How nice."

Tyler halted the horse at a red light, and he shared an awkward smile with Charity as they both ran out of things to say. *This is going to be a long ride home.*

"Do you and Michelle bake together often?" he asked.

"We do every once in a while."

"That's great. What do you like to bake?" He guided the horse through the intersection while Charity listed a variety of cookies, cakes, pies, and breads that she and Michelle had baked together.

Too soon Charity ran out of items to list, and the buggy fell quiet once again.

"Have you seen the milk cans Michelle has painted?"

Charity turned toward him. "No, but she's told me about them."

"You need to see one. I had no idea how talented she was. She never told me that she painted."

"Oh *ya*. She's always loved to draw while her *mamm* and *schweschdere* quilted."

Tyler nodded slowly. "How interesting. I've known her all my life, but she never shared that before."

"I like to quilt."

"Do you sell your quilts?"

"*Ya,* or donate them to fundraising auctions."

Charity spent the remainder of their journey to her house discussing her favorite quilt patterns. Tyler tried to focus on her words, but his mind kept wandering to thoughts of work and his to-do list for tomorrow.

Soon they arrived at her farm, and he

walked her to her back porch with his flashlight illuminating their path.

"*Danki* for giving me a ride home," she said as they stood by her back door.

Tyler shook her hand. "I enjoyed it. *Gut nacht.*"

"I hope to see you soon, Tyler."

He nodded and then loped back to his buggy.

After making the short trip home, he stowed his buggy and horse and ambled into the house. He was surprised to find *Dat* sitting in the family room, reading a book.

"I thought you'd be in bed by now," Tyler said as he sat on the sofa across from him.

Dat set his book down on the end table beside him. "I wanted to hear how your night went."

"It was fine." Tyler rested his right ankle on his left knee.

"Just fine?"

Tyler chuckled. "What do you want me to say?"

"Did you have a *gut* time? Do you want to see her again?"

"I guess so." Tyler drummed his fingers on his shin. "I'm just not sure we have anything in common."

"Why do you say that?"

"We had a tough time keeping the conversation going. It was pretty awkward."

Dat smiled. "Well, that's what dating is all about — becoming acquainted and seeing if you might want to continue getting to know each other and then build a future together."

Tyler leaned back in the chair. "She's really eager and has a crush on me."

"And why is that a bad thing?"

"What if I don't live up to her expectations? I feel like I'm going to let her down when she really gets to know me."

"Why don't you just give her a chance? You only gave her a ride home. Spend some time talking to her. Go visit her. After you've made an effort to get to know her, then you can decide if you're right for each other."

Tyler nodded. "All right." Then he stood. "Well, *danki* for waiting up. I'll see you in the morning."

"Gut nacht, sohn."

Tyler's footfalls echoed in the stairwell as he made his way to his room. He contemplated the day and grinned when he recalled how Michelle had given him a thumbs-up.

He got ready for bed and wondered how the rest of Michelle's evening went, and he pondered what Charity might tell Michelle about him. He couldn't wait to talk to Michelle again.

126

■ ■ ■ ■

"Tell me everything about your ride home with Tyler last night," Michelle said to Charity as they sat in Charity's kitchen the following afternoon.

Michelle had finished her chores quickly and then rushed over to Charity's house to spend the remainder of the afternoon visiting with her.

Charity picked up her mug of tea and grinned. "Tyler is just as wonderful as I imagined he would be."

"And . . . ?"

"And we had a nice conversation. We talked about hobbies and things like that." A dreamy sigh escaped her lips. "He's so friendly and good-looking. Oh, I like him so much. I can't wait to see him again."

Michelle reached across the table and gave her hands a gentle squeeze. "I knew you two would get along well. Did he say when he'll see you again?"

"No." Charity cupped her hands around her blue mug. "I was thinking we should double-date."

Michelle nodded and then sipped her tea. "*Ya.* I'd like that."

"Did everything go well with Korey

last night?"

"It did." Michelle held her warm mug. "He insists he's going to invite me over for supper one night this week, and he promised to call me soon."

"I'm glad to hear that." Charity smiled as she lifted her mug, and they toasted each other. "Everything is going well for us."

"It is." Michelle smiled, but she still couldn't stop herself from worrying that Korey might stand her up for his friends once again.

Later that evening, Tyler scooped some rice onto his plate beside his breaded pork chop and mixed vegetables and then handed the bowl of rice to Jayden. "So, *Dat,*" he began while cutting up his pork chop, "we'll finish the job in Ronks on Wednesday and then start on the job over in New Millton. I can go tomorrow and give the customer in Bellemont an estimate if you'd like."

Dat nodded and swallowed. "*Ya,* that's a good plan. You can handle the estimate."

"*Danki.*" Tyler bit back a grin. He was beginning to regain *Dat*'s confidence. This was a step toward running his own crew.

Korey cleared his throat and peeked over at Crystal. "May I invite Michelle for supper this week?"

"Of course." Crystal gave him a sweet smile. "She's always welcome here."

Tyler lifted his glass of water as Korey continued to frown at Crystal. His father and Crystal had been married for nearly a year, and his middle brother still treated Crystal like an unwanted stranger. Korey needed to grow up — *fast.*

"What are you going to cook for Michelle, Kore?" Tyler asked with a smirk.

"Oh, I know!" Jayden teased, holding up his fork. "How about hot dogs and potato chips?"

Tyler snorted, and Korey fixed each of his brothers with a foul expression.

"Korey doesn't need to cook. I don't mind cooking for Michelle at all. Just let me know what you'd like me to make, Korey," Crystal said.

With a shrug, Korey turned his attention back to his dish, and irritation threaded through Tyler. When would his middle brother treat Crystal with respect? Sometimes Tyler longed for his father to scold Korey, but he had a feeling that Crystal had encouraged *Dat* to stop correcting Korey and allow him to come around on his own. But Korey had had a year to adapt to their stepmother, and he still behaved like a spoiled child who hadn't gotten his way.

Dat wiped his beard with a napkin and smiled over at his wife. "How about your parmesan chicken?"

"That sounds *appeditlich,*" Tyler said.

Jayden nodded. "I love your parmesan chicken, Crystal."

"Does that sound okay to you, Korey?" Crystal's voice and expression were almost too eager.

"Sure. *Danki,*" he muttered while he studied his pork chop as if it held all of the answers to his problems.

"How about Thursday?"

Korey met her gaze and nodded. "*Ya, that's gut.*" Then he cast his eyes back down at the plate. "*Danki.*"

"*Gern gschehne.* I look forward to seeing her," Crystal said.

Tyler took another drink from his glass of water. He would get to see Michelle on Thursday, and he looked forward to it too. He hoped to get a moment to talk to her about Charity.

"Michelle!" Jorie called as she burst through the mudroom into the kitchen after supper. "*Dat*'s calling you. Korey's on the phone."

"Oh!" Michelle turned from the counter where she had been stowing dishes. Korey had kept his promise!

Jorie joined her. "Go take the call. I'll finish the dishes."

"Danki!" Michelle rushed out to the barn and found the receiver sitting on the little desk next to the pad and pencil where she and her family members wrote down voice mail messages. She smiled as she held the receiver to her ear. "Korey?"

"Hi. I wanted to invite you to join my family and me for supper Thursday night."

She smiled. "I'd love to. I'll bring dessert."

"No, I believe I owe you dessert."

"Don't be *gegisch.*" She laughed as she sank down onto the stool in front of the small desk. "I've wanted to make a banana cream pie for some time. How does that sound?"

"Perfect. We should be home from work by six."

"I can't wait to see you."

"You too."

Michelle hung up the phone and grinned. Perhaps she and Korey would be all right. If only she could convince her heart to trust him completely once again.

CHAPTER 10

While balancing a pie plate in one hand, Michelle knocked on the Bontrager family's back door Thursday evening.

After a few moments, the door opened, and Crystal smiled at her. "Hi, Michelle. I wasn't expecting you until six."

"I wanted to help cook."

Crystal shook her head and stepped back from the storm door. "You are just so sweet and thoughtful. Come on in."

Michelle followed her into the kitchen, where she set the pie in the refrigerator. "Put me to work."

Together they gathered the ingredients and began breading the chicken.

"It was very kind of you to cook tonight," Michelle said as she placed a chicken breast on a plate. She tried to mask the frustration that rolled through her. She had told Korey that she didn't want Crystal to cook for her, but here Crystal was preparing the meal. If only Korey would put more effort in . . .

Crystal smiled at her. "I could tell Korey wanted to have you over, and I didn't think it was necessary for him to have to come home from work and cook for you."

"I appreciate that you're doing this, and I'm so grateful I could help." Michelle finished breading the chicken while Crystal prepared a pan with oil.

"I'm glad that you and Korey could work things out after he forgot about your plans. I'm sure that hurt your feelings, but I know he didn't mean to."

"*Danki. Ya,* I know. I could tell he was distracted the night I mentioned it."

Soon all of the chicken was breaded and the pieces were sizzling in the hot oil.

"I can't wait to be married and have my own home," Michelle said as she set the table for six.

Crystal placed a basket of rolls in the center of the table. "I'm certain it will happen in God's perfect timing. I had begun to believe I wouldn't have the chance to become a *fraa,* and then I met Duane when I least expected it. Tomorrow is our first wedding anniversary."

"Oh my goodness!" Michelle said. "Happy anniversary."

"*Danki.* The year has gone by so quickly."

Michelle began filling the drinking glasses with water from a pitcher. "By any chance, does Korey ever talk about marriage?"

"Not to me, but that doesn't mean he hasn't said anything to Duane about it. Korey doesn't talk to me unless I ask him a direct question, and then I sometimes receive only a nod or a grunt for a response."

Michelle frowned. "I had hoped he had matured by now. I'm so sorry he's still behaving that way."

"It's not your fault. I pray every night that Korey will accept me and not see me as a threat to his *mamm*'s memory, but that will happen when God sees fit to warm his heart toward me."

"You are such a blessing to this family."

"Danki." Crystal opened the refrigerator. "Would you please help me put together a salad?"

"Of course."

Tyler walked up the porch steps and into the mudroom, where he removed his work boots and hung his straw hat on a peg. The sound of women talking and laughing, along with the delicious smell of Crystal's parmesan chicken, floated over him as he entered the kitchen.

Michelle placed a platter of chicken on the table and then smiled over at him. "Tyler! I didn't see you standing there."

"I just got home." He admired her bright smile and took in how beautiful she was. Her blue eyes reminded him of the clear sky, and her pink dress complemented her rosy cheeks and lips.

Then he mentally shook himself. Michelle was Korey's girlfriend!

Tyler cleared his throat and peered over at his stepmother. "Supper smells fantastic."

"*Danki.* Where are your *bruders* and *dat*?"

"On their way in."

"How was your day, Tyler?" Michelle placed a large bowl of salad in the center of the table.

"*Gut.* We finished up a small project today. How was yours?"

"I had a very productive day. I finished my chores, did some painting, and came here to help Crystal with supper."

Crystal carried a bottle of homemade dressing over to the table. "I just love that milk can you painted for Korey. You're so talented, Michelle."

"*Danki.*" Michelle gave her a sheepish expression, and she looked charming.

Stop it, Tyler! She's Korey's girlfriend, not yours!

He crossed to the sink and began scrubbing his hands. "How many milk cans did you paint?"

"I finished one and started on a second one." She leaned against the counter beside him. "And I spoke to Charity this week . . ."

Tyler lifted his eyebrows as he dried his hands. "Oh yeah? What did she have to say about me?"

"Well, she said that —"

"Michelle!" Korey grinned as he walked in. "You're here early."

Michelle pushed off the counter. "Hi, Korey. I made your banana cream pie."

"Danki." His brother's smile was warm and held something in it just for her.

Disappointment and an unexpected jealousy slithered through Tyler's veins as he watched Michelle focus all of her attention on his middle brother. Tyler tried to dismiss this strange awakening, but it continued to surge like a noxious weed, entwining his insides.

Dat and Jayden came in, and *Dat* kissed Crystal's cheek before scrubbing his hands at the sink.

After all of the men had washed their hands, everyone sat down to supper. Michelle and Korey sat across from Tyler and Jayden, while Tyler's father and stepmother

136

took their places at each end of the table.

After a silent prayer, they all began to fill their bowls with salad and their plates with the scrumptious chicken, rolls, and broccoli. Utensils scraped the dishes while they passed the serving platters around the table.

"This is fantastic, *mei liewe,*" *Dat* told Crystal.

"*Danki,* but Michelle gets the credit too. She helped cook," Crystal said.

Korey looked up from his plate and turned toward his girlfriend. "*Danki,* Michelle. I didn't expect you to come and help."

"You know I didn't want Crystal to cook for me." Michelle blushed. "It was fun."

"It's *appeditlich,*" Jayden said.

Tyler nodded. "*Ya,* it is."

"I'm so glad you like it," Crystal said. "So, tell me about your day."

Dat began talking about the project they had finished while Crystal peppered him with questions about the work.

Tyler tried to keep his focus on his father's words, but his eyes kept defying him and sneaking peeks at Michelle. Whenever her gaze tangled with his, she'd bless him with a sweet smile, and his heart hammered. At first he was certain he was losing his mind, but he just chalked it up to enjoying their new friendship.

At least he hoped that was what his visceral reaction to her meant.

After supper, Michelle and Crystal stacked the dirty dishes in the sink, and then Michelle carried her banana cream pie to the table while Crystal brewed coffee.

Michelle, Tyler, and his brothers reminisced about when they were younger while they enjoyed the scrumptious dessert.

Once their plates were clean, Michelle began stacking up their empty dessert plates, and Crystal gathered up their mugs.

Korey touched Michelle's arm, and she looked up at him. "I need to go help take care of the horses, but I'll meet you on the porch."

"Of course," Michelle said.

Tyler lingered in the doorway for a moment before forcing his feet to carry him outside and away from the strange feelings he felt brewing in his chest for Michelle.

Michelle stepped out onto the porch after she and Crystal had finished cleaning up the kitchen. She sat down on the porch swing and pushed it into motion while breathing in the comforting scent of animals and listening to the happy sounds of cicadas and frogs while a dog barked in the distance.

Above her the sun began to set, sending

its beautiful, vivid streaks of light across the sky. She hugged her arms to her waist and looked out toward the barn just as Tyler started up the rock path toward the house.

He smiled and waved as he picked up his pace. After trudging up the porch steps, he leaned back against the railing and lifted his straw hat before pushing his hand through this thick, dark hair. "You know, Michelle, it's not fair that you say you're going to tell me what Charity said about me and then you don't. In fact, I think in some cultures, that's considered cruel and unusual punishment."

She laughed, and when he grinned, she couldn't help but think he was handsome. All three of the Bontrager sons were tall like their father, but Tyler and Korey both had dark hair while Jayden's hair was sandy blond. Still, Tyler and Jayden had both inherited their mother's sparkling hazel eyes while Korey had his father's brown eyes.

Tyler also had a strong jaw with chiseled features that looked as if they were carved out of fine granite, a wide chest, muscular arms, and a trim waist. And then there was that boyish look about him . . .

"So, tell me now. What did Charity say about me?" Tyler pressed.

Michelle shrugged. "Not much."

"Michelle . . ."

"All right, all right." She held up her hands. "She really likes you. She had a nice time, and she hopes to see you again soon."

He studied her. "Are you holding back information? I thought we could trust each other."

"Well, I have to hold some information back since she's my best *freind.* I'm sure you would protect Jonah as much as I protect Charity."

He rubbed his jaw and his face filled with exasperation, making her laugh once again.

"Okay, Tyler. Stop making me laugh. She also said she wants to double-date."

Korey appeared on the steps and divided a look between them. "Who wants to double-date?"

"Tyler wanted to know what Charity said after he took her home Sunday night, and Charity wants the four of us to double-date," Michelle explained.

"Oh." Korey nodded. "That's fine with me."

Tyler held up his hands. "Hold on there now! I haven't asked her out yet."

"But you're going to, right? You told me that you liked her, and she obviously cares for you very deeply," she said.

"I don't know. I have so much going on at work."

"You're almost thirty, Tyler," she said. "Don't you want to get married?"

Tyler shrugged. "I guess someday, but I'm not in a hurry. And, by the way, I have five years before I'm thirty." He held up his hand. "Five."

"Don't you have somewhere to be?" Korey frowned at Tyler.

"Sorry, Kore." Tyler started toward the house and then turned and smiled at Michelle. "Keep me posted on what Charity says about me." Then he pulled the storm door open.

Michelle called after him, "Are you going to ask her out or not?"

He hesitated. "Yeah, I think so. I'll have to talk to her *dat.*" Then he pointed at her. "Don't you tell her."

"My lips are sealed." Michelle made a motion like she was locking her lips.

Tyler chuckled as he disappeared into the house.

Michelle laughed a little and then looked up at Korey. "Sit with me." She patted a spot on the swing beside her.

He sat down beside her and looked out toward the barn.

"You okay?" she asked. "You seem lost in

141

thought."

Korey angled his body toward her. "I was just thinking that I never imagined I'd double-date with *mei bruder.* It's a little strange."

"Why is it strange?"

He shrugged. "We've never been that close."

"Maybe this will bring you two closer together. I would have loved to have double-dated with Lainey, but she was dating before I was because she's older. I like spending time with Jorie. Double-dating with her would be fun, but she's not dating yet. Wouldn't you like to be close to Tyler?"

He pursed his lips. "I suppose so, but I don't know if we'll ever be. We're at odds too much."

"I think you two could be close if you both put in the effort." She touched his hand.

He shrugged, and they both turned their attention to the barn.

The pasture was now cloaked in darkness as the evening crept in, bringing with it cooler air.

"I had so much fun this evening cooking with Crystal. She's very sweet. She's such a blessing to your family."

Korey snorted.

Michelle turned toward him and touched

his hand once again. "Korey, I know you miss your *mamm.* I miss her, too, but you need to accept Crystal. She makes your *dat froh,* and she's so *gut* to you and your *bruders.*" She kept her tone warm, hoping to touch his heart.

"That's easy for you to say, Michelle, but you don't understand. You still have both of your parents."

"Your *mamm* was wonderful. I have many special memories of the times we spent with her. I do miss her very much, and I'm not saying that I completely understand how you feel. But I know your heart hurts for her, and I loved her, too, Korey."

His milk-chocolate eyes glistened in the light of the lantern. "It's not the same thing, and you have no right to tell me to just get over it."

"I'm not telling you to get over it. I would never be that cruel or insensitive." She gave his hand a gentle squeeze. "I'm just saying that Crystal is trying, and maybe you should too."

He looked out toward the barn again, and silence fell between them.

After several minutes, she stood. "I should get going. Would you please walk me home?"

"Of course."

After retrieving her pie plate and the portable dishes she had left at their house after she delivered the last meal, she and Korey started down the street toward her house.

Korey remained quiet, and she tried to think of something to say.

"Are you upset with me?" she finally asked him.

"No. I just have a lot on my mind."

She nudged him with her shoulder. "Penny for your thoughts?"

"Tyler asked *Dat* if he can hire a second crew to run, and I feel like he's trying to take over the company and leave me in the dust. He never wants me to be in on the decisions. He's eighteen months older than I am, but he acts like he's five years older and is entitled to everything. It's like he thinks the company is going to be solely his one day."

Michelle shook her head. "I'm sure he's not doing that."

"You really don't understand my relationship with Tyler." Korey stopped walking and studied her. "He has always tried to take things from me. He started this when we were little kids, and he hid toys we were supposed to share. That's why he and I could never be close."

"I understand that you had issues when you were *kinner*. All siblings do. I argued with *mei schweschdere,* but we're close now. Surely you two can work out your issues if you just try, Korey."

"Tyler and I aren't like you and your *schweschdere*. Not every family is like yours. He's always wanted the things that we were supposed to share, and *mei dat*'s business is no different."

"I think maybe you should talk to Tyler instead of just assuming he wants to steal the company out from under you. Maybe he wants to be close, but you assume he doesn't. Don't give up on your *bruder.*"

Korey remained silent for the remainder of the journey to her house. They walked up the driveway together and then stood by the back door.

"Gut nacht," he said before kissing her cheek. "I'll see you Sunday."

As Michelle walked into the house, she contemplated her discussions with Korey during the evening and found herself questioning her devotion to him. Was he even mature enough for marriage if she had to lecture him about both how he treated his stepmother and how he felt about his older brother in one night?

But if he wasn't ready for marriage, then

that meant their relationship wouldn't last the test of time. What kind of husband or father would he be if he was disrespectful to his stepmother and didn't trust his older brother?

She swallowed a groan as worry whirled through her. The idea of giving up on Korey and starting over with a new relationship made her limbs weary. She wouldn't give up on Korey just yet, but doubt still crept into the back of her mind, taunting her.

CHAPTER 11

"So, I've been thinking about what you said about expanding the company," *Dat* told Tyler while they sat on the roof of a large flea market in New Millton the following morning.

Tyler set his hammer down and sat back on his heels. "And?" He held his breath, awaiting his father's decision.

"I think it's time to let you try to run your own crew."

Excitement built in Tyler's chest. "*Danki, Dat.* I won't let you down."

"You can start interviewing to hire a crew, but I want final say in who you hire. The employees represent us." *Dat* pointed to his chest. "They have our company's reputation on the line. That means don't hire your *freinden* just because they're your *freinden*. You want to hire *gut,* reliable workers who will arrive at work on time and work, not sit around just to receive a paycheck. Understand?"

Tyler nodded. "*Ya,* I understand."

"I want to be part of these decisions," Korey said, stalking over to them. "I'm part of this company, too, and Tyler and I are almost the same age."

Tyler looked at *Dat* and then back at Korey. "Of course. You and I could run the crew together. I just didn't think you were interested."

"Of course I am," Korey said. "It's not just your company, Ty."

Dat smiled. "I'd like to see you two working together for once. That's a *gut* idea."

"I thought we could ask around at youth group to see if any of our *freinden* are interested in trying roofing as a career," Tyler suggested. Then he held up his hands. "But we'll only hire *freinden* that we know are truly interested in roofing and not just a job. We'll be sure that they really want to work and take it seriously. And we could run an ad in the paper too."

Korey pushed his mirrored sunglasses up on his nose. "I think that's a great idea."

Dat tapped Tyler's shoulder and then Korey's. "I'm *froh* to finally see you two work together toward a common goal. Keep it up and let me know when you've decided who to hire. I suggest you get two workers to help you, and I'll need two also."

"Danki, Dat." Tyler grinned. He couldn't wait to run his own crew and make his father proud.

Later Tyler finished hammering a shingle and then swiped his forearm over his sweaty brow.

"So, are you going to ask Charity to be your girlfriend?" Jayden asked.

Tyler picked up a box of nails. "Probably."

"What are you afraid of, Ty?" Korey's tone held the hint of a challenge.

"I'm not afraid of anything." Tyler recalled his conversation with Michelle and grinned. He enjoyed teasing her and hearing her sweet laugh. "Hey, Kore, if I do ask her out, what do you think about Charity's idea of you and Michelle going on double dates with us?"

Korey sat back on his heels. "Sure. Why not?"

Tyler returned to hammering, and while he worked, he recalled Michelle's confession about hoping Korey would propose. "Hey, Kore."

"Ya?" Korey turned toward him.

"When are you going to propose to Michelle?"

Korey froze and swallowed. "I don't know. Why?"

"You've been together more than a year. Haven't you at least thought about it?"

Korey opened his mouth and then closed it. "A little."

"Just a little bit?" Tyler studied him.

"The thought has crossed my mind, but I'm not ready for that. Did she say something to you about it?"

Tyler suddenly felt caught between Korey and Michelle, and for some reason, he couldn't betray her confidence. "No, she hasn't. I was just thinking that you two have been together so long that maybe you were making plans. Haven't you talked about marriage?"

"She makes comments, but I don't think it's the right time."

Tyler nodded. "I understand."

As Tyler returned to hammering, he wondered if maybe Korey and Michelle weren't in tune with each other, which meant Korey would break sweet Michelle's heart.

And for some strange reason, that bothered Tyler to his very core.

Michelle smiled across the kitchen table at her older sister, Lainey, and her husband, Noah. She was so excited that her sister and her family had joined them for supper that evening. It seemed as if it had been too long since she'd spent time with them.

"Brot," Jana Beth, her two-year-old niece, said as she sat in her booster seat beside Michelle. *"Brot!"*

Michelle smiled down at her sweet niece, who looked as if she'd grown since the last time Michelle had visited their home in Ronks. With her light-brown hair and bright blue eyes, she looked just like her pretty *mamm.* "Did you say you'd like some more *brot*?"

Jana Beth nodded and grinned.

"Okay, *mei liewe."* Michelle buttered a roll and handed it to her. *"Ich liebe dich,"* she whispered while touching her hair.

"How are you feeling, Lainey?" *Mamm* asked as she passed a platter of pot roast.

Lainey touched her distended abdomen. "Fine. Just a little tired." She smiled at her husband. "Only three more months. We're excited, right, Noah?"

"Of course we are." Her husband gazed at her with love in his dark eyes, and Michelle felt a tug at her heart as she wondered if she'd ever see that same love for her in Korey's eyes.

"How's the furniture business, Noah?" *Dat* asked.

Noah scooped a pile of mashed potatoes onto his plate and then passed the bowl to Jorie. "We're taking a lot of orders for Christmas. It's keeping us busy, which always makes *mei dat* and *bruders froh.*"

"It's *gut* to be busy," *Dat* said.

Michelle cut up pieces of meat for Jana Beth and set them on her plastic plate. Then she added a few green beans and a small pile of potatoes. Jana Beth grinned before digging into her food. Then Michelle began eating her supper while Noah and *Dat* discussed their work.

"Lainey, you need to see what Michelle has been working on," Jorie suddenly said.

Michelle's head popped up at the sound of her name, and she found her family watching her.

"What have you been doing, Shell?" Lainey's pretty face filled with curiosity.

Michelle set down her fork and wiped her mouth with a napkin. "I started painting old milk cans with farm scenes."

"Oh my goodness. I can't wait to see them," Lainey said.

"It's really not a big deal."

Jorie held up a finger. "Don't listen to her. They're fantastic. Right, *Mamm* and *Dat?*"

"They are," *Dat* agreed.

Mamm added, "Spectacular."

152

Michelle's cheeks heated.

"I want to see them after we clean up the kitchen," Lainey said.

Noah smiled. "I do too."

"Okay," Michelle said.

After finishing supper and then enjoying apple pie, vanilla ice cream, and coffee for dessert, Michelle, Jorie, *Mamm,* and Lainey cleaned up the kitchen. *Dat* and Noah sat in the family room while Jana Beth played with a doll and a plastic tea set.

Jorie and *Mamm* joined *Dat* and Jana Beth in the family room while Michelle led Lainey and Noah out to her small room in the barn, which she had transformed into her painting studio. The scent of paint mixed with animals and hay filled Michelle's nose.

"You are so talented, Michelle," her brother-in-law said while examining the shelf that held her completed milk can paintings.

Lainey touched Michelle's arm. "I agree. Are you going to sell them?"

"*Dat* said I could look into it," Michelle said. "There's a little gift shop up on Old Philadelphia Pike that I thought might be interested in them. I just need to make the time to go up there."

Noah tapped Michelle's worktable. "Well,

I think you'll sell them all when you do." Then he kissed his wife's cheek. "I'll let you two get caught up." He nodded at them and then left the room.

"I'm so proud of you, Michelle." Lainey gingerly sat on a nearby stool.

Michelle sat down across from her. "*Danki.* Jorie told me I should find a way to sell my paintings, and the idea came to me while I was doing chores."

"It's brilliant." Lainey rested her elbows on the tabletop. "So, how are things with Korey?"

Michelle smiled. "Fine."

"Just fine?"

Michelle played with a loose piece of wood on the edge of the table while she told Lainey about how Korey had forgotten about their date but now seemed to be more attentive than he had been in the past.

"Korey is making an effort, but I can't help but feel like something is missing." An ache expanded in her chest as she said the words aloud for the first time.

Lainey nodded slowly as if pondering her response.

"Just tell me what you think, Lainey. I value your opinion."

"Do you think you and Korey have a future together?"

"I want to believe it, but sometimes I don't know if he truly wants a future with me. Then I find myself wondering if he's mature enough for a future." Michelle shared her conversations with Korey regarding his stepmother and Tyler, and then she shook her head, trying to dislodge her doubts. "But maybe now he'll wake up and see that it's time for him to grow up and think about a future. That might prompt him to realize how much I mean to him."

Lainey sat up straight and rubbed her abdomen. "It took Noah longer than I expected to propose. You remember that we dated almost two years, and there was a period of time when I doubted how he felt about me."

"I forgot about that."

"*Ya*, that was tough, and it wasn't something I wanted to discuss." Her older sister chuckled. "But it all worked out. If you truly love him, then be patient with him. Some men take longer than others to make that commitment because they're *naerfich* about the responsibility of being the head of a family. That could be what's keeping him from making the commitment just yet."

Michelle nodded as a new hope expanded in her heart. "That makes sense. *Danki.*" She smiled. "This is why I need time with my older *schweschder*. I've missed you."

"I missed you too." Lainey reached across the table and touched Michelle's hand.

Michelle pointed at Lainey's belly. "So, what names have you and Noah been discussing?"

"If I tell you, you can't share with anyone."

"Of course I won't." Michelle smiled as Lainey began sharing the names.

Later Michelle hugged her niece and kissed her head while she stood with her family by her sister's horse and buggy. "I hope to see you again soon, Jana Beth."

Her niece wrapped her arms around Michelle's neck and kissed her cheek.

"My turn." Jorie took Jana Beth from her arms and kissed her too. "Love you."

Lainey hugged Michelle and whispered in her ear, "Don't give up on Korey. If it's meant to be, the Lord will guide you two toward a life together."

"I'm so glad we got to talk," Michelle whispered back.

Her older sister released her from the hug and touched her cheek. "You need to come visit me so we can talk more often."

"And me too," Jorie chimed in.

Lainey laughed. "Of course."

Noah took Jana Beth, and Michelle's parents each kissed her goodbye while

Lainey hugged Jorie.

"I'll talk to you soon," Lainey said before climbing into the buggy.

As Lainey's family buggy moved down the driveway toward the road, Michelle smiled. She was so grateful for her older sister.

CHAPTER 12

Tyler's eyes roved over the unmarried women's section during the service on Sunday, and he quickly found Charity sitting a few rows back from the front. She looked pretty in a bright yellow dress and white apron.

He had already decided last night that he was going to ask her to ride to the youth gathering with him and also to ride home with him. He wanted to get to know her better and see where their relationship might lead. Yet he still found himself on the fence about asking her to be his girlfriend. Something was holding him back.

His gaze drifted, and when it met with Michelle's, he took in her pretty face and how her pink dress complemented her lips and cheeks. And when she smiled, happiness pulsed through him.

He tried to focus on Charity once again, but it was as if his eyes were glued to

Michelle's.

What's wrong with me?

He cast his eyes down toward his hymnal and tried to concentrate on the minister's holy words. Then he began to pray: *Lord, please guide my heart toward the woman you've chosen for me and help me sort through my confusing feelings.*

When the service was over, he and Jonah helped convert the benches into tables for lunch. Then he and Jonah took a seat across from each other.

"Do you happen to know anyone who might be interested in working as a roofer?" Tyler asked as he piled lunch meat onto a piece of bread.

Jonah's dark eyebrows rose. "Why? You hiring?"

"Yup."

Jonah grinned and leaned forward. "So you finally convinced your *dat* to let you run your own crew?"

"I did." Tyler held up a pretzel. "He told Korey and me to start interviewing."

"That's fantastic. Congratulations."

"*Danki.* So, do you know anyone?"

Jonah nodded while smothering a piece of bread with peanut butter spread. "*Mei bruder* isn't too fond of working in the store. He's much more outdoorsy than the rest of us.

159

He might want to give roofing a try."

"Perfect. I'll talk to Dennis." Tyler felt as if someone was watching him, and he turned toward the far end of the table where Charity and Michelle stood close together as if they were whispering and peeking over at him.

When Tyler nodded at them, Charity waved and Michelle grinned.

"You really need to ask her out."

Tyler spun to face Jonah once again. "Who?"

"Charity, of course." Jonah rolled his eyes.

"Oh, right." Tyler took a bite of his sandwich while trying to imagine dating Charity. She was sweet, outgoing, and definitely eager.

But did they have enough in common to sustain a relationship? He'd have to give it a try in order to find out.

Michelle lifted a full coffee carafe in the Fisher family's kitchen and started toward the door, nodding to other women on her way back toward the barn.

"Wait!" Charity called as she caught up to Michelle. She balanced a tray with bowls of pretzels and looked behind her. "I caught Tyler looking at me. I'm hoping he'll ask me to ride with him to the youth gathering."

"I'm sure he will."

"Michelle! Charity!" Kendra rushed over to them. She also held a coffee carafe. "I have to tell you all about the decorations I picked up for my wedding. They're going to be just gorgeous."

Michelle forced a smile on her face as Kendra droned on about votive candles while they walked together to the barn. When they stepped inside, Michelle slipped to the far side of the barn and then began moving down the table, greeting the men and refilling their coffee cups. Once her carafe was empty, she padded toward the barn exit and almost walked right into Tyler as he entered.

"Whoa!" He held up his hands and stepped back. "Excuse me."

Michelle's cheeks burned. "I'm so sorry. I wasn't watching where I was going."

"It's no problem. I'll walk with you."

"Don't you need to finish your lunch?"

"I have a question for you."

Michelle shrugged. "Okay," she said as they started down the path toward the house. "What's your question?"

"Were you and Charity talking about me earlier?"

Michelle stopped walking, placed her hand on her hip, and looked up at him. "Tyler Bontrager, are you one of those men who think that all *maed* are talking about you?"

"No." He chuckled. "Do I seem like that type of man?"

She tapped her chin with her finger. "I don't know. You do seem to have a big head."

"I thought it was normal sized." He touched his head, and she rolled her eyes. "Well, now that you mention it, I suppose it is a bit inflated."

She laughed.

"Seriously now, you and Charity were whispering and pointing at me."

"What if we were?" she teased.

"Aha!" He pointed at her. "So you admit you were."

"I didn't say that."

"But you did."

She took a step toward him, and she breathed in his scent — soap mixed with a woodsy cologne or aftershave — and she felt a strange stirring in her chest. "So, you're right, Tyler. We were talking about you."

"And what did you say?"

She held up her free hand. "I can't betray

my best *freind*'s confidence."

He lifted his dark eyebrows, and she huffed out a breath.

"Fine. She's hoping you'll take her to the youth gathering, and more than that, she's hoping you'll ask her to be your girlfriend."

"Oh." His smile dimmed a fraction.

"Are you going to?"

"Yes and maybe."

"Maybe?"

He rubbed his chin.

"You like her, don't you?"

Tyler hesitated. "*Ya,* I do."

"Was iss letz?" she asked.

"Nothing is wrong, but I'm preoccupied with work. *Mei dat* finally agreed to allow me to hire my own crew."

"Tyler!" she exclaimed. "That's amazing. That's what you wanted, right?"

"*Ya,* but it's a lot. I have to stay focused on proving to *mei dat* that he can trust me. If I'm focused on work, then I can't be much of a boyfriend."

A few of their friends walked past and nodded a greeting.

"Why don't we talk over there?" Tyler asked before they moved over to the stable, and he leaned against the wall.

"First of all," she began, "I'm so *froh* that you convinced your *dat* to let you run your own crew. I knew you could do it."

"*Danki.*" Something unreadable flashed across his face.

"*Gern gschehne,*" she said. "But second, if you're running your own crew, that means you might be ready to settle down soon, and you don't want to miss out on an opportunity with the right *maedel.*" Michelle realized what she had said, and she blushed once again. "I'm so sorry, Tyler. That was very forward of me. Forgive me. Excuse me. I should really get back to the kitchen to refill the carafe."

She started to walk away, but he took her arm and gently pulled her back to him.

"It's okay, Michelle," he said. "I like talking to you because you're so open and honest with me."

Her throat dried as she took in his hazel eyes that sparkled in the afternoon sunlight. She felt something unspoken pass between them, something strong and magnetic. Perhaps a special friendship?

"How about I make you a promise?" Tyler offered.

"What promise?"

"I already decided I'm going to ask Charity to ride with me to the youth gathering and then home." He paused for a beat. "I'm still not sure about asking her out, but I promise I'll let you know when I'm ready to ask her father for permission to date her."

"Okay." She smiled. "She'll be so excited."

He grimaced. "Can we keep this between us?"

"Of course."

"Great."

They studied each other, and Michelle suddenly felt awkward.

She cleared her throat. "I'll see you later, Tyler." Then she scurried toward the kitchen.

"Go ask her, Ty." Jonah gave Tyler a shove toward Charity when they walked out of the barn after the women finished lunch and filed out.

Tyler scowled at him. "Calm down." Then he sauntered over to where Charity talked with Michelle. "Charity? Could I please talk to you?"

Michelle grinned at him and took a step back. "I'm going to go look for Korey." Then she winked at Tyler and traipsed away.

Tyler bit back a chuckle at her wink. She was just so cute!

Charity blushed as she looked up at him. "Hi."

"Would you like to ride to the gathering with me?"

"*Ya,* I would love to. I just need to stop home to change and pick up the dessert I made yesterday."

"Great. Let's go."

They climbed into his buggy and started the short journey to their homes to change their clothes.

"How was your week?" he asked as he guided his horse down the road.

She folded her hands on her lap. "It was *gut.* I did my chores and also started working on a new quilt."

"How nice. What does the quilt look like?"

"Oh, it's a Lone Star."

"What color?"

Charity spent the remainder of their trip describing the colors in her quilt. While he tried to concentrate on her words, his mind wandered to his discussion with Michelle. Their conversations were always so pleasant and delightful. Words flowed between them with ease, but his talks with Charity were stilted, awkward, and forced. And that baffled him.

Charity, however, was sweet and pretty, and he liked her well enough. Perhaps he expected too much out of their relationship when they were still getting to know each other better. Perhaps love was a feeling that grew over time, and he needed to allow his feelings for her to flourish naturally.

After dropping Charity off at home, Tyler continued to his house, where he changed out of his church clothes. Then he picked Charity up again, and they spent their short journey to the Byler farm discussing the weather and Tyler's work schedule for the upcoming week.

When they arrived at the gathering, he spotted Korey and Michelle, and Michelle waved at him and Charity. Tyler's stomach clenched when Michelle took Korey's hand before they strolled toward the volleyball game.

Tyler forced his lips into a smile and turned toward Charity. "We're here. Let's go have fun."

"Okay!" Charity pushed open the door and gathered up her box of peanut butter chocolate chunk cookies before stepping down from his buggy.

As Tyler climbed out, he looked forward to fun with his friends and hoped to get to know Charity better.

Later that evening, Michelle helped Mary Byler and a few of her other friends clean up after the youth gathering. She set a stack of serving bowls in Mary's cabinets and smiled while Kendra talked on about the menu for her wedding reception. Michelle was happy for Kendra, but her mind was stuck on Tyler and Charity and how their day had gone. She hadn't been able to get Charity alone to ask her about their ride in his buggy. She couldn't wait to find out if Tyler had decided to ask her out.

"*Danki* for helping me pick up," Mary Byler told Michelle once the kitchen was cleaned up.

"*Gern gschehne.* Have you seen Charity?" Mary glanced around at their friends in the kitchen, and they all shook their heads. "No."

"I thought she was outside talking to Jorie and a few of the other *maed,*" Kendra said.

Michelle nodded. "*Danki.* I'll look for her there. *Gut nacht.*"

Her friends said good night, and then she walked out onto the porch. The sun had set, and the dark sky was clear and peppered with shining stars. The late September air had cooled off and held the promise of fall weather. She pulled her small flashlight from her pocket and flipped it on while breathing in the aroma of fresh air and honeysuckle.

Michelle started down the porch steps and scanned the area for both Jorie and her boyfriend.

"Hey."

She gasped and spun, finding Tyler grinning at her. "You startled me. Hey yourself."

"Sorry." He pointed his flashlight beam toward the ground. "Have you seen Charity?"

"No, I haven't, and I was looking for her, too, as well as Korey. I was in the kitchen helping Mary clean up. Kendra said she saw Charity talking to *mei schweschder.*" Michelle smiled up at him. "I saw you and Charity talking and laughing earlier. It looks like you two are getting close, huh?"

He shrugged. "*Ya,* she's sweet."

"She is, and she's sweet on you."

"Can you blame her?" A smile played on his lips.

She laughed. "Have you made a decision about asking her father's permission to date her?"

"Maybe." He leaned in close to her. His familiar scent of soap mixed with sandalwood sent a strange awareness zinging through her veins. "Do you think I should get to know her better or ask her out?" he whispered, his voice close to her ear.

It took Michelle a moment to catch her breath. "You're asking for my advice?" she managed to say as she took a step back, needing to put some distance between them.

"Yeah. Is that *gegisch*?" He looked embarrassed. "Forget I said anything."

"No, it's okay. I'm glad you're comfortable enough to ask me for my opinion. I think you should ask her out and see how it goes. I'm certain you'll be glad you did." She touched his arm and then grimaced and stepped away. "I'm so sorry. I don't know why I did that."

He shook his head. "It's okay." Then his eyes focused on something behind her, and his smile dimmed as he took a step back.

"What are you two discussing?" Korey asked, looking curious or possibly concerned.

"I was just giving your older *bruder* relationship advice."

"Oh." Korey turned to Tyler. "Was she helpful?"

"Yup." Tyler took a step away from them. "I'll see you at home, Kore."

"All right." Korey turned toward Michelle. "Let's go. I'm getting tired." He started toward the field of buggies, leaving Michelle and Tyler.

Michelle turned toward Tyler. *"Gut nacht."*

"Wait." Tyler reached his hand out toward her and then pulled it back. *"Danki* for talking with me. I'm sorry if Korey is upset that we've been talking so much lately."

170

"You don't have to thank me, and I've told Korey that you and I are *freinden.* I look forward to hearing about you and Charity."

"Michelle!" Korey called. "Are you riding home with me?" She could hear the impatience in his voice.

"Ya," she called. "I'm coming." She looked back at Tyler once more and then scurried to catch up to her boyfriend.

After Korey hitched up the horse and buggy, Michelle climbed in beside him. With the glow of his lantern illuminating the buggy, she took in his rigid posture and the glower etched in his face, and guilt swarmed in her chest.

"Korey," she began softly. "I'm sorry if I —"

"Do you like *mei bruder?*" He nearly spat the words at her while keeping his eyes trained on the road ahead.

Michelle blanched. "As a *freind?* Of course I do. Besides, he might be my family someday, right?" She tried to laugh, but it came out as a squeak.

Korey continued to study the road with his jaw clenched.

"Are you seriously jealous that I'm *freinden* with Tyler?"

He finally turned his glare on her. "I'm jealous that my girlfriend is talking to *mei bruder* more than to me."

"He's funny, Korey, and when we're together we talk about his relationship with Charity. You shouldn't be jealous." She took a deep, shuddering breath as the truth hit her hard and fast — she felt something special developing in her heart for Tyler. But even as the realization came, she immediately fought to bury it. He could only ever be her friend — a special friend, but just a friend. "Korey, *you're* my boyfriend. You're the man I'm with. We've been together for so long and I don't plan to give that up, okay?"

Korey looked unconvinced.

The hum of the buggy wheels and the rhythm of the horse's gait filled the buggy. Silence stretched between them, and it felt like a giant chasm that might swallow them whole. Remorse and embarrassment slithered through her as reality splashed cold water on her — she had hurt him, and she might lose him, which meant she could lose her dream of marriage and a family.

"Korey, I never meant to upset you by talking to your *bruder*. I honestly didn't think it was a big deal. Please forgive me, okay?"

He breathed out a heavy sigh that seemed to bubble up from his toes, and his posture relaxed — slightly. "It's okay. I just got so jealous when I saw you laughing with him. I haven't seen you laugh like that with me in a long time."

"Oh." She blinked. "The truth is that he's easy to talk to, and I feel like you don't talk to me anymore. It hurts me when you don't open up to me."

Korey reached over and touched her hand. "I'm sorry I've been so closed off. I didn't think about how much that would hurt you. I'll work on opening up to you."

She smiled at him as relief rushed through her. They were going to be okay. *Thank you, God!*

She turned toward the window as cars rumbled by and road noise filled the buggy. When a car whizzed by a little too close for comfort on the passenger side, she gasped. She turned toward Korey, where he sat in the driver's seat on the side of the buggy closest to the shoulder.

"I can't stand when cars illegally pass buggies," she said. "*Mei dat* read about another bad buggy accident in the paper last week. A little boy and girl were hurt when their parents' buggy was rear-ended."

Korey grunted in response.

When she peeked over at Korey, he once again was focused on the road, and she searched her mind for something to say to start a conversation with him. While he had promised to open up to her, he still remained quiet, as if he were lost in thoughts he refused to share.

"Are you still helping Dwight work on his *haus*?"

"*Ya.*"

"How's it going?" she prodded.

"It's going well, but there's a lot of work to be done."

"Kendra has been talking about their wedding." When Korey didn't respond, she began listing all of the details Kendra had shared, from the color of her dress to the menu and the table decorations.

Instead of commenting, Korey nodded without meeting her gaze.

"Do you want to get married?" she asked.

Korey winced and then recovered. "Uh. Sure. Someday."

"Oh." Michelle's posture slumped. "Someday, but not anytime soon?"

"Right. I'm-I'm not ready."

Michelle nodded and tried to smile, but his confession felt like a smack in the face. Perhaps Lainey was right and Korey was afraid of the responsibility of being a husband and perhaps someday a father.

She sat up straighter. "That's okay. There's

no rush." While she said the words as a way to comfort him, deep down she dreaded the thought of waiting much longer. She was ready to start her future as a wife sooner rather than later!

Michelle fingered the hem of her apron and peered out the window. Once again her thoughts turned to Tyler, and she contemplated how different the two brothers were.

And then a thought struck her — Would Tyler be ready to marry before Korey? And if so, would he marry Charity? For some reason, that idea sat cold and heavy over her heart.

CHAPTER 13

"Now that I have three guys to join the crew, I'm ready to branch out and start working on my own jobs," Tyler told *Dat* while they stood by the large water cooler at the fitness center they were roofing in White Horse on Wednesday afternoon.

A gentle breeze moved past Tyler's face, bringing with it the scent of rain. Above him the sky was overcome with gray clouds. Vehicles rumbled past them on the street, and knots of people meandered by on the sidewalk.

Dat sipped his cup of water and then licked his lips. "Are you sure you're ready?"

"*Ya, Dat.* I've been preparing for this. You can trust me."

The ladder beside them rattled as Korey climbed down. He removed his mirrored sunglasses and poured himself a drink from the large cooler. "What's going on?"

Tyler lifted his straw hat and raked his

hand through his sweaty hair. "I was just telling *Dat* that the men we spoke to accepted our offers to join our crew."

"We're going to run the crew together, right, Ty?" Korey seemed to watch him with distrust.

Tyler pursed his lips. Ever since Sunday, he had a feeling that Korey was giving him the silent treatment. On one hand, Tyler had chalked it up to just another one of his middle brother's foul moods, but deep down he had a feeling it had to do with his conversation with Michelle.

"I thought we already agreed we were going to run the crew together, Kore," Tyler said, working to keep his tone even in order to avoid one of Korey's blowups. After all, he didn't want to get into an argument with Korey in front of *Dat* and destroy all of the hard work and effort he'd put into getting his own roofing crew.

Korey's eyes narrowed at Tyler for a fraction of a second and then recovered. "Just making sure you didn't change your mind and take this over like you do everything else."

Tyler balled his hands into fists and let his brother's snide comment go as he turned his attention back to their father.

"Well, since you two are going to run your

own crew, that means you'll have to pay a driver. And you'll need a business cell phone. Have you thought about that?" *Dat* asked.

"Ya," Tyler said. "I'll go to the cell phone store on my lunch break. Also, I have the name of a driver who is available. I was going to call him after we had a start date. His name is Jack Damon."

Dat tapped the side of his cup. "That also means I'm going to need a couple of guys to replace you two."

"I thought about that too. Since we have three candidates, you can take one or two of them."

"I'll start with one and see how it goes," *Dat* said.

"Duane?" Their conversation was interrupted when the fitness center owner called *Dat*'s name.

Dat looked his direction and waved. "Brett." He joined him by the sidewalk and began to update him on the project, leaving Tyler and Korey by themselves.

"So, Ty," Korey began, his expression impassive. "I've been meaning to ask you something. Is it true that you and Michelle were discussing your love life on Sunday when I caught you two together?"

Tyler scoffed as he refilled his cup.

"Caught us? I wouldn't say that you caught us doing anything but talking."

"Answer the question. Is that what you were discussing?"

"*Ya,* it was. It was an innocent conversation, and that's all. If it seemed like something else, then I'm sorry. All right?" Tyler snuck a look over to where *Dat* stood talking to Brett. "You need to calm down and stop blowing this out of proportion."

Korey's jaw was rigid as he took a step toward him. "You aren't going to tell me to calm down. This *is* a big deal. I'm *not* comfortable with you and Michelle talking so much. It seems like it's all the time. She's *my* girlfriend. Just back off."

Tyler hesitated. He opened his mouth to tell his brother that Michelle could talk to anyone she wanted to, but then he stopped. Instead, he took a deep breath. "Michelle has been encouraging me to ask Charity out."

"Then quit beating around the bush and do it. We can stop at Charity's *haus* on the way home if you want, so you can just get it over with and move on."

Tyler shook his head. "No, I'll go there myself."

"*Gut.*" Korey tossed his empty cup into the trash can, grabbed a box of nails, and climbed back up the ladder.

Tyler's hands trembled as he stood on Charity's porch later that evening. He looked out toward Michelle's farm, and his chest squeezed. He'd much rather talk to her, but he recalled his brother's suspicions, and renewed guilt filled him. The last thing he wanted to do was ruin his fragile relationship with his middle brother or cause a rift between Korey and Michelle. He cared about them and wanted them both to be happy.

Squaring his shoulders, he knocked on the door and then sucked in a breath.

Footfalls sounded from beyond the door before it squeaked open, revealing Charity. She was lovely in a purple dress. Her pretty face lit with a smile as she pushed open the storm door. "Tyler. What a surprise."

"Hi." He turned his straw hat in his hands.

"Would you like to come in for some *kichlin* and *kaffi*?"

"Actually, I was wondering if I could talk to your *dat*."

Charity beamed. "*Ya*, of course. He's in the barn."

"*Danki*." Tyler loped down the porch steps and strode toward the large dairy barn as the smell of animals and wet hay wafted over him. His mouth dried when he approached the barn, and he longed to stop his heart from thundering in his chest.

The barn door opened, and Hans Swarey stepped out. His green eyes lit up as he grinned. "Tyler. *Wie geht's?*"

"Hi, Hans. I was wondering if I could speak to you for a moment."

"Of course. What can I do for you?"

"Charity and I have been spending some time together, and I'd like to get to know her better." Tyler jammed his trembling hands in his pockets. "I wanted to ask for your permission to date her, and of course, I promise to always be respectful."

Hans gave Tyler's shoulder a gentle pat. "I've known you your whole life. You're such a nice young man. Of course you have my permission."

"Danki." Tyler breathed a sigh of relief.

"The way you thank me is to treat my Charity right."

"Oh, I will."

"Gut, gut."

Tyler thanked him again before returning to the back porch. He raised his hand to knock on the door just as Charity appeared at it.

She pushed the door open wide. "Would you like to come inside?"

"*Ya,* I would."

He followed her into the large kitchen, where the table was set with a platter of assorted cookies and two empty mugs. The delicious smell of coffee filled his senses.

Charity gave him a shy smile as she made a sweeping gesture toward the table. "I didn't know what your favorite kind of *kichli* was, so I brought out all of them."

"I've never met a *kichli* I didn't like."

She chuckled and then picked up the percolator. "I made decaf so it doesn't keep you up at night."

"*Danki.*"

He washed his hands and then carried the cream and sugar to the table before they sat down across from each other. He chose a gingersnap and a snickerdoodle before adding cream and sugar to his coffee and stirring it.

When his eyes moved to Charity across the table, he found her watching him expectantly. His hands began to sweat, and he set down his spoon. "I came here to ask you a question."

She nodded and her eyes widened.

"Would you be interested in being my girl —"

"Yes!" The word burst from her lips before he could finish the question. Then she laughed as her cheeks flushed bright red. "I'm so sorry. I'm just thrilled. I've liked you for a while, and I never imagined you'd like me back."

"I do like you, and I look forward to getting to know you better."

"I'm so *froh* to hear that."

For the next hour, they discussed their week while they ate cookies and drank coffee. The conversation flowed a little better than the last time they had spoken, and Tyler finally felt himself relax with her.

Charity walked him out to the porch when it was time for him to go home. She smiled up at him and touched his arm. "I'm really glad you came tonight."

"I am too." He shook her hand, and he was almost certain he detected disappointment in her expression. *"Gut nacht."*

"Gut nacht, Tyler."

"I'll see you soon."

"I hope so."

Tyler felt the weight of her gaze as his flashlight guided him down her driveway and onto the road that led to his house. He smiled and looked up at the stars twinkling in the sky as an orange barn cat scurried across the road and into a field.

As he breathed in the cool fall air, he hoped he had made the right decision by asking Charity to be his girlfriend. Only time would tell.

"Michelle! Michelle!" Charity burst into Michelle's painting studio the following afternoon, beaming as she rushed over to the worktable. "Guess what happened last night?"

Michelle set her paintbrush down and blinked at her. "Uh. I have no idea, but I'm guessing it was exciting."

"He asked me! He asked me!" Charity danced around.

Michelle hopped down from the stool. "Tyler asked you to be his girlfriend?"

"Ya!" Charity explained how he'd arrived at her home unexpectedly, spoke to her father, and then stayed for cookies and coffee. "It was so sweet."

Michelle reached for her best friend to hug her and then looked down at the paint splattered on her apron and pulled her arms back. "I'm so *froh* for you. I would hug you, but I'll get paint all over you." She forced a smile on her lips, but a strange jealousy wriggled through her.

"I didn't think he'd ask." Charity sighed as she sat on the stool across from Michelle. "Do you think we can set up a double date soon?"

Michelle sat on her stool and nodded. "*Ya,* of course. We could make them supper."

"Great. How about this Saturday? I can host this time, and then you host next time."

"Perfect." Michelle smiled as Charity began discussing a menu. She couldn't wait for the four of them to start spending time together.

A knock sounded on the back door Saturday evening just as Charity set a platter of baked potatoes on the table next to the large bowl of salad. "Oh! They're here. I'll get it."

Michelle used tongs to place the pieces of fried chicken on a platter and then set it on the table while voices sounded from the mudroom. She added a bowl of corn to the table just as Charity walked in holding a bouquet of colorful fall flowers.

"Our guests are here," Charity sang.

Tyler waved as he stepped through the doorway. *"Wie geht's?"*

"Hi, Michelle." Korey presented her with an identical bouquet. "These are for you."

Michelle smiled as she took them. "How thoughtful. *Danki*!"

Charity found two vases in the cabinet and set their bouquets in water.

"Supper smells amazing. What can we do

to help you?" Tyler rubbed his hands together.

Charity touched his arm. "Everything is ready. Let's eat."

After washing their hands, they each took a seat at the small, square table. They bowed their heads in silent prayer and then began filling their bowls with salad and their plates with fried chicken, corn, and a baked potato.

"How was work today?" Michelle asked the men as she shook homemade dressing onto her salad.

Korey cut his potato in half. "It went pretty well."

"When do you start with the new crew?"

"Next week." Korey added butter to his potato.

Michelle handed the bottle of dressing to Charity. "Are you excited?"

"*Ya,* but they will need training," Tyler said. "It's going to be slow going in the beginning."

Michelle peered across the table at Tyler. "But it will be worth it once you get them up to speed."

"That's right." Tyler smiled at her, and she silently admired how his green shirt brought out the flecks in his hazel eyes.

The thought took her by surprise, and she ducked her head, dropping her focus to her plate as embarrassment crept up her neck.

"What new crew?" Charity asked.

Tyler explained how he and Korey planned to start running a second roofing crew on Monday. Charity kept the conversation going through supper, asking questions about who they hired, where their first job would be, how they planned to train their employees, and where the idea to start a second crew had come from.

Michelle was grateful her best friend was so curious about their work because it gave her time to try to douse the confusion and embarrassment that continued to heat her face and neck.

"We made cupcakes for dessert," Charity announced when their plates were clean.

Tyler leaned forward. "Oooh. What kind?"

"Vanilla with chocolate icing." Charity stood and picked up the bottle of dressing, and it slipped, dousing her burgundy dress and black apron. "Oh no!"

Michelle dove for a dish towel and handed it to her. "Here you go." Then she grabbed a roll of paper towels.

"*Danki.*" Charity shook her head and laughed as she began mopping up the mess. "I'm such a klutz."

Michelle pointed to the doorway. "Go get changed, and I'll clean this up."

"I got it." Tyler pulled the trash can over and gathered up the used paper towels.

"Danki," Charity said as she swept past him and out of the kitchen toward the stairs that led up to her bedroom.

While Tyler cleaned the floor with paper towels, Michelle wiped up the mess on the table, and Korey carried the dirty dishes, glasses, and utensils to the sink.

Korey touched Michelle's arm. "I need to use the restroom."

"Okay," she told him as she moved to the sink and began filling one side with hot, sudsy water. She scrubbed the dishes, rinsed them, and set them in the drainboard.

Tyler appeared beside her. "Where are the dish towels?"

"You don't need to help me."

"I want to."

"The bottom drawer to my left."

He retrieved a dish towel and dried and stacked the dishes. "How's painting going?"

"I have a dozen milk cans completed."

"Wow. You've been working hard. When are you going to take them to a gift shop?"

"I don't know." She shrugged. "I'll probably just give them away as gifts. Maybe for Christmas or something."

"You should sell them, Michelle. They're too *schee* to just give away. They will bring joy to so many more people if you put them in a store. You could even add a Scripture verse to them and use them as a way to spread the gospel. It could be your ministry." He touched her shoulder, and the contact sent a trill dancing down her spine. "I'm serious."

She looked up at him, and he was standing so close that her body heat mixed with his.

Oh no.

"Maybe I will sell them," she mumbled as she took a step away from him, limbs trembling, and busied herself with scrubbing their utensils.

When she started to rinse them, a fork slipped from her hand and bounced onto the floor. She leaned down to retrieve it the same time as he did, and when their hands brushed, heat tingled up her arms.

She gasped and jumped away from him.

"Are you okay?" Worry seemed to etch his face.

"*Ya.*" She stepped back from him. "I-I need to sweep the floor."

Tyler's brow furrowed, and he opened his mouth to say something just as Charity entered the kitchen wearing a pink dress and fresh black apron.

"Oh, you're so sweet, Tyler," Charity

cooed. "You don't need to help with the dishes. Michelle and I will handle it after we have dessert."

Tyler's smile seemed forced. "I don't mind helping."

Korey returned, and they all sat down at the table for cupcakes while they discussed friends in the community. Michelle worked to keep her focus on Korey, Charity, or the cupcake, but her eyes kept betraying her and fixating on Tyler instead.

After cleaning up the kitchen, Michelle said good night to Charity and Tyler and retrieved her bouquet before she and Korey started down the road toward her house.

"Did you have a *gut* time tonight?" she asked Korey as they walked down the street by the light of his flashlight.

"Ya." He nodded and threaded his fingers with hers.

She released the breath she hadn't realized she'd been holding. Korey hadn't noticed anything unusual. *"Gut."*

"Maybe we can do it again sometime." When he smiled down at her, she nodded. His brow crinkled. "You okay?"

"Of course. I'm just tired." Michelle tried to ignore the guilt that popped up and smacked her. Her sweet boyfriend was concerned about her, but she couldn't possibly tell him about the way her body had reacted when his older brother touched her hand. She couldn't admit that Tyler's warm skin had sent heat crashing through her veins!

Lord, please rid me of my strange feelings for Tyler! Don't allow me to hurt Korey!

"How did you like the fried chicken? Charity used her *mammi*'s recipe." Michelle kept Korey talking about the menu while they continued toward her house.

When they reached it, he walked beside her up the back steps.

"*Danki* again for the flowers," she told him.

He smiled and touched her cheek. "*Danki* for the meal." He kissed her cheek and started down the steps. "See you soon."

"*Gut nacht.*" She watched him disappear down the driveway and then dashed into the house, grateful her parents and Jorie weren't in the kitchen so she could deal with her confusing feelings alone.

Michelle rushed up to her room and sank down on her bed. Covering her face with her hands, she took deep breaths.

"Lord, please erase my feelings for Tyler from my heart. Help me find my way back to Korey and the future I desperately want," she whispered.

191

CHAPTER 14

Michelle pulled her wagon carrying two large plastic containers into the Country Quilts and Gifts shop located on Old Philadelphia Pike in Bird-in-Hand. The welcoming fragrance of vanilla washed over her as she scanned the store, finding an array of quilts, signs, figurines, candles, ornaments, postcards, T-shirts, and dolls.

Englishers roamed around the store, browsing the gift items and filling handheld, plastic shopping baskets with their choices.

Michelle pulled her wagon over to the counter, where a young woman with bright red hair and a nose ring stood by the cash register. Her name tag said "Addie."

"Hi," Michelle said. "I have an appointment with Lola."

"Oh, you must be Michelle. Come with me." Addie led Michelle to the back of the store and into a hallway that led to a storeroom and an office. "Lola, Michelle is here."

"Great. Thanks, Addie." Lola, an attractive woman in her mid-forties with dark-brown hair and turquoise glasses, stepped out of the office. "Hi, Michelle! It's so nice to meet you. I can't wait to see your milk can paintings."

Michelle shook her hand. "I appreciate that you're taking the time to meet with me." She opened up the lid on the top container. "So, here they are."

"Oh my goodness. These are spectacular." Lola held one in her hands and turned it over, inspecting every inch. "You are a very talented young lady."

"Thank you."

Lola examined the bottom. "Oh. John 3:16. You added a Scripture verse."

"My friend suggested that."

"It's lovely." Lola set the milk can back into the container. "I hope you're planning to paint some more, because I think these will sell quickly."

Michelle's lips tipped up in a smile. "You think so?"

"Are you kidding? I won't be able to keep these on the shelf, especially since they are Amish-made." She picked up another milk can. "Did you sign your name to them?"

"No, I'd rather stay anonymous."

"I understand, but I'll add a sign saying

that they are authentic Amish creations." Lola picked up another can. "So, what were you thinking about a price?"

Michelle and Lola agreed on a price, and then Michelle left the two containers by Lola's office before Lola walked her out to the front of the store.

"I'm so glad you came by," Lola told her. "I'll give you a call when I'm running low on stock. In the meantime, you keep painting."

Michelle shook her hand. "Thank you again." Then she set out on the sidewalk, towing her wagon behind her. She walked to the corner and waited for the light to change so she could cross the street.

When she glanced down the sidewalk, she did a double take when she realized Tyler was sauntering toward her. His gaze met hers, and his handsome face lit up in a smile as he quickened his pace.

"Michelle!" He waved. "What are you doing here in town?"

She closed the distance between them. "I just met with the manager of Country Quilts and Gifts."

"About your milk cans?" His face flashed with excitement.

She nodded. "*Ya,* she's going to start selling them."

"Michelle! You did it!" Reaching out, he touched her hand, and heat rushed to the spot where their skin collided. "I'm so proud of you."

The affection in his eyes stole her breath. *No, no, no! He's Korey's brother!*

"Danki," she whispered, pulling her hand away.

"I'd love to see the display."

"Lola has to set it up."

"Oh." He peered down at her wagon. "Are you heading home now?"

"No, not yet. I told *mei mamm* I'd run to the grocery store while I'm here. Then I need to call my driver."

"Oh." He nodded and seemed to be working through something in his mind. "Do you have time for lunch?"

Michelle hesitated as her emotions tangled up in a knot. While she longed to spend more time with Tyler, she was aware of how her body reacted to him. She'd never felt so drawn to a man before, but she tried to convince herself that the emotions were all in her head. Staying away from him was the best way for her to avoid her feelings, and more importantly, not upset Korey. The last thing she wanted to do was break Korey's heart.

"Oh, well. I-I don't know," she stammered.

"It's okay." His smile fell away. "I didn't mean to be so forward." He took a step away from her. "Well, have a *gut* day." He turned to go.

"Tyler, wait!"

He spun to face her.

"What's wrong with lunch, right?"

His smile was back. "Is that a yes?"

"Ya."

"So you had an estimate in town this morning?" Michelle asked Tyler as she sat across from him in a booth at the Bird-in-Hand Family Restaurant.

Tyler smiled over at Michelle. He'd been so surprised to see her when he walked out of the bookstore and spotted her standing on the corner with her wagon. She was effortlessly beautiful wearing a green dress and black apron, and he had been disappointed when she turned down his offer of lunch. He was so grateful she'd changed her mind. Having time to talk with her was such an unexpected blessing.

"Ya, the bookstore needs a new roof, and I'm grateful that they called us for an estimate."

Their server, a middle-aged Mennonite

woman with glasses, appeared at their table and set their BLTs and chips in front of them before leaving.

They bowed their heads in silent prayer and then picked up their sandwiches.

Michelle swallowed a bite of her sandwich and then picked up a chip. "How are things with Charity?"

"Gut." He picked up his glass of water. "But I suspect you already knew that. I know how you *maed* talk." She chuckled, and he loved the sound. "Well, now you just have to tell me what she's been saying about me."

Michelle popped a chip into her mouth and then swallowed. "You already know that she really likes you — a lot. It's pretty obvious, Tyler."

He rubbed his chin. *"Ya,* that is true. It's obvious."

"And you care about her, too, right?"

"I do." He did, but sometimes he wasn't sure he cared about her enough. "How are you and Korey?"

"Fine." She said the word a little too quickly and then ducked her head.

Tyler leaned toward her, curiosity nipping at him. "Fine?"

"Ya." She shrugged. "It's obvious he's really trying to make things work."

"But . . ." he prodded.

Michelle sighed. "I shouldn't be discussing this with you."

"Because I'm his *bruder*?"

"Exactly."

"I'm sorry. I shouldn't have pried." He picked up half of his sandwich.

She shook her head. "You're not prying. The problem is you're so easy to talk to. I feel like I could say any anything to you." She blushed and focused her eyes toward her plate.

"The feeling is mutual."

She peeked up at him. "I'm sorry. This is just so awkward."

"Maybe this was a bad idea." Guilt tightened his chest.

"I didn't mean it that way." Her expression warmed. "This just shouldn't be so awkward. We're *freinden,* right?"

"Of course."

She fingered the edge of the table. "I'm ready for marriage, but he's not. When I brought it up, he actually looked terrified. But I'm willing to wait for him since we've already invested so much time together. It seems wrong to give up on our relationship after more than a year. *Mei schweschder* said that some men aren't ready because they are intimidated by the responsibility of

198

being the head of the family, which I understand." She seemed to study him. "Are you intimidated by that?"

"Honestly, I haven't thought too much about it." He shrugged. "I sort of always assumed I'd know when I was ready for marriage. I figured when it felt right, then I'd know it was time to get married."

She nodded slowly. "Exactly."

"And you're sure God is leading you to marry Korey?"

She opened her mouth and then closed it.

"I'm sorry. That's none of my business — again. So, tell me about the gift shop. How many milk cans did you bring to sell?"

"I brought her a dozen. And I took your advice."

"What advice?"

"I added a Scripture verse to the bottom of each can."

Tyler grinned. "That's fantastic."

They spent the rest of lunch discussing her painting. When the server brought the check, Tyler fetched his wallet from his pocket.

"How much is it?" Michelle opened her own wallet.

Tyler shook his head. "I'll pay it. This was my idea."

"I can't let you do that. After all, we're

two *freinden* sharing a meal."

She was right. This wasn't a date. "Fine."

She handed him a few bills and then slipped her wallet into her apron pocket while he put his back into his trouser pocket.

Then they walked up to the cashier together, and he paid the bill while she retrieved her wagon.

He pulled his business cell phone from his pocket. "I'm going to call my driver. Would you like a ride?"

"No, *danki*. I need to go to the grocery store and then call my driver."

"Okay." He felt a twinge of disappointment that their time together was coming to an end. "I'll see you Sunday."

"You will since church is at my house. Have a *gut* day."

"You too."

As he dialed his driver's number, Tyler watched her pull her wagon toward the grocery store. Sunday couldn't come soon enough.

"Did you get lost, Ty?" Korey joked when Tyler returned to the jobsite.

Tyler picked up his hammer. "Not exactly. I gave the estimate and got the job."

"*Gut.*"

"Then I ran into Michelle, and we had

lunch together."

His brother blinked. "Did I hear you correctly? You had lunch with my girlfriend?"

"Ya."

"Why would you do that, Ty?" Korey's face pinched.

Tyler held up his hands. "Please calm down. It was a friendly lunch, Kore. There's nothing to get upset about. We're *freinden.*"

"I'm not a *dummkopp.* You always have to have everything, don't you?"

"What does *that* mean?"

"You heard what I said. I still remember when you were six and I was five, and *Mammi* and *Daadi* brought us that metal Tonka dump trunk. We were supposed to share it, and you hid it in your room so that I couldn't have it."

Tyler grimaced. "That was so long ago, Korey, and I've apologized for that several times. I was a *kind.*"

"*Ya,* but you haven't changed!" Korey gestured around the jobsite. "You wanted to run your own crew and leave me out of it."

"That's not true. I didn't think you were interested."

"You act like the company will be all yours when *Dat* retires because you're eighteen months older than I am."

"Korey, I don't feel that way."

"*Ya,* you do! And now you're going behind my back and meddling with my relationship with Michelle."

Tyler peered up toward the roof, where their two crew members, Dennis and Roger, stood staring at them. Frustration burned through him as he took in his brother's sneer. "Korey, you're making a scene. I'm sorry if I upset you. We had an innocent lunch. That's it. I have a girlfriend, and Michelle is yours. I would never dream of getting between you two. So, please, calm down."

"Don't tell me to calm down. I've had to deal with your selfishness my entire life, and I've had it."

"Selfishness?" Tyler's frustration morphed into anger.

"*Ya,* selfishness." Korey pushed his finger into Tyler's chest. "You've always needed to be the center of attention and can't stand if you're not. You always pushed me out of the way when *Mammi* and *Daadi* were alive and came to visit. If I was in the middle of a story, you'd interrupt me. You couldn't stand it if anyone else had a better story than yours."

"That's not true," Tyler growled.

"It is! That's why I'm sure you're after Michelle. You realized you should have

202

asked her out before I did, but you're not going to win because I'm onto your schemes."

"There's no scheme! You're *mei bruder,* and I would never deliberately hurt you," Tyler insisted.

Korey snorted. "Right." He headed for the ladder. "Leave me alone. I've had enough of you today."

Tyler rubbed his hands down his face and sat on a pile of shingles. He had managed to completely ruin his relationship with his brother in less than five minutes. He had to find a way to repair what went wrong between them quickly as well as find a way to get Michelle out of his head.

Lord, please guide my heart and help me find a way to prove to Korey that I value his friendship and would never deliberately hurt him.

Then he picked up his hammer and a box of nails and began to climb the ladder.

Later that evening, Tyler stood in the hallway outside of Korey's bedroom door. He had endured the afternoon full of Korey's dirty looks and terse responses to his questions. Korey's attitude hadn't changed during the ride home or at supper. He had avoided Tyler's gaze, ignored his questions, and just brooded his way through the ride home and the meal.

And the giant abyss expanding between Tyler and Korey was slowly eating away at Tyler. He couldn't lose his brother this way. Although they frequently bickered, Tyler loved his brother and wanted him in his life.

Raising his fist, Tyler knocked on the door.

"Ya?" Korey called from inside.

"Could we please talk about this?" When Korey remained silent, Tyler continued. "Please, Kore. I want to apologize and make things right between us. You're important to me."

A beat of silence passed before Korey finally said, "Come in."

Tyler opened the door and found Korey lying on his bed, glaring at him. He took a deep breath and then bared his soul to his brother. "Look, Kore, I spent all afternoon pondering what you said, and I'm sorry if I've always acted like I need to be the center of attention. I never realized I made you feel like we were in competition for anyone's affection. I always felt like I was supposed to be the one learning the business because I thought you wanted to move on to something else."

"Why would you think that?" Korey sat,

hanging his long legs over the edge of the bed.

Tyler shrugged. "You just never seemed to be that interested in roofing. You've always behaved as if it was expected, not that you want to do it."

Korey nodded. "I like it."

"*Gut.* Then we can stay in business together after *Dat* retires. We can be partners with Jay if he wants to stay too."

"All right." Korey folded his arms over his wide chest. "What else?"

"And I never meant to make you feel like I was trying to steal Michelle away. That's not the case. We're *freinden.* I enjoy talking to her, and I would never do anything to come between you and her."

Korey studied him, his eyes narrowing as he moved his tongue over his teeth.

"I want to clear the air between us, so please just say what's on your mind."

"You act like you care for her."

Tyler swallowed. "I'm sorry if I act that way."

"Do you care for her?"

"I do as a *freind,* and I'm concentrating on making it work with Charity."

"If you want to clear the air between us, then you need to back off from Michelle."

"Okay." Tyler nodded. "I will."

Korey's expression relaxed slightly.

"So are we okay then?" Tyler asked.

"Ya."

Tyler breathed a sigh of relief. *"Danki."*

As he stepped out into the hallway, he hoped he could convince his heart to let go of Michelle. After all, his relationship with his brother depended on it.

"You had lunch with Tyler?" *Mamm* asked while they cleaned the kitchen after supper that evening.

Michelle set the dry dishes in the cabinet while *Mamm* scrubbed the remaining dirty dishes.

Jorie stopped sweeping and turned toward Michelle. "Why would you have lunch with Tyler?"

"He's so funny and easy to talk to." Michelle shrugged as she dried a handful of utensils. "I saw him on the street, and he suggested we have lunch."

"Are you having doubts about your relationship with Korey?" *Mamm*'s brow pinched.

Michelle hesitated and then said, "No."

"Michelle," *Mamm* said slowly. "Are you sure?"

Jorie clucked her tongue. "You and Korey are having problems?"

"Tyler is with Charity, and I'm with Korey," Michelle said. "It's the way it's supposed to be."

Mamm looked unconvinced. "If you're having doubts, then you need to be honest with Korey."

"Everything is fine," Michelle said. "So, what else do we need to do before church on Sunday?"

While their conversation turned toward their chores, Michelle tried to push all thoughts of Tyler out of her mind.

But the harder she tried to dismiss Tyler, the more thoughts of him persisted.

CHAPTER 15

"Gude mariye," Michelle greeted a few of her friends Sunday before the church service. She had helped her mother and sister scrub the house from top to bottom as well as clean out their largest barn for the service. And now the day had arrived!

She glanced toward the line of horses and buggies moving toward her parents' farm and breathed in the cool early October air. She spotted a few squirrels chasing one another toward the bird feeder in her mother's garden while the sun was high in the bright blue sky.

She looked over toward the driveway just as the Bontrager family arrived. Her parents greeted Duane and Crystal while Korey, Tyler, and Jayden smiled and nodded.

When her eyes locked with Tyler's, her breath stalled in her chest. He nodded, and she returned the gesture before she turned toward her group of friends. Her mother's words echoed in her mind as she fought to catch her breath:

If you're having doubts, then you need to be honest with Korey.

But she couldn't be honest with Korey. She couldn't imagine breaking up with him. They'd been together for more than a year, and she couldn't give up on him. She also couldn't see herself betraying him, especially for his older brother. Besides, Tyler was dating Charity, her best friend. She'd never forgive herself if she broke Korey's heart as well as Charity's! They both meant too much to her.

"Michelle."

She turned as Korey approached her. "*Gude mariye.* How was your week?"

"*Gut.*" He shrugged. "Yours?"

"Great. My painted milk cans are now available at a gift shop in Bird-in-Hand, and the manager called me yesterday to tell me she already sold three. I'm so excited." She rubbed her hands together. "I'm hoping I can keep up with the demand. I've been busy painting more of them."

"*Gut.* I'm sorry I haven't called in a few days. We've been working long hours."

"It's okay. We were busy getting ready to host the service."

Korey's dark eyes scanned the nearby

knots of people and then focused on her once again. "Could we please talk in private for a moment?"

"Of course," she said.

Korey nodded and then took her hand and gently led her to a nearby tree.

"Was iss letz?" She studied his serious expression, and worry curled in her chest.

"Why didn't you tell me that you had lunch with *mei bruder* on Thursday?"

She blinked. "I'm sorry. We haven't spoken much this week, but I wasn't trying to keep anything from you. I ran into Tyler while I was in town visiting the gift shop, and he asked me if I had time to have lunch, and that was it — just lunch."

"Just lunch?"

"*Ya,* we were two *freinden* having lunch. Does that bother you, Korey?"

"Michelle, do you have feelings for *mei bruder?*" Korey's expression crumpled, and she was certain she found pain in his eyes. "Just be honest with me, okay? I need to know how you truly feel about him."

Guilt nearly broke her apart as she took in his expression. Oh no. The last thing she ever wanted to do was hurt him. She reached up and cupped her hand to his cheek. "Korey, I am telling you the truth when I say that you're the man I'm planning a future with. I want to get married and have a family." And she craved those things more than ever!

He nodded.

"Do *you* see a future with me?"

He swallowed. "Yes, but I'm not ready for it now."

"That's okay." She touched his hand despite her disappointment in having to continue to wait for him. "We agree that we'll take our time, right?"

He nodded. Then he took her hand in his. "It's time to go into the barn for service. I'll see you later." He gave her hand a gentle squeeze and then released it.

Michelle walked over to her friends.

"I can't believe my wedding is two months away," Kendra exclaimed as their friends gathered around her. "Before I know it, I'll be changing my last name."

Michelle turned toward the line of young men walking into the barn for the service, and she found herself wondering if Korey would ever be ready to marry her.

Then Tyler's words about marriage echoed in her mind: *"I sort of always assumed I'd know when I was ready for marriage. I figured when it felt right, then I'd know it was time to get married."*

What if Korey wouldn't ever be ready to

marry her? Then what would she do? Having to start over with another relationship would be difficult. And what if she never found someone else? The thought of being alone while watching Charity and Tyler get closer and eventually marry made her stomach sour.

Charity appeared at her side. "Are you ready to walk into the barn?"

"Ya." Michelle plastered a smile on her face and tried to shake off her worries about her future and turn her thoughts toward worshipping the Lord.

Jonah glanced behind the bench where he sat beside Tyler. "Korey and Dwight are sitting three rows behind us. Did you and Korey have an argument?"

"Sort of." Tyler traced his finger on his hymnal, the *Ausbund.*

"Uh-oh. What's going on?"

Tyler sighed. "I thought we worked it out, but he's still not really talking to me."

"Just tell me what happened."

While carefully keeping his voice low, Tyler explained that he'd had lunch with Michelle, and Korey was upset. "I apologized, but he's still been standoffish with me. We're not arguing, but we're not really talking either. He's giving me the cold shoulder."

"Does Korey have any reason to be jealous of you and Michelle?"

Tyler shook his head. "I'm dating Charity."

"That doesn't answer my question, Ty."

Turning his attention to the other side of the barn, Tyler's eyes found Charity and Michelle sitting in the second row with the other unmarried women. He took in Charity's pretty face as she whispered something to Michelle. Then, when Michelle's eyes met his, he felt the air rush from his lungs. And the truth hit him — he was drawn to Michelle as if an invisible magnet pulled him toward her against his will. It wasn't a choice — it was a fact — a fact that he could no longer deny.

And that was why he had to do his best to stay away from her. He had to save his relationship with his brother and also his relationship with Charity.

"Tyler," Jonah said, leaning toward him. "Do you have feelings for Michelle?"

"She's a really *gut freind,* but I would never betray *mei bruder* that way. Besides, I'm seeing Charity, and we're still getting to know each other."

Jonah gave him a knowing look, but before Tyler responded, the song leader started the first line of the hymn and the rest of the congregation joined in the singing.

Tyler turned his attention to the service and tried to erase all thoughts of Michelle from his mind, but deep down he knew that she had somehow already carved out a piece of his heart.

Michelle shivered and hugged her sweater against her body as she rode beside Korey in his buggy later that evening.

Korey reached behind the seat and re-trieved the quilt he kept in the back of his buggy to use for impromptu picnics and to keep warm during cool nights. "Here you go."

"Danki." She smiled over at him before wrapping the quilt around her shoulders. She ran her hands over the beautiful stitch-ing of the burgundy, black, and gold Mari-ner's Compass patterned quilt that his mother had made him years ago.

Memories of his mother drinking tea and talking with her mother reeled through her mind. She could almost hear his mother laughing while she and Jorie played with Tyler and Korey in the family room. Grief battered her heart as she recalled her funeral and watching Korey, his brothers, and his father wiping their tears as Michelle, her sisters, and her mother wiped their own.

"Something on your mind?" His question broke through her thoughts.

She forced a smile on her face and looked over at his handsome profile. "Did you have fun today?"

"Ya." He gave her a sideways glance. "Did you?"

"Of course." The events of the youth gathering floated through her mind — playing volleyball, eating snacks and later supper, and then singing hymns until it was time to go home. She'd enjoyed time with her friends, but she'd been disappointed that Tyler had kept his distance from her.

Although Tyler had nodded from afar, he never approached her or spoke to her. And as much as she tried to pretend his silence hadn't hurt her, the truth was that it had cut her to the bone. She missed him, and she longed to chase those feelings away.

"Do you have a busy week planned?" she asked, hoping to fill the buggy with something other than her frustration and disappointment.

"I'll be working."

"Where?"

Michelle nodded while Korey listed the projects and the towns where his jobs were located, but her thoughts drifted back to her confusing feelings for Tyler. Guilt weighed heavily on her shoulders. She was sitting next to her wonderful boyfriend and thinking of his brother. She was a terrible sinner!

"What about you?"

"Huh?" She spun toward him, and he lifted a brow.

He gave her a concerned expression. "You okay, Michelle?"

"*Ya,* of course. What did you ask me?"

"I asked about your plans for the week."

"You know. The usual." She shrugged. "I'll have my chores, and then I hope to do some painting since my milk cans are selling so well. Did I tell you that I added a Scripture verse to the bottom of each milk can as sort of a ministry?"

Korey kept his eyes focused on the road. "That's nice."

Michelle felt her enthusiasm deflate like a balloon when she realized Korey wasn't interested in hearing about her milk can paintings. It was then that it occurred to her that he never asked about them.

Tyler, however, constantly asked about them and encouraged her to pursue selling them.

But Tyler was with Charity.

And that was why Michelle had to stop thinking about him. But she needed to find

216

a way to evict him from her mind, which seemed impossible.

"So, how is your crew working out, Korey and Tyler?" Crystal asked as they sat around the supper table Thursday evening.

"I'll let Korey answer," Tyler said as he cut up his piece of tilapia. "Supper is *appeditlich,* by the way, Crystal."

His stepmother beamed. *"Danki."*

Tyler nodded. He tried to be extra kind to his stepmother, especially since Korey refused to accept her. He turned to Korey. "How's our crew going?"

"Fine." Korey kept his eyes trained on his plate filled with seasoned tilapia, rice, and mixed vegetables.

Tyler looked over at his stepmother and found that her smile had lost some of its luster. "They're doing even better this week. Dennis has really caught on and is working faster. Roger is working hard to catch up, and he gets better every day." He glanced over at Korey, who frowned at him.

Ignoring Korey, Tyler looked over at *Dat.* "How are Tom and Andy doing?" he asked about his father's two new crew members.

"They're doing great. I'm glad you convinced me to add two new crew members instead of just one. We definitely work faster with a crew of four."

"*Gut.*" Tyler added a small pile of rice to his plate. "Kore, I'm going to see Charity tonight. Did you want to walk over with me and see Michelle?"

Korey shook his head. "Dwight asked me to come by and help him with the renovations to the *daadihaus.*"

"Are you sure?"

"*Ya.* Why?"

"It seems you make more time for Dwight than you do for Michelle."

Korey stopped chewing and glowered at Tyler. Then he swallowed. "Are you criticizing my relationship with my girlfriend?"

"No." Tyler worked to keep his tone even. "I'm just surprised you haven't gone to see Michelle this week. That's all."

Korey studied Tyler for a few moments and then returned to eating and keeping his eyes focused on his plate.

After supper Tyler took a shower and changed into fresh trousers and a clean shirt before pocketing his flashlight and walking down the road toward Charity's farm.

When he trudged past Michelle's farm, he spotted lanterns glowing in the house. He imagined her helping her mother and sister clean up the kitchen after supper.

He yearned to see her and talk to her. It

had nearly broken his heart to avoid her during the youth gathering on Sunday, but he needed to respect his brother and keep his distance. Still, he missed their conversations. If only he weren't so drawn to her, then they could have possibly been friends.

Tyler did a mental head slap. He needed to focus on Charity, his lovely girlfriend. She was sweet, friendly, intelligent, and beautiful. And she clearly cared for Tyler. He needed to cultivate his relationship with her and forget his confusing feelings for Michelle.

He quickened his pace and continued on to Charity's father's dairy farm. When he reached the rock driveway that led to her large, two-story white house, he strode to the porch and then stopped dead in his tracks when he found the house was dark.

Tyler climbed the steps and knocked on the front door. He waited for a few moments and listened for the sound of voices and footsteps but heard nothing.

He moved to the back door and knocked again, but the house remained silent.

With a sigh, he started down the driveway and back toward his house. His eyes took in the lights glowing in Michelle's family's home, and the urge to see her gripped him once again. He longed to go and say hello, but he couldn't allow himself to violate his brother's trust.

Still, he and Michelle were friends, and there was no harm in stopping by to say hello . . .

Tyler considered what the consequences might be if he visited Michelle. Perhaps if he was honest with Korey and told him that he visited her, then the repercussions would be less dramatic. After all, their families were close, and they'd known each other their entire lives.

Who was Tyler kidding? Korey would be upset if he knew that Tyler had stopped by to see Michelle, but his feet still kept moving forward as the urge to say hello to her gripped him. He just needed to see her. He would keep the visit brief and then return home.

By the time he reached Michelle's driveway, he had convinced himself that there was no harm in just stopping by to say hello. Tyler once again felt the invisible magnet pulling him to her. Could that be a sign from God? But God wouldn't want him to ruin his relationship with his brother.

He scrubbed his hands down his face as more confusion spiraled through him.

But friendship wasn't a sin, and he craved her friendship.

He just hoped Korey would agree as he headed up Michelle's driveway.

CHAPTER 16

The warm yellow glow of the lanterns in the studio illuminated Michelle's worktable and the milk can she painted. After supper she'd finished her chores and then grabbed a sweater and retreated to the barn to lose herself in her favorite hobby and pray.

Lord, help me work through my bewildering feelings for Korey and Tyler. Please lead my heart on the path you've chosen for me. Erase my emotions for Tyler that have hijacked my thoughts. Help me love Korey the way I should. I don't want to hurt him. He's too important to me and the future I crave.

Michelle dipped her brush in blue paint and began working on the sky above the patchwork of rolling fields. Then she added puffy white clouds. When she heard the door behind her squeak open, she frowned.

"I know it's getting late, Jorie . . . Tell *Mamm* I'll be in soon. I just need to finish this up, okay?"

222

"I'm not Jorie."

Michelle stilled, and heat ricocheted up her neck as her nerve endings started to thrum. She peered over her shoulder, and her breath caught in her lungs as she drank in the sight of Tyler highlighted by the glow of the lanterns. He was handsome in a gray shirt. His strong jaw looked freshly shaved, and his hazel eyes sparkled.

"Hi," she managed to say, her voice soft and quavering.

Tyler fiddled with his straw hat in his hands. Then he pointed to the door. "I can go."

"No!" Her quick response only caused her cheeks to burn hotter. She took a deep breath. "You can stay."

He nodded and took another step into the small room.

"What are you doing here?"

"I went to see Charity, and she wasn't home." He crossed to the table and stood beside her. "So, I saw the lanterns in your *haus,* and I thought I'd come by to say hi. When I went to the door, Jorie told me that you were out here."

"Charity and her family are visiting her cousins who came to town for a wedding. Didn't she tell you?" Michelle asked.

He rubbed his chin. "I don't recall her

mentioning it."

"She might not have since it was last minute. She told me that she wasn't sure that the cousins were going to make it."

"Oh." He smiled. "I guess I should have called her before heading over to her *haus,* but her visit with her cousins sounds like it was just as unplanned as my visit."

"Sometimes the unexpected visits are the best ones." She felt her body relax as they studied each other. She breathed in his scent — soap and sandalwood — and her hands trembled.

Then a vision of Korey's handsome face flashed in her mind, and guilt grabbed her by her throat.

"Where's Korey?" she asked.

Tyler hopped on a stool. "He's helping Dwight work on his *haus.*"

"Their wedding is coming in just a month and a half." She once again wondered if Tyler would marry Charity someday, and she felt her lips flatten.

Tyler pointed to the milk can she'd been painting. "That's beautiful."

She smiled as warmth swirled in her chest. Tyler once again showed interest in her hobby, and her heart felt as if it might burst.

"Would you like to help?"

Tyler scoffed. "Oh no. I'm better working

with wood than a paintbrush. I would ruin it."

"No, you won't." She dipped the paintbrush in the white paint and then held it out to him.

"If you say so."

She placed the paintbrush in his hand and pushed the milk can over to him. "Now, add some clouds."

His hand trembled as he held the brush over the can. Then he pulled his hand away and frowned. "I can't do it. I'll mess it up and ruin your hard work."

"What if I helped you?"

"Okay . . . How?"

Michelle placed her hand on his, and heat zipped up her arm as her mouth dried. She guided his hand over to the milk can and helped him add a few more fluffy clouds.

"You got it," she said, releasing his hand. Her skin was cold from the absence of his touch.

Tyler added another cloud and then gave her a sheepish expression. "I ruined it, right?"

"Stop being ridiculous. It looks great."

He studied it. "You're so talented, Michelle." His voice was reverent, sending another shock wave of heat through her.

"*Danki,*" she whispered.

"Have you added a Scripture verse to this one?"

She shook her head. "No, not yet."

"I'm sure you've sold more since we last spoke."

"*Ya,* Lola said she has only a few left, so I need to bring her more cans soon."

Tyler folded his arms over his wide chest. "That's not a surprise to me at all. I told you they would sell." He surveyed the shelf where the finished milk cans sat. "Those are ready to go?"

"*Ya.*"

"May I look at them?"

"Of course."

Tyler sauntered over to the shelf and gave a low whistle as he examined the milk cans. "Wow. I think you need to learn to paint faster to keep up with the demand."

She blushed at his compliments and pondered why Tyler was more interested in her painting than Korey was.

Stop comparing them!

"Are these dry?" he asked.

"*Ya.*"

He reached for one. "May I . . . ?"

"Stop asking for permission," she said with a laugh. "Go ahead."

He lifted one, examined it, and then turned it over. "Psalm 23." He smiled at her. "I like it."

"It was your idea."

He took the time to pick up each milk can, compliment her on the work, and then read the verse inscribed on the bottom before he returned to the stool. "Your parents must be so proud."

"I suppose so."

"They like them, right?"

She nodded. "They do." She fingered her paintbrush and wondered why Tyler had decided to visit her today when he never approached her on Sunday.

"What's on your mind?" he asked.

Michelle started to ask him why they hadn't spoken on Sunday, but she couldn't allow herself to be so forward with him. "What are your hopes and dreams for the future?"

"Wow." He snorted. "You get right to the heart of things, huh?"

"I was just thinking about my own future, which made me wonder what other people hope for." She laughed nervously. "Sorry if that's too personal."

"No, it's okay. I don't mind answering." He rested his elbows on the worktable. "I hope to take over the roofing company when *mei dat* retires." He held up his hands. "Not to steal it from Korey, as he seems to think."

Michelle shook her head. "I don't understand why he would think that."

"He believes that I've always tried to overshadow him, and I'm trying to prove that I'm not." He seemed to study her. "Do you and your *schweschdere* bicker often?"

"Not since we were little. I'm close to both of them and grateful for them. In fact, I miss having Lainey close by. I feel like I don't see her enough. I miss our heart-to-heart talks."

Tyler held a clean paintbrush. "I hope Korey and I have that relationship someday."

"You and Jayden are close?"

Tyler nodded. "*Dat* calls Jay the peacekeeper. He goes out of his way to be a *gut bruder.*"

"So, your hope is to run the roofing company after your *dat* retires, and your dream is to have a *gut* relationship with Korey."

Tyler smiled. "Sure. That sounds *gut.*"

"What about a family and a home?"

"Well, that goes without saying. I hope to meet a *maedel* who warms my heart and then build a future with her."

"What about Charity? Could she be that *maedel*?"

He hesitated and then nodded. "She could be. I think I need to get to know her better." He rested his chin on the palm of his hand. "Now it's your turn to answer. What about your hopes and dreams?"

She dipped her brush in a cup of water and swirled it around. "I want what all Amish *maed* want — a husband, a home, and a family — if the Lord sees fit. And I'd like to keep painting as long as my husband is supportive."

"I hope you marry someone who is supportive of your painting."

She peered over at him, and his intense stare made the air whoosh from her lungs. Their eyes locked, and she felt as if time had stopped for a moment.

Tyler shifted on the stool. "Korey is jealous of my friendship with you."

"I know."

"That's why I didn't talk to you on Sunday — as much as I longed to. I don't want to hurt *mei bruder.*"

"I understand."

"But it's not easy staying away from you. I enjoy talking with you."

She smiled. "I feel the same way, but I would never want to hurt Korey. He means too much to me."

Tyler nodded.

"Michelle? Are you still out here?" Jorie appeared in the doorway, and she blinked, looking startled. "Tyler. I didn't realize you were still here."

He cleared his throat and stood. "I really should get going."

"I'll walk you out." Michelle stood, picked up her flashlight, and ignored the confused look her younger sister gave her as she followed Tyler through the barn.

They walked out into the dark night together and flipped on their flashlights. She took in the vast sky and the stars that seemed to twinkle only for them. The air was cool and smelled like pine. It was the perfect autumn night. She glanced over at Tyler and longed for more time to talk with him.

"I'm glad you stopped by," she said, hoping she didn't sound too eager for his attention.

Tyler nodded. "I am too." He held his hand out to her, and when she shook it, she yearned to keep holding on, thread her fingers with his, and pull him back into the barn to talk for the remainder of the night.

But that would be wrong. Tyler was her friend, and that was all they could ever be.

Don't hurt Korey!

"I'll see you Sunday," she said.

"Enjoy the rest of your week." Tyler began walking backward down the driveway.

"Keep painting."

"I will." She stood in the driveway until the beam of his flashlight disappeared from view.

Then she returned to the barn, where Jorie sat at the table, eyeing her with suspicion.

Her younger sister tapped the tabletop with emphasis. "What was going on in here?"

"What do you mean by that, Jorie?" Michelle asked as she began cleaning up the paint and brushes.

"Why was Tyler here?"

"He went to visit Charity, and she wasn't home. So he stopped by to say hello." Michelle cleaned off her brushes and stowed them.

"He was here for a long time."

Michelle shrugged as she continued cleaning up. "We were talking."

An awkward silence fell between them, and Jorie finally asked, "Are you cheating on Korey with his *bruder*?"

"What?" Michelle gasped as she faced her sister. "Do you honestly think that about me?"

Jorie shrugged. "I don't know what to think. You two were out here all alone. Why would he come to visit you?"

"We were talking, Jorie. That's it. We're

freinden. I would never cheat on Korey. I'm offended that you would even think that about me."

Jorie grimaced. "I'm sorry. I was just surprised that he was here. That's all. I didn't think you'd hurt Korey that way." She stood. "Let me help you clean up."

They finished tidying up the studio, and then Jorie walked toward the door.

Michelle stood by the table and studied the milk can that Tyler had helped her paint, and more confusion gushed through her. She wanted to be his friend, but she felt so much more than friendship for him. And she knew it was a sin to have feelings for a man who wasn't her boyfriend.

Jorie stood in the doorway. "You look upset, Shell. *Was iss letz?*"

"Nothing is wrong." Michelle flipped on her flashlight and then turned off the lanterns before exiting the barn.

Michelle strode beside her sister toward the house, their shoes crunching along the rock path. When she looked up at the clear sky, she sent a silent prayer up to God. *Please, Lord, remove the feelings for Tyler that have overtaken my heart and replace them with my love for Korey. Guide me toward a path that pleases you. I don't want to hurt Korey or be a sinner.*

232

"You okay?" Jorie asked as they climbed the porch steps.

"I will be." *With God's help.*

CHAPTER 17

Tyler climbed the porch steps and reached for the storm door and then stilled. Breathing in through his nose, he worked to calm his frayed nerves and stop his pulse from zooming. He dropped onto the porch swing, which creaked under his weight. After pushing it into motion, he switched off his flashlight and gazed up at the sky and the stars twinkling above him.

His mind spun like a cyclone as he recalled how easy and natural it had felt to sit with Michelle in her barn studio and talk about everything from her art to their hopes and dreams. The truth was that he felt more comfortable talking to Michelle than talking to Charity — *his girlfriend.* And that reality had his insides twisted up in knots.

Why would God lead his heart to someone he couldn't have — someone who could cost him his relationship with his brother?

Tyler rubbed his eyes with his fingertips.

Perhaps he was misreading his feelings, but the way his pulse galloped every time he saw her was as real as the heat he felt when she held his hand and helped him paint the clouds on the milk can.

Psalm 51, verse 10, echoed in his head: *Create in me a pure heart, O God, and renew a steadfast spirit within me.*

"Tyler?"

He jumped at the sound of his name and turned toward the doorway where his stepmother stood watching him. *"Ya?"*

"Why are you sitting out here in the dark?"

"I-I was just thinking."

Crystal nodded slowly. "Would you like some company?"

Not really. "Sure."

Carrying a lantern, Crystal took a seat on the rocker beside the porch swing. The soft scraping sound of her chair moving back and forth filled the porch, along with the hum of traffic along the highway in the distance.

"Is Korey home?" Tyler asked, his voice sounding too loud as it broke through the quiet.

"No. Jayden is in his room, and your *dat* is in the barn."

"Oh."

The silence stretched between them, and

235

out of the corner of his eye, he spotted her watching him.

"Is everything all right, Tyler?"

He brushed his hands down his trousers while debating his response. While he trusted Crystal, he wasn't sure that revealing his inner turmoil was an appropriate confession for him to make to anyone — especially his family members.

"Sometimes it helps to talk to someone," she said. "But I'm not pressuring you to open up to me. Just know I'm here if you need someone to listen."

He smiled over at her. "*Danki,* Crystal." If only Korey could see the good in her.

Korey.

Guilt crawled up on his shoulders and clawed at his already sore muscles.

He turned toward Crystal. "I'm confused," he blurted.

"About what?"

"My feelings for . . . Charity." That wasn't exactly a lie. He was just as befuddled about Charity as he was about Michelle.

"Okay. Tell me about your confusion." Crystal's expression was open and encouraging. "Do you think you love her?"

"I-I don't know. Well, I don't think I do." He swallowed. "Is love a feeling that grows over time, or is it something that hits you fast like a lightning bolt?"

"It's difficult to say. I believe it can be either. With your *dat,* we sort of were *freinden* first, but it quickly turned to love for me when I got to know him better."

Tyler looked out toward the barn.

"Are you doubting your feelings for Charity?"

He sighed. "You could say that."

"Do you think she may not be the *maedel* for you?"

Tyler stopped the swing from moving and turned toward Crystal. "I'm not sure. Right now, all I feel is confusion."

"Have you prayed about it?" She faced him, and he appreciated the sympathy and compassion he found in her expression.

"*Ya,* and I keep praying about it. I don't want to hurt Charity, but I also don't want to lead her on."

"Would you like my advice?"

"Very much."

"If I were in your situation, I would keep praying about it and listen to my heart. If the relationship doesn't feel right, then it most likely isn't. It's not fair to you or Charity to keep the relationship going if you don't see a future with her. Honesty is always the best choice. Breakups are tough, but they also mean that you're more likely to find the right person."

"You sound like you speak from experience."

Crystal gave a soft laugh. "*Ya,* I do. I dated a man whom I was certain I would marry someday, but he chose to move to Ohio to start a business with his cousin instead of staying here and marrying me. I couldn't go with him because I was caring for my ill *daed.*"

"I'm so sorry." Tyler shook his head. "That's terrible."

"*Danki,* but it worked out the way it was supposed to. If I had married him, then I never would have met your *dat.*" She held up her hand. "Don't get me wrong. The breakup was painful, and I had emotional scars for a long time. But I had to get through that relationship before I met your *dat.* If it doesn't feel right with Charity, then it may not be, and that's okay."

He nodded slowly. *"Danki."*

The barn door opened, and *Dat* walked out, the beam of his flashlight bouncing along the path.

"Could we please keep this between us?" Tyler asked Crystal.

"Of course. And I'm grateful you trusted me with this, Tyler. I'm always here if you need someone to talk to."

238

Dat smiled as he climbed the porch steps. "What are you two up to?"

"Just talking." Crystal smiled up at *Dat.*

"Did you have a nice visit with Charity?" *Dat* asked Tyler.

"She wasn't home."

"Oh. Well, I'm sure you'll see her soon." *Dat* looked down at Crystal, his expression filled with love.

It was then that it occurred to Tyler that perhaps *Dat* had felt as if he couldn't stay away from Crystal, which was the same way Tyler felt about Michelle.

That idea rocked Tyler to his core because he couldn't have Michelle. And that truth hurt the most.

"I can't believe I'm due in a month." Lainey rested her hands on her protruding abdomen while sitting at her kitchen table on a Wednesday afternoon two weeks later.

Michelle picked up her mug of tea. "That's why Jorie and I wanted to come to help you with chores today."

"*Ya.*" Jorie nodded.

"*Danki* so much," Lainey said. "My back and feet have been so sore."

Jana Beth yawned and rubbed her eyes before picking up her cup of milk.

Michelle pointed to her little niece. "I

239

think someone needs an n-a-p."

"*Ya,* I can put her in," Lainey said. She grasped the edge of the table and then pushed herself up.

Jorie stood. "No, no. You sit, Lainey. I'll take her up and then clean the upstairs bathroom before I sweep and dust."

"Would you like me to do your laundry?" Michelle asked.

"Oh, that would be such a blessing."

While Jorie took Jana Beth upstairs, Michelle set to work on the laundry in the utility room. After running the clothes through the wringer washer, she carried the large basket out to the porch and began hanging Noah's trousers on the line.

The late-October air held the hint of a chill, and Michelle was grateful she had worn her heavy sweater. The golden-brown leaves fluttered in the breeze while two chattering squirrels chased each other up a nearby tree.

She fetched another pair of Noah's trousers and then lost herself in thoughts while she worked. For the past two weeks, she had pondered her conversation with Tyler when he had come to see her in her painting studio. She had cherished their time together and longed to see him again; however, since then, they had only shared nods

240

of hello at youth gatherings. They both had kept their distance, and as much as she'd begged God to remove her feelings for Tyler from her heart, they had only expanded.

She had done her best to keep her focus on Korey, but Tyler still resided in the back of her mind — lurking in her thoughts like an uninvited visitor.

The storm door creaked open, and Lainey stepped gingerly out onto the back porch. "Need some help?"

Michelle peeked over her shoulder at her older sister. "No, I need you to rest. Just sit on the rocker and supervise."

"I can definitely do that." Lainey slowly lowered herself down on the rocker.

Michelle hung up another pair of trousers. "How are you feeling?

"Ready to meet this little angel."

"I am too." Michelle smiled over at her. "Do you think you're having a boy or a girl?"

Lainey rubbed her abdomen. "I honestly don't have a feeling either way. We'll find out soon."

Michelle picked up one of Noah's shirts and hung it out.

"So, how are you?"

Michelle shrugged. "Fine."

"*Mamm* told me that you've sold quite a

few of your milk can paintings. That's such great news, but I'm honestly not surprised that they're doing so well."

"*Danki.* I've been busy painting more. I delivered another dozen to the store last week."

"I'm so proud of you and your talent."

Michelle smiled over at her sister. *"Danki."* She was so grateful for her sisters. She hung out two more of Noah's shirts on the line.

"And how are things with Korey?"

"Fine." Michelle kept her back to her sister as she worked.

"Just fine?"

Michelle avoided eye contact as she retrieved one of Lainey's dresses. *"Ya."*

"Shell."

"What?" Michelle hung the dress on the line.

"Look at me, Shell."

With a sigh, she turned toward her older sister. There was no hiding her feelings from Lainey. They knew each other too well. Often just Michelle's tone of voice would tip Lainey off that Michelle was holding something back from her.

"You know you can always be honest with me. What's going on between you and Korey?"

Michelle leaned back on the railing. "How

did you know Noah was the one God had chosen for you to marry?"

"*Ach* no. You're having problems?" Lainey's pretty face filled with sympathy. "I'm so sorry."

Michelle peered down at her apron. "I wouldn't say we're having problems. I'm just . . . unsettled about our relationship."

"Shell, please look at me," Lainey said, and Michelle complied. "What are you unsettled about?"

Michelle took a deep breath. "I don't think Korey is mature enough to become a husband and eventually a father."

"So, you're still concerned about how he treats his stepmother and Tyler?"

"*Ya.*"

"Do you want to move on?"

"I-I don't know. Every time I imagine breaking up, my heart hurts. I've cared about him for so long, you know? I don't want to think about not having him in my life, but at the same time, I'm not sure he's ready for a future with me. I want to get married and have a family, and I don't know if I have the patience to wait for him to grow up."

"Have you asked him how he feels about getting married?"

"Not in those words."

Lainey pursed her lips and absently rubbed her belly.

"What are you thinking?"

"Sometimes it's necessary to have those tough conversations to see if you're on the same page."

"Did you and Noah go through this?"

"Sort of. I was ready to settle down before he was. We talked about it and were honest. He said he wanted to have a *haus* first, and then his grandparents offered him this farm. It all worked out in the end, but for a while I began doubting his feelings for me." Lainey rested her hands on the arms of the rocker. "Have an honest conversation with Korey and tell him how you're feeling. It might clear things up and make you feel better if you tell him where you stand and ask him how he feels."

Michelle nodded as some of the worry coiling in her chest relaxed. "So, I'll be honest with him and see where he stands."

"*Ya,* I think you should."

"*Danki,* Lainey."

"It will all be okay, Michelle. I can feel it."

Michelle smiled, hoping her sister was right.

CHAPTER 18

Sunday afternoon Michelle stared out the side window of Korey's buggy at the traffic rumbling past. The sky was clogged with dark, threatening clouds, and the smell of rain wafted over her.

"I wonder if Ray made any indoor plans for the youth group today." She angled her body toward Korey and took in his handsome profile.

He nodded. "Ray said he would set up the Ping-Pong tables in one of the barns just in case we couldn't play volleyball since the forecast called for rain today."

"When did you talk to Ray?"

"I ran into him at the hardware store yesterday."

"Oh," she said.

A stiff silence overtook the buggy, and her conversation with her sister echoed through her mind. Now was the perfect time to discuss their future. If she could only form the right words.

Korey halted the horse at a red light, and she took a deep breath.

"So, I've been thinking," she began.

He faced her, his forehead wrinkled. "About what?"

"Us."

Something unreadable flickered around his face.

"Are we okay?"

"I think we are. Don't you?"

"Well, it's just that I'm perplexed about something."

He frowned.

"I don't understand why you never want to talk about the future."

He turned away from her just as the light turned green, and then he guided the horse through the intersection.

She waited for him to respond, but he kept his eyes focused on the road ahead.

"Korey?" she asked.

He remained stoic.

"Korey, why won't you answer me?" Her voice quavered as worry sat like a boulder in the pit of her stomach.

A muscle flexed in his jaw, but he kept his eyes trained on the road ahead.

"Do you want to break up?" she asked, her hands trembling.

He finally glanced over at her. "No. Do you?"

"No, but I don't understand why we're stuck in the same pattern after fourteen months. Why aren't we talking about a future together?"

"Why does everything have to follow a precise schedule?" His voice was pinched as he turned back toward the windshield. "Does every couple have to get engaged after a year and then get married a few months later? Can't we do what's right for *us*?"

She huffed out a breath as the boulder began to dissolve. "Does that mean you want to get married?"

"Eventually." He swallowed. "Maybe."

The word sent a shaft of ice through her heart. And just like that, the boulder was back, and a sick, shaky feeling swept through her. "Maybe?"

A deafening silence overtook the buggy as he guided the horse onto the road that led to Ray Esch's family's farm.

"What does *maybe* mean, Korey?" Her voice shook.

His posture was ramrod straight as he pursed his lips. "It means I'm not ready to get married."

"Are you waiting to save up enough money

for a *haus,* or do you simply not want to marry me?"

"Why do we have to discuss this today, Michelle?" Frustration vibrated in his tone.

Her frustration snapped her to attention in her seat. "Because I need to know where I stand with you."

Korey's nostrils flared as he guided the horse up the driveway toward a sea of buggies parked in the Esch family's field. He halted the horse at the top of the driveway and faced her. "Why don't we get together one night this week, and we can talk this out."

"No." She hugged her arms to her chest as if to shield her crumbling heart. "I want to talk about this now. You always avoid discussing the future with me. Insisting we talk about the future later this week is just another way for you to put off telling me how you truly feel."

Korey rubbed his hands over his face. "Michelle, I'm not in the mood to talk about getting married. It's not something that I can just snap my fingers and decide to do. I'll know when I'm ready to marry you. Someday I might be, but not now. If you want me to tell you that we can get married this fall, you're going to be disappointed because I can't say that. I'm just not ready, and I don't understand why that's not *gut* enough for you." He held up his hands. "There's really nothing else to say, so let's go have fun with our *freinden.*" Then he pushed open the door.

"Wait," she said, and he stilled. "Do you care about me?"

"Of course I do."

"Do you love me?"

He nodded. "Yes."

"Then why don't you ever tell me that you love me anymore?"

Korey sucked in a deep breath through his nose. "I'll say it, okay? Can we go now?"

"No." She shook her head. "I can't go and pretend to have fun when we're in the middle of an argument. We need to work this out right now." She pointed to the floor of the buggy.

"Michelle, there's nothing more to say," he hissed. Then he closed his eyes. "I care about you, and I want to be with you. I'm just not ready to get married." He hesitated. "I'm *froh* with how things are now. I hope you can accept that."

She tried to swallow past the sand in her throat.

"Can we please go now?" He pushed his door open and climbed out.

Michelle remained cemented in place, her

heart shattering as he stood outside the buggy, frowning at her.

He leaned back inside, his expression resigned. "You're upset with me."

"Of course I am! I don't feel that we've resolved anything. You just told me that you're not ready, but you didn't even ask me how I feel. Apparently all that matters is how you feel, but you're not the only person in this relationship."

He looked down at the buggy floor and then back up at her. "Michelle, I think we should save this conversation for later when we can really talk alone, okay?"

"I'm talking now."

Korey shook his head. "Let's enjoy our afternoon, and we'll discuss this later. We can talk on the ride home and then sit on your porch too. All right? Let's have fun with our *freinden* today."

Her eyes began to sting as his words cut her like shards of glass, but she sat up taller. She wouldn't let him see how much he'd hurt her.

"I need to put the horse in the barn."

She lifted her apple pie from the floor and climbed out of the buggy. Then she marched up to the Esch family's back door.

After forcing her lips into a smile, she entered the kitchen and nodded greetings to the women gathered around the table full of desserts. She breathed in the delicious smells of a variety of cookies, cakes, and pies, but her stomach still felt queasy as her heartbreaking conversation with Korey echoed in her mind.

Kendra stood nearby and talked on about how the renovations on her future house were coming along quite nicely.

Michelle tried to listen, but only the sound of her shattering future filled her ears. She lingered by the edge of her group of friends for a few moments, smiling and nodding as Kendra went on and on about her wedding. But Kendra's words pummeled her heart as she began to accept the hard truth — Korey might not ever want to marry her. She'd been kidding herself for months, convinced that he would propose to her soon.

Perhaps it was time for her to set him free. Maybe their relationship had ended a long time ago but she'd been too focused on getting married to accept that truth.

Grief hit her hard and fast. She needed to get back outside before her sadness leaked from her eyes and her friends began asking questions that she wasn't ready to answer out loud.

Michelle padded to the door, grateful no one stopped her before she stalked out into the late-October chill. She hoped the cold air might cool her warm cheeks.

When she heard voices sounding from the large barn, she followed the hooting and hollering until she reached the door. Maybe Korey was feeling as miserable as she was and would reconsider his decision to postpone their conversation. The sooner they worked this out, the better for her breaking heart.

Inside, she spotted members of her youth group gathered around the Ping-Pong table, and her eyes immediately focused on Korey, talking and laughing with Dwight over in the corner. He acted as if nothing was wrong while she was drowning in disappointment and despondency.

Frustration exploded through her veins as she spun and made for the grove of apple trees that led to a small pond.

Grateful to find the area empty, Michelle sat on a lonely bench and stared out toward the water. She hugged her sweater against her body and held her breath, hoping to keep her tears at bay.

Tyler turned toward the entrance of the barn just as Michelle appeared in the doorway, and his heart gave a little bump. As she scanned the crowd, he took in the sadness etched in her pretty face, and worry flooded him. Something was wrong.

He peered across the barn to where his brother stood engrossed in a conversation with his best friend. Korey laughed at something Dwight said and then turned his attention toward the Ping-Pong game.

Tyler glowered. So, instead of checking on his girlfriend, his middle brother was more interested in enjoying time with his buddies.

Setting his cup of water on the hay bale beside him, Tyler stood.

"Where are you going?" Jonah asked beside him.

Tyler nodded toward the barn exit. "I'll be right back."

He stepped out into the yard and breathed in the overwhelming scent of rain while surveying the area for Michelle. When he didn't spot her by the house or the buggies, he turned toward a path that led through a grove of apple trees to a retention pond.

"That's where I would go to be alone," he whispered before hiking down the rock path toward the trees.

He entered the clearing by the pond and found her sitting on the bench with her back toward him, her shoulders hunched and her head bent.

Tyler sucked in a breath as doubt suddenly swarmed him. If he sat down with her, he risked overstepping his bounds with both his brother and Charity.

But it was clear Michelle was hurting, and he couldn't walk away when she needed someone.

Against his better judgment, he started down the well-worn path toward her.

Michelle's chin lifted, and she sniffed before her lips turned up into a manufactured smile. "Hi, Tyler." She dabbed her eyes with a tissue. "Fancy meeting you here."

His chest pinched as he took in the puffiness around her beautiful eyes. "Are you okay?"

"Of course I am." She looked as if she tried to laugh, but no sound came out.

He stood by the bench and pointed to the empty spot beside her. "May I join you?"

"Ya." She scooted over and then patted the empty seat beside her.

He sat, and then they both looked out over the pond. He remained silent, waiting for her to share the root of her sadness.

Instead of speaking, she sniffed once again.

"Do you want to talk about it?"

She shook her head. "No."

"Do you want me to leave?"

"No." She looked over at him. "Just sit with me, okay?"

Tyler nodded. "I'm happy to." He kept his focus on the small ripples in the water, holding his breath and hoping she'd open up to him.

After several moments, she cleared her throat. "I didn't see Charity in the kitchen or the barn. Is she still not feeling well?"

"No, she said she still has an upset stomach."

"I'm sorry to hear that. I was hoping she'd feel better soon."

"I offered to visit her, but she said she didn't want me to see her that way." Tyler picked up a pebble and tossed it toward the pond. It landed in the water with a plop, creating tiny waves that fanned out.

He picked up another pebble and ran his fingers over the smooth edges while he waited for her to say something else.

"On the way over here, I told Korey that I wanted to discuss our relationship," she began softly, her voice vibrating. "It didn't go well."

He rested his elbows on his thighs and tried to calm the anger burning in his gut when he thought of his brother causing sweet Michelle's emotional pain. He threw the pebble into the water, but the motion offered no relief. "I'm sorry."

"It's definitely not your fault." She looked down at the black apron that covered her blue dress. "Sometimes I feel like Korey prioritizes his *freinden* over me."

Tyler stopped himself from nodding at her astute observation. Instead, he kept his focus on the pond.

"I don't know what to do. I envision a future with him, but he doesn't want to discuss it. I care for him, but I . . ."

His eyes snapped to hers. "But what?"

"I'm sorry. I shouldn't be talking about this with you." She rubbed her hand down her apron. "You're his *bruder,* and it's not appropriate for me to discuss our relationship issues with you."

Tyler understood, but he couldn't stop his disappointment. He wanted to relieve her anguish and help her. "Is there anything I can do?"

"You're such a *gut freind.*" She covered his hand with hers, sending a spark that ignited his skin.

Unable to speak for a moment, he simply nodded and then looked out over the water once again. They sat in a comfortable silence for several minutes, and he enjoyed the feeling of her warm skin against his. He breathed in her scent — vanilla mixed with soap and something uniquely Michelle.

While he longed for her to open up to him, he was satisfied just offering his silent support, and he hoped their time together meant as much to her as it did to him.

"Did you feel that?" she suddenly asked, turning toward him. "It's raining."

Droplets peppered his shirt and trousers and sprinkled over the pond.

They stood and darted down the path toward the barn as the rain increased. When Michelle stumbled, he grabbed her hand and righted her. She threaded her fingers with his as they continued through the grove.

They came out the other side, and he noticed that more than half of the buggies had disappeared.

Michelle released his hand. "What are you looking at?"

"Did a bunch of people leave?" He pointed toward the field.

She shrugged. "I don't know, but we're getting wet." She jogged toward the barn.

He took off after her, and they stepped inside the barn, where nearly half of their youth group had disappeared.

Jonah sidled up to Tyler. "There you are! I thought you left with everyone else." He pointed at Tyler's clothes. "You're soaked."

"Where did everyone go?" Michelle asked, hugging her arms to her middle and shivering.

"They decided to go over to John Fisher's *haus* to play board games," Jonah said.

Michelle's blue eyes roamed the barn. "Where's Korey?"

"He left with Dwight and Kendra," Jonah said.

"He left without me?" Michelle's voice broke.

Jonah grimaced. "I'm sorry."

"It's okay." She swallowed back her threatening tears. "Did you see Jorie leave?"

Jonah nodded. "She was with a group of her *freinden.*"

She shrugged. "I'll just walk home." She pivoted toward the Ping-Pong table. "Ray, do you have an umbrella I could borrow?"

"No," Tyler said, and she spun toward him. "I'll give you a ride."

Jonah lifted his eyebrows, but Tyler ignored his best friend's silent accusation.

Tyler removed his straw hat and handed it to her. "You can hold this over your head. Let's go."

Michelle nodded, and then they scooted back out into the rain.

As they bolted toward his buggy, renewed

fury simmered through Tyler. He would never understand how his brother could take such a wonderful young woman like Michelle for granted.

CHAPTER 19

Michelle settled on the seat beside Tyler and rubbed her hands over her soaked sweater while raindrops pelted the windshield of his buggy.

Tyler halted the horse at the end of the Esch family's driveway and reached behind him. "Wrap yourself in this," he said, handing her a blue, gray, and green quilt in a Mariner's Compass pattern, similar to the one Korey kept in his buggy.

"Danki." She wrapped the quilt around her shoulders and hugged it against her, closing her eyes as she breathed in Tyler's scent.

Tyler glanced over at her. "You okay?"

"Ya. Danki for the ride."

He smiled and shook his head. "There was no way I was going to let you walk home in this weather." He held up his hand. "I'm not saying I'm the boss of you. I just meant that I didn't want you to walk home in the rain."

260

She chuckled. "I know what you mean, and I appreciate it, Tyler."

"It's so *gut* to hear you laugh again."

Michelle looked out toward the passing trees, hoping he couldn't see her blush.

"How's your painting going?"

"It's going well. I took another dozen milk cans to the store this week."

He grinned over at her. "*Gut.* I'm glad people are recognizing your talent and buying them up."

Warmth and appreciation overtook her chest. Tyler seemed interested in what she had to say and in her life. If only Korey were that engaged in their conversations . . .

Stop comparing them!

"How's your family doing?" he asked.

"Everyone is fine. Lainey's second *boppli* will be here soon, and we're all excited."

"That's right. When is she due again?"

"Next month. Jorie and I went to visit her and help with chores this week."

Michelle and Tyler talked on about their families and his work for the remainder of the ride to her house, and Michelle felt herself relax. Talking to him was easy, and conversation flowed like the raindrops trailing down his windshield.

By the time Tyler halted the horse in front of her porch, the rain had dissipated, leaving the sky bright blue with happy rays of sunshine.

Disappointment drenched her as she untangled herself from the quilt. She dreaded having to say goodbye.

"I hope you have a nice evening," he said.

"Would you like to stay and visit?" she asked as she pushed the door open.

He looked down at his damp clothes. "*Ya, if I could possibly borrow a towel.*"

"Absolutely not," she teased and then laughed. "I'm kidding."

They walked up the porch steps together and entered the kitchen.

"Michelle? Jorie?" *Mamm* asked as she padded in from the family room. Her gaze swung between Michelle and Tyler, and then her expression turned curious. "Oh, Michelle. Tyler. What a surprise."

Tyler lifted a hand in a wave. "Hello, Elaine."

"Hi, *Mamm.*" Michelle tried to smile.

"Where's Jorie?"

"She's with some of her *freinden,*" Michelle said.

Her mother studied them. "Did you two get caught in the rain?"

"We sure did. Would you please give Tyler a towel to dry off?" Michelle started toward the stairs. "I'm going to get changed, and

262

then I'll meet you on the porch," she told Tyler.

She hurried up the stairs and changed into a fresh purple dress, black apron, and dry stockings before fixing her hair and covering it with a dry prayer *kapp*. She pulled on a clean black sweater and then slipped on dry shoes before zipping down the stairs and into the kitchen, where her mother stood by the counter.

"Why are you with Tyler and not Korey?" *Mamm* asked.

"It's a long story." Michelle began digging through the refrigerator and found the cut-up vegetables, cheese, and dip she had saved from Saturday, and then she turned to the pantry and chose a box of crackers.

Mamm appeared behind her and touched her shoulder. "What's going on?"

"Everything is fine," Michelle said while loading the food onto a serving tray. "Tyler brought me home." She poured two glasses of apple cider and added them to the tray.

"Please look at me."

Michelle met her mother's concerned gaze. "I promise everything is fine."

"Didn't Korey pick you up this morning?"

Michelle nodded.

"Where is he?"

"I don't know." Michelle picked up the

263

tray. "We had a disagreement on the way to the youth gathering. When we got there, I went for a walk to clear my head. When I came back, Korey and some of our *freinden* had gone to John Fisher's *haus.* So Tyler offered to bring me home."

"He left you there?" *Mamm* asked, her voice rising.

Michelle shrugged as if his abandonment hadn't sliced at her soul. "In his defense, he didn't know where I was."

"Did he even bother to look for you before he left?"

"I don't know." She nodded toward the mudroom. "Would you mind opening the back door for me?"

Mamm hesitated as if contemplating something, but then she crossed to the mudroom and opened the back door.

"Danki," Michelle said.

Mamm looked over at Tyler and smiled before disappearing into the house.

Tyler smiled up at her from a bench, a blue towel sitting in a heap at his feet. "Those snacks look scrumptious."

"Would you like a sandwich too?"

He shook his head. "No, *danki.* This is perfect." He slid all the way over to the far right side of the bench. "Please join me."

She moved a small table over in front of

264

them, set down the tray, and then sat on the bench beside him. After they both bowed their head in silent prayer, they began drinking cider and eating the vegetables, cheese, and crackers.

"Your *mamm* seemed very surprised to see me."

"She asked me why you were here instead of Korey. I summarized what happened without giving many details."

Tyler swirled a piece of celery in the dip and took a bite.

"It's turned into a pretty afternoon." She set a piece of cheese on a cracker and ate it.

Tyler nodded and finished the celery. "It sure has."

She took a sip of cider.

"Do you think you and Korey can work things out?"

She settled back on the bench and sighed. "I hope so."

Tyler seemed unconvinced. "I know it's our way to forgive, but why do you allow him to take you for granted over and over again?"

She studied her glass, running her fingers through the condensation. "We've known each other for so long that I can't give up on us. I don't want to hurt him."

"But, Michelle, he's hurting you. I saw

the pain in your eyes."

She smiled over at him. "Why don't we talk about something else? How do you like running your own crew?"

"It's going well," he began.

She ate a few vegetables and listened while he talked about work. The afternoon wore on as they moved on to discussing friends in the community. When it grew late, she gathered up the empty plates and their glasses.

"Would you like some supper? I can warm up some of *mei mamm*'s leftover meat loaf," she offered.

"No, *danki.* I don't want to impose."

"Tyler, you're not imposing. You're a dear *freind.* In fact, you're one of my best *freinden.*"

He touched her hand. "*Danki.* I feel the same way."

Above them, the sun had begun to set, bringing with it a glorious, vivid light show of colors.

"I enjoyed the snacks and the company." He picked up the towel. "Let me get the door for you." He held open the back door, and they both walked into the kitchen.

Michelle set the tray on the counter.

"Where would you like me to put the towel?"

She reached for it. "I'll take it."

Tyler stood in the doorway to the family room and waved to her parents, who were each reading books. "*Gut nacht,* Elaine and Simon. Have a *gut* week."

"You too," *Dat* said.

Mamm waved. "Tell your folks we said hello."

Then Tyler turned to Michelle. "I hope to see you again soon."

"Me too," she said.

As she watched him leave, she wasn't sure how she'd ever expel him from her heart.

Tyler sat out on the porch later that evening and stared down toward the road. He drummed his fingers on the rocking chair arm and waited for his middle brother to arrive home. He was going to give Korey a piece of his mind, whether he wanted to hear it or not.

When the sound of hooves and the flashing headlights of a buggy started up the driveway, Tyler began popping his knuckles. He tried to gather his thoughts despite his boiling anger with his brother's thoughtlessness.

The horse halted at the barn, and Jayden climbed out, his lantern guiding him as he unhitched the horse and led it to the barn.

267

Tyler leaned back on the rocker and pushed it into motion, hoping the movement would relieve some of his pent-up energy.

After several moments, Jayden stowed the buggy and started toward the house. "Ty?"

"Yeah."

"I was wondering where you were. You didn't go to John's *haus* with us," Jayden said, jogging up the porch steps.

"Is Kore on his way?"

"Ya." Jayden leaned back against the railing. "He wasn't far behind me."

Tyler nodded slowly, breathing through his nose.

"Is everything okay?"

"Ya." Tyler rubbed the side of his neck in an effort to relieve his coiling muscles.

Jayden pushed off the railing and rubbed his hands together. "Well, I'm starved, so I'm going to go see if Crystal has any of that mac and cheese casserole left that she put together yesterday." Then he disappeared into the house, the storm door clicking shut behind him.

A few minutes later, Korey's horse and buggy moved up the driveway. Tyler stood and walked over to the railing while Korey unhitched his horse and led it to the barn. Once his horse was settled, Korey started up the path toward the house with his flashlight beam pointed toward the ground.

"How was your afternoon?" Tyler asked him.

"Fine," Korey said. "Why?"

"Well, I was just wondering, since you left your girlfriend crying in the rain."

Korey stopped at the bottom of the steps, his face illuminated by the lantern at Tyler's feet as he looked up at the porch. "How do you know that?"

"Because I'm the one who found her crying and gave her a ride home since you were nowhere to be found." Tyler leaned forward on his elbows. "Did you even think about her when you left with your buddies?"

Storm clouds gathered across Korey's face. "If it's any of your business, she was angry with me, and I couldn't find her. So I figured she walked home."

Tyler studied him. "Why do you treat her so badly?"

"I don't treat her badly." Korey's mouth pinched.

"Do you even care about her?"

"Of course I do."

Tyler stood up straight. "So then, tell me, why do you treat her so badly?" he asked, his voice tinged with anger.

"I didn't mean to." Korey took a deep

breath. "We argued on the way to the youth gathering. She was upset, and I figured I should let her cool down. I thought we'd talk about it later. When John invited us all over to his *haus* to play games, I couldn't find her. So I thought she had already walked home. I never thought I was abandoning her. I figured she gave up on me."

"First of all, when you were letting her cool down, she was off crying by the pond and you were playing Ping-Pong and having a fantastic time with your *freinden.*" Tyler took a step toward him. "Secondly, you figured she had walked home, right? Well, did it ever occur to you to make sure she was okay?"

Korey climbed the steps and his mouth dipped. "And where was your girlfriend when you were taking care of mine?"

"She's home sick today. She wasn't at the youth gathering, but that's beside the point. Michelle needed a *freind,* and I was there when she needed one."

Korey set his flashlight on a rocking chair. "Why are you interfering in my relationship again?"

"Is that all you're worried about?" Tyler demanded. "You're more concerned that I'm interfering than about the fact that you left your girlfriend behind with a broken

270

heart in the rain. You should be more concerned about losing her than the fact that I was there to save her."

Korey stepped over to him and poked Tyler in the chest. "Are you threatening me?"

"No, I'm not threatening you. I'm trying to get you to open your eyes, Kore. You're going to lose her if you keep taking her for granted."

"And you're saying that you hope Michelle and I do break up so that you can ask her out, right? Because you can't stand the fact that I'm dating her."

"Korey, that's not what I'm saying at all!"

"Whoa, whoa!" *Dat* burst out onto the porch and nudged Tyler and Korey apart. "What's going on here?"

"Nothing!" Korey spat the word at Tyler and then stomped into the house, slamming the door behind him.

Tyler took deep breaths, trying to calm his frayed nerves.

Dat rubbed his hand down his beard and heaved a deep sigh. "What's going on between you two now?"

"Korey is going to lose Michelle. That's what's going on." Tyler explained how he found Michelle by the pond and then took her home in the rain since Korey had left

271

with his friends. "He doesn't appreciate her. I'm trying to tell him that he needs to treat her better or he's going to lose her. He needs to grow up and realize that his actions hurt others, and today he hurt Michelle deeply."

"I know you mean well, Tyler, but you need to let him figure it out for himself. That's what growing up is about — learning from your mistakes and changing your behavior."

"You should have seen how upset she was."

Dat shook his head. "I hate to say it, but he'll figure it out when he loses her. Sometimes you have to fall down and hit rock bottom before you suffer the consequences of mistakes you've made." He patted Tyler's shoulder. "Everything you've said is correct, but he's not going to listen to you. He needs to realize it on his own. Just let him live his life, and you live yours, all right?"

Tyler nodded. *"Ya, Dat."*

"Come inside. It's getting late, and we all have to work tomorrow." *Dat* started for the door and then stopped and turned around. "Are you coming?"

"Ya, I'll be there in a minute." Tyler picked up his lantern and felt this strange awakening of his heart at the idea of Korey

and Michelle breaking up.

Then guilt doused him with a dose of reality. How terrible would it be for him to even imagine dating his brother's ex-girlfriend? And how much worse would the issues between them become if Tyler considered dating Michelle?

But deep down, Tyler longed to date Michelle, and the more he tried to stop imagining it, the more vivid the image became in his mind.

CHAPTER 20

Tyler stood by the ladder at the jobsite the following morning and looked up toward where Korey spoke to their crew members, Dennis and Roger. Renewed remorse billowed through him as he considered how he had attacked Korey last night.

He had stayed awake most of the night contemplating all of his actions the day before — how he had come to Michelle's rescue and then spent the afternoon visiting with her, how he had argued with Korey, and then how he had considered the idea of asking Michelle to date him if she and Korey ended their relationship. He realized that while he cared deeply for Michelle, he didn't want to lose his brother. He also agreed that *Dat* was right, and Tyler needed to let Korey make his own decisions.

Now Tyler just had to find a way to smooth things over with Korey before he did lose him.

The ladder began to rattle, and Korey climbed down.

"How are things going up there?" Tyler asked.

"Fine." Korey pushed his mirrored sunglasses up on his nose. "They're doing a *gut* job."

Tyler nodded.

"I'm going to see Michelle after work," Korey said as he poured water from the large cooler into a cup.

"I'm going to check on Charity, too, since she hasn't been feeling well. Why don't we walk over there together?"

Korey took a drink of water and hesitated.

"I'm sorry I overstepped last night," Tyler began. "You were right when you said that I was interfering. Your relationship is your business, and I was out of line lecturing you. I promise I'll mind my own business in the future. You're *mei bruder,* and I don't want any animosity between us. I'd like to work things out so that we can be close."

"I'd like that too." Korey shook his hand. "We can walk to their houses together."

"Gut." Relief fluttered through Tyler. He had his brother back. Now he just had to work on eliminating his feelings for Michelle.

Michelle opened the back door later that evening and found Korey standing on the porch holding a bouquet of pink roses. "Korey."

"I'm here to grovel." He held the flowers out to her. "I'm really sorry for being such a *dummkopp* yesterday. I never meant to make you feel bad, and leaving things unresolved was selfish and cruel. You deserve better than that. I'm also sorry I left without checking on you. I thought you had gone home, but I should have made sure you were safe."

Michelle took the flowers and breathed in their fragrance. "They're gorgeous."

"Please forgive me," he continued. "Tyler told me that he brought you home in the rain, and he made me realize that I've really taken you for granted."

"He did?"

Korey nodded. "*Ya*, he let me have it when I got home last night, and he was completely right." He paused. "So, I'm here to beg you for your forgiveness."

She swallowed as admiration for Tyler swelled in her heart, but then she came crashing back to the present when she recalled her painful and unfinished discussion with Korey. "What about our conversation yesterday? You decided to go laugh with your *freinden* while I was hanging by a thread and holding back tears."

Korey nodded. "You're right. I was completely wrong." He touched her shoulder. "I know that you're eager to get married since we've been together so long, and I know it's disappointing to you that I'm not ready yet. I've been pondering it all night, and I finally realized what the problem is."

"Okay." Her lungs constricted as she awaited his explanation.

"The reason why I'm not ready is that ever since I lost *mei mamm,* I've struggled with change. She's gone, *mei dat* has remarried, and everything has changed." He paused, sucking in a deep breath. "I care about you deeply. But right now, I just want to keep things the way they are." His dark eyes glistened with unshed tears. "I know it's a lot to ask, but I just need you to give me more time."

She sniffed as her own eyes filled with tears. "That makes sense. *Ya,* of course I'll give you time." Although she longed to get married soon, her heart swelled with understanding for Korey's grief and his yearning to keep his status quo for a while longer.

"Danki." His expression seemed relieved. "I promise I'll do better. I'll make an effort to put you first, and I promise that someday soon I will be ready to settle down. I just need more time. I hope and pray you'll wait for me."

"Of course I will, Korey."

He kissed her cheek.

"Would you like to come in and have some dessert? I baked a lemon cake today."

"Oh, that sounds perfect."

He followed her into the kitchen, where she put the roses in water and served lemon cake and decaffeinated coffee.

"This is fantastic," he said after taking a bite.

She smiled. "I'm so glad you like it." She added cream and sugar to her coffee.

"Tyler and I walked over together. He's next door seeing Charity. He said she hasn't felt well for a few days."

"Oh." Michelle smiled, imagining Tyler next door. "I spoke to her earlier, and she was doing much better."

"I'm glad to hear it." Korey took another bite of cake as silence fell over the kitchen. She tried to think of something to say while contemplating why conversations were so much easier with Tyler. Could it be because there was no pressure for her and Tyler to maintain the perfect relationship, or was it something more, something deeper?

"How was work today?" she asked as she forked a piece of cake.

"The usual. We're roofing a grocery store in Gordonville."

"Which store?"

As Korey talked on about work, Michelle wondered how Tyler and Charity were enjoying their visit and if they had more interesting subjects to discuss than the Bontrager brothers' roofing jobs.

"Are you sure you're not too cold?" Tyler asked Charity while they sat together on her porch.

She smiled over at him. "I'm comfortable. I'm so glad you came by tonight. I've missed you."

"I'm just *froh* you're feeling better. I'm sorry you were *krank* for so long."

"*Ya,* that stomach flu was terrible. My parents had it too."

"I'm sorry to hear that." Tyler sipped the hot cocoa she had made for him.

"How was the youth gathering?" she asked. "I was so disappointed I missed it."

"It was okay. It rained and about half of our youth group left to go to John Fisher's *haus* to play games. I wound up giving

Michelle a ride home."

"Did Korey not attend the gathering?"

"Well, Michelle and Korey had a disagreement, and she went for a walk." He explained how he found her by the pond and it started to rain. Then he told her that Michelle had realized that Korey had left her at the youth gathering, so he gave her a ride home.

"Oh." Charity nodded. "Well, I'm glad you were there to give her a ride home."

"I am too."

Charity watched him for a moment and then picked up a brownie from the plate she had carried out to share. "Kendra and Dwight's wedding is coming up fast. It's only about a month away now."

Tyler nodded and chose a brownie.

"It will be so nice when they get married, won't it? I know they'll be so *froh* together." Charity sighed.

Tyler nodded again and swallowed a bite of brownie. Then he took a sip of cocoa to wash it down.

"I've been thinking about how nice it would be to get engaged."

Tyler froze in place and blinked. Perhaps he'd heard her wrong.

"I mean, I know it's early, and we're still getting to know each other. But I really care about you, Tyler. I've cared for you for a long time now. I was just delighted when you finally asked me out. Now I can't stop thinking about our future together."

Tyler's stomach cramped, and when he opened his mouth, his words were lodged in his throat.

"Are you okay?" she asked. "You look a little pale."

He suddenly felt hot, as if his skin were on fire. The truth was that he didn't feel the same way about her, but he didn't want to hurt her. He also didn't want to live a lie.

"Tyler?"

"Charity, I like you, and I'm enjoying getting to know you. But the truth is that I'm not ready to get engaged. Let's give it time and see where this goes, okay?"

"Okay." Her smile flattened. She cleared her throat and then plastered another smile on her face. "Did I tell you about the quilts I've been working on for the Christmas bazaar?"

While she talked on about quilting and the Christmas bazaar, Tyler tried to think of an excuse to go home.

Michelle carried their plates and mugs to the counter after she and Korey had finished eating their cake and drinking their coffee.

"I'm going to use the restroom," Korey said.

"Okay." She began washing their dishes and then stopped when she heard a knock at the back door.

She walked out through the mudroom, opened the door, and found Tyler standing on the porch. "Hi."

"Hi." He rocked back on his heels. "I wanted to see if Kore was ready to walk home."

"He'll be out in a minute." Michelle stepped into the mudroom and pulled on her sweater before joining him on the porch. "Would you like to sit and wait for him?"

"Sure."

They sank down together on the bench. Then they both started to talk at once and ended up laughing.

"You first," he said.

"I just wanted to thank you for talking some sense into Korey last night. He apologized and said he's going to work harder at not taking me for granted."

"I just told him how I felt." Tyler shrugged. "But I'm glad I could help."

"Don't act like it was no big deal, because it was. *Danki.*"

"Gern gschehne."

"How did it go with Charity?"

"It was *gut.*"

Michelle tilted her head as a mixture of curiosity and jealousy raged through her. "Is everything all right?"

He sighed. "She wants to get engaged."

"Isn't it a little soon?"

Tyler scoffed. "*Ya,* you could say that. I feel like we're still getting to know each other, and I'm not ready to get married."

A strange relief filtered through Michelle.

"Please don't tell her I told you any of this. I don't want her to think I'm betraying her, but it's so easy for me to tell you how I'm feeling. Sometimes I tell you things without even thinking about it."

She smiled. "I feel the same way."

"Did you do any painting today?"

"A little bit. I was busy with chores, but I was able to work on one milk can."

"Well, that's something, right?" Tyler asked.

The storm door opened with a loud creak, and Korey walked out onto the porch, his expression stoic.

Tyler stood. "Hey, Kore. I was on my way home and wanted to see if you were ready to go home too. I thought we could walk together."

"Sure," Korey said. "I was just about to say good night."

283

"All right." Tyler turned to Michelle and held out his hand. *"Gut nacht."*

"I'll see you Sunday," Michelle said before shaking his hand.

Then Tyler looked at his brother. "I'll meet you at the end of the driveway." He flipped on his flashlight and hopped down the porch steps.

Korey touched Michelle's hand and then kissed her cheek. "*Danki* for giving me another chance. I won't let you down."

"*Gut nacht,* Korey," she told him before he left.

She hugged her arms to her chest and hoped she could sort through her confusing feelings.

"Did everything go okay with Michelle?" Tyler asked Korey as they walked down the street together, their flashlights guiding their way through the dark.

Korey nodded. *"Ya."*

"Then why are you so quiet?"

Korey eyed him. "I was standing at the door when you confessed to Michelle that you tell her things that you don't tell anyone else. It's obvious that you care for her."

"Kore, I've told you numerous times that we're just *freinden.*" Tyler paused to gather his thoughts. While he was aware that he wasn't telling Korey the whole truth, he refused to ruin his relationship with his brother. "We have a close friendship, but that's all it is. Right now I'm concentrating on getting to know Charity better."

"That might be true. But I see how you look at Michelle, and it's not like a *freind*. You don't look at Charity the same way as you look at Michelle."

Tyler hesitated, certain his brother was right, and he couldn't bring himself to deny the truth.

"You say you don't want any animosity between us, but it's not true. You enjoy making me angry. That's why we argue all the time."

Tyler found true pain and disappointment in his brother's eyes, and guilt threatened to obliterate him. "I'm sorry. I never meant to hurt you. If it will save our relationship, I won't talk to Michelle at all anymore. I'll stay away from her. I don't want you to feel threatened by me. I want to be your *bruder*, not your enemy."

Korey stopped walking and stared at him. "Do you honestly mean that, Tyler?"

"Of course I do. You said that you've always felt like I was trying to overshadow you, and I haven't been. But it's obvious that I've been doing something wrong if you've always felt that way. I want us to get along, and I'll do what I have to in order to preserve our relationship."

Korey nodded. "Okay. Then please stay away from her and don't talk to her."

Tyler patted his shoulder. "I promise you I won't." As Tyler said the words, he knew he would miss Michelle.

But Korey was his brother, and he had to put his family first — no matter how difficult and heartbreaking that sacrifice would be.

Crystal looked up from a cookbook and smiled at Tyler and Korey when they stepped into the kitchen. "How was your evening?"

"It was *gut,*" Tyler said. "*Danki* for asking."

"Fine," Korey mumbled on his way to the stairs.

Tyler sighed and shook his head. Would his brother ever grow up?

"Is everything okay?" Crystal asked.

Tyler stopped in the doorway and faced her. He wanted to tell her that no, nothing was okay since he had agreed never to speak to Michelle again, but he couldn't admit that out loud. What would Crystal think of him if she knew he had feelings for his brother's girlfriend? She would call him a sinner, and he might have to confess that sin in front of the congregation and then lose his brother forever.

"Were you ever at odds with your *bruder*?" Tyler asked instead — careful to keep his voice soft.

Crystal frowned. "I'm not sure I know what you mean."

"Never mind. *Gut nacht,*" he said, and he took a step toward the stairs.

"Tyler, I've said this before, but you can talk to me. I'm always *froh* to listen and offer advice if I can. I might actually be able to help you if you give me a chance."

He walked back into the kitchen and sat down across from her. "Sometimes I feel like I don't belong with Charity, but I don't want to hurt her. Tonight she admitted that she wanted me to propose to her, but I don't see myself marrying her. She's sweet, intelligent, and *schee,* but I'm not sure we're meant for each other."

"That's a tough situation. Have you prayed about it?"

He nodded. "I pray often about it."

"Well, you don't want to hurt her, but you also shouldn't lead her on. You should trust God and follow your heart. If you decide that you and Charity should break up, then it would be tough on both of you. But you and Charity will heal, and God will guide both of you to the right person." She paused as if to gather her thoughts. "I told you what happened with me and my ex-boyfriend. It was painful when he broke my heart, but I was so grateful when I met your *dat.* I've never been happier, and I'm certain God led us to each other."

"How did you know *mei dat* was the one?" Tyler drew invisible circles on the tabletop.

Crystal smiled. "God put love for your *dat* in my heart, and I couldn't deny it. I couldn't stop myself from thinking of him and wanting him in my life."

Tyler nodded as clarity filled his mind. Crystal had described how he felt about Michelle, but not Charity, and that was the root of all of his problems.

"Is there something else on your mind, Tyler?"

"No," he said, his voice sounding hoarse. He stood. "*Danki* for talking to me. *Gut nacht.*"

"Sleep well," she said.

Tyler ascended the stairs to the second floor, and as he walked past Korey's door, his remorse was as sharp as a blade.

As he slipped into his room, Tyler decided to pour all of his emotion into his relationship with Charity and somehow banish Michelle from his mind.

Help me, Lord.

CHAPTER 21

"Well, here we are," Tyler said as he halted the horse by the field full of buggies at the Yoder farm the following Sunday afternoon.

Since it was a church Sunday, Tyler and Charity had attended the service at the Stoltzfoos family's home, eaten lunch, and then gone home to change their clothes before heading to the Yoder farm for the youth gathering.

The service had been excruciating as he tried to avoid looking at Michelle in order to keep his promise to Korey, but his eyes had defied him, sneaking glances every few minutes. He had no idea how to convince his heart to let her go when he felt the continuous urge to be with her. No matter how hard he prayed, she was still a constant companion in his thoughts. It was as if she'd taken up permanent residency there.

He had tried to pour his feelings for Michelle into his relationship with Charity, but so far it had been in vain. They seemed to be too different, which was evidenced by the quiet ride to the youth gathering. Every question he asked Charity and every joke he made was met with a one-word response or a baffled expression.

"Tyler?"

He turned toward her and found her staring at him with the same confusion she had displayed earlier. *"Ya?"*

"You seem a little preoccupied today. Is everything all right?"

He shrugged. *"Ya.* Let's go have some fun, okay?"

They climbed out of the buggy, and Charity stood nearby while he unhitched the horse. The early November sky was dotted with white, puffy clouds, and the aroma of a wood-burning stove permeated the chilly air.

"Oh look. There are Michelle and Korey." Charity pointed toward the barn, where his brother and Michelle spoke to mutual friends.

Tyler tried to ignore the tug he felt in his heart when he heard Michelle's name.

"How do you and Korey like working together?"

Tyler shrugged. "Some days are better than others."

"You two don't get along all the time?"

"You're joking, right?" He snorted as he looked over his shoulder.

She blinked at him. "No."

"You honestly didn't know that Korey and I bicker constantly?"

"You do?"

Tyler laughed as he unhitched his horse. "*Ya,* we disagree often, but I've been working on it, trying to improve our relationship."

"Oh." Charity still looked discombobulated. "I knew that you argued when we were *kinner* in school, but I assumed you both grew up."

"Well, even grown-ups bicker sometimes, right? Don't your parents argue at times?"

She shook her head. "Not much at all."

"They must hide it from you, because all family members bicker sometimes. We all have our off days, but Korey and I seem to have them more often than not." He held on to the reins. "You're lucky to be an only child. You never had to share toys or clothes. And you never had to work to get your parents' attention. I think Korey has some middle-child resentment, but I'm trying to be a better older —"

Tyler stopped speaking when her mouth dropped open in a gasp.

"How could you say that?" she demanded. "What did I say?"

Charity lifted her chin. "How could you talk so terribly about your *bruders*? You're blessed to have them. And you think I'm spoiled because I'm an only child? Well, let me tell you that my parents tried for years to have *kinner*, and they could only have me. You don't appreciate what you have."

"I'm sorry. You're right. I wasn't thinking."

"You should think before you speak, Tyler," she said with a huff before stomping off toward the barn where the youth were already gathered.

Bewildered, Tyler stared after her. He rubbed his cheek and then strolled toward the barn as more frustration and confusion spilled through him.

When he reached the barn, Tyler stood just inside the door and surveyed the crowd. Games were in full swing at two Ping-Pong tables while groups of young people stood around talking, eating snacks, and watching the players.

Tyler spotted Charity in the far corner, where she had pulled Michelle aside and was frowning and speaking animatedly. He blew out a deep, regretful sigh. He could only imagine what Charity would say about him now.

"Hey, Ty," Jonah exclaimed as he sidled up to him. "Why so glum?"

"Have you ever had one of those days where everything you said was taken wrong?"

Jonah shook his head. "Uh, not really."

"Let's just say I'm having an off day."

"I'm sorry to hear that."

Tyler looked over at Michelle, and his heart sank.

"Is there anything I can do to help?"

"No, thanks." Tyler glanced around the room and spotted his brothers laughing with a group of friends. If only his life could be that carefree, but he felt trapped in a dungeon created by his complicated emotions. He longed to go home and relax alone in the solace of his room, but he wouldn't leave Charity stranded like Korey had done to Michelle.

"How about a drink?" Jonah offered. "There's cocoa."

"That sounds perfect. *Danki.*" Tyler followed Jonah over to pick up a cup of hot cocoa, then stood nearby sipping the warm, chocolaty drink while Jonah made conversation with a few friends.

He couldn't wait for the youth gathering to end so he could go home and be alone with his thoughts.

"Michelle." Charity's voice vibrated with urgency as she approached the group of friends where Michelle stood. "I need to talk to you alone. Please."

"Was iss letz?" Michelle asked Charity as she pulled her over to an empty corner of the barn.

"It's Tyler."

Michelle searched Charity's pretty green eyes as worry threaded through her. "What do you mean?"

"During the ride over here, he acted like he was in his own world. We hardly talked. Then when we got here, he started complaining about his *bruders* and then said I couldn't relate because I never had to deal with things like sharing toys and trying to get my parents' attention. He made it sound like I'm a spoiled brat! As if it's fun to be an only child. He apologized, but he really offended me."

"Charity, I know Tyler, and he would never deliberately hurt your feelings."

"I don't like when he says things like that. He's so blessed to have siblings when I have none." Charity shook her head. "What if he's not the man I thought he was?"

"I'm sure he didn't mean to hurt you.

He's not a mean-spirited man, Charity."

Kendra walked over toward them. "Charity! Michelle! There you are. Can you believe my wedding is only a month away? It's coming so fast! I can't wait for you to see *mei haus*. It looks so *gut*."

As a few more of their friends joined them as Kendra bragged about the renovations to her future home, Michelle took a few steps away. She looked across the barn just as Tyler walked outside into the cold afternoon air.

Michelle muttered, "Excuse me," and then made a beeline for the barn exit. When she reached outside, she hugged her sweater to her chest and took off after Tyler.

"Tyler! Tyler, wait!" she called.

He turned toward her, nodded, and kept walking toward the pasture.

"Wait! Tyler!" she chased after him. "Please stop!"

He spun toward her while continuing to walk backward.

"Was iss letz?" she asked.

He stopped moving. "Nothing."

She caught up to him and touched his arm. "I need to talk to you."

He looked behind her and then took a few steps away from her. "It's better if we don't talk."

"Why?"

"It's causing problems with *mei bruder,* and we already have issues."

She blanched as if he'd struck her as her heart began to crumble.

He looked stricken. "Don't look at me like that, okay?"

"Like what?"

"I'm sorry, Michelle, but I can't do this anymore." He held up his hands and starting moving forward again.

"Are you sure you're okay?" she called after him.

He stopped in his tracks and faced her. *"Ya."*

"I'm worried about you." She took a step toward him.

"I'm sorry, Michelle." He looked behind her and then shook his head. "I need to go. Take care of yourself."

As he walked away, she felt as if he took a piece of her heart with him.

Michelle sat beside Charity later that evening in the barn while they sang hymns. She spotted Tyler in the back of the men's section, staring down at his hymnal, and her heart gave a bump. She'd spent the last couple of hours trying to figure out what he'd meant when he said, *"I'm sorry, Michelle, but I can't do this anymore."*

She had a feeling he meant that he couldn't be her friend, and if so, then that nearly broke her in two. She couldn't imagine not being able to talk to him anymore.

"Do you really think Tyler didn't mean to hurt my feelings?"

Michelle's eyes flitted to Charity's. "*Ya,* of course. He would never deliberately hurt you or anyone else." *But losing his friendship is eating me up inside!*

Her best friend sighed. "Maybe you're right."

Michelle studied her hymnal.

"Maybe we should do another double date."

Michelle turned toward Charity.

"We could bring casseroles and desserts to their house on Sunday since there's no service next week. We can prepare the food on Saturday. What do you think?"

Michelle shrugged. "Sure."

"Perfect," Charity said. "I'll tell Tyler that we're going to do it. They can invite Duane, Crystal, and Jayden to stay too. We'll spend the day with the Bontragers. It will be so fun."

"*Ya.* Fun." Michelle tried to smile, but the idea of spending the day with Tyler

when he wouldn't speak to her sounded
more like torture.

CHAPTER 22

"*Danki* so much for bringing lunch over today," Crystal announced Sunday afternoon. "This Italian meatball casserole is fantastic."

Tyler mumbled in agreement, careful not to look across the table at Michelle, but once again, his eyes defied him and landed on her. She looked pretty this afternoon, wearing a pale blue dress that accentuated her gorgeous sky-blue eyes. Her cheeks and lips looked pinker than usual.

It had been a week since he had told her that it was better that they didn't speak, and his heart wilted like a plant without any water or sun more with each passing day. He missed her friendship so much that his chest ached.

Michelle nodded across the table at Crystal. "I'm glad you like it. Charity and I put all of the food together yesterday."

"Wait until you try the dessert," Charity

said, leaning toward Tyler. "We made a new recipe. I'm sure you'll love it."

Tyler looked up at her. *"Danki."*

He was grateful Charity had decided to forgive him for hurting her feelings Sunday. Still, their relationship had been nothing but strained since then. He felt as if he had to walk on eggshells around her — always worried that he might say something to offend her. But he was going to keep trying to make it work.

"So, Michelle," Crystal began, "how are your milk can paintings selling?"

"I'm staying busy. I brought more to the store last week," Michelle began.

Tyler kept his focus on his casserole and his roll while Michelle talked on about her milk cans. Listening to her voice was both a blessing and a curse as he once again longed to pull her into an empty room and talk to her in private.

"What is the name of that gift shop where you're selling them?" Crystal asked.

"Country Quilts and Gifts," Michelle said.

"Where is it again?" his stepmother asked.

"It's on Old Philadelphia Pike in Bird-in-Hand," Korey snapped. "I pointed it out to you the other day, Crystal."

"Oh, right," Crystal gave a nervous laugh. "Silly me. I'm so sorry."

301

"You don't need to apologize, Crystal. It's okay," Michelle said.

Tyler peeked up from his meal as Michelle shot Korey a look.

"It's a nice little store," Charity chimed in. "You have to see the display with her milk cans. They look amazing. Have you seen them, Korey?"

Korey shook his head. "I haven't made it down there yet, but I'm sure it's nice."

Tyler didn't miss the hurt expression that overtook Michelle's face. His brother was still taking her for granted, but it didn't surprise Tyler.

But it wasn't Tyler's business how Korey treated his girlfriend. Tyler had to find a way to stay out of Michelle's life. He had no idea how to let go though. His heart wouldn't allow it.

"How are your folks doing, Michelle?" *Dat* asked as he picked up his glass of water.

Michelle nodded and wiped her mouth with a napkin. "They're doing well and eager for their second grandchild to arrive."

"Oh, how nice!" Crystal said.

Jayden grinned. "Good for Lainey. That's so exciting."

Michelle beamed, and she looked even more lovely. *"Danki."*

Tyler gave himself a mental head slap. He

needed to concentrate on Charity, not Michelle!

Tyler directed his gaze on his girlfriend. "Everything is positively *appeditlich.*"

"*Danki.* I had hoped you'd enjoy it." Charity touched his hand, and he waited to feel the explosion of heat that Michelle's touches brought, but instead, he felt nothing.

"Kendra and Dwight's wedding is coming up soon, right?" Crystal asked.

Dat swallowed a bite of casserole. "No kidding."

"It's in two weeks," Charity said. "Kendra is so excited, and I can't blame her. I would be, too, if I were getting married."

Tyler didn't miss the side-eye Charity gave him, and he found it confusing. On one hand, Charity told him that his comments about her being an only child hurt her feelings, but on the other hand, she constantly hinted about marriage. It was pretty obvious that she just wanted to get married, but she didn't necessarily want to marry Tyler. Instead, she just wanted to marry *someone.*

"Korey," Crystal began, "are all of the renovations done at Dwight's *haus?*"

His middle brother kept his eyes focused on his plate and nodded.

In response, Crystal seemed to be working hard to keep a pleasant expression on her face.

Tyler frowned. If only Korey could just accept their stepmother. He gave his father a quick glance and noticed that he pursed his lips as if he were strangling his irritation to save humiliating Korey in front of their company. Surely *Dat* would give Korey a piece of his mind later in private.

"I believe Kore said they finished everything up last week, and it looks really nice," Tyler said, hoping to ease Crystal's embarrassment.

"Korey," Michelle drew out his name. "Why don't you give Crystal the details." Her words were measured as if she were speaking to a four-year-old.

Tyler studied her, taking in the frustration in her expression. It seemed she was just as aggravated with Korey's behavior as he was. When she met his gaze, his breath paused and his heart did a funny little dance while she stared at him, her expression unreadable.

Tearing his eyes away, Tyler focused on his remaining casserole.

"The work is done," Korey muttered. "It looks really nice."

Crystal nodded with too much enthusiasm for Korey's lame response. "Oh, *gut*." She looked at Charity. "How are your folks doing, Charity?"

"Oh, they're doing well," Charity began. "*Mei mamm* and I have been quilting to try to fill all of the Christmas orders we received." She snapped her fingers. "That reminds me, Tyler. Are you and your *dat* working on those trains for the toy drive?"

Tyler nodded. "*Ya,* we are."

"We've made about two dozen so far, but we're just getting started," *Dat* said.

"I'd love to see one of those trains," Charity said. "Maybe you can show me sometime."

"Sure," Tyler said.

"How's your *dat* doing, Charity?" *Dat* said.

"He's doing well. The farm keeps him busy," she began.

While his girlfriend talked on about her family, Tyler kept eating and hoping that this meal would end soon.

"Those pumpkin spice cupcakes were scrumptious," Crystal said while drying a serving platter after supper. "The cream cheese icing was perfect."

Charity scrubbed a dish. "I'm so glad you liked them. Michelle and I enjoyed preparing everything yesterday. Right, Michelle?"

"*Ya.*" Michelle wiped the table and worked

to keep a smile on her face despite the frustration and grief brewing in her chest.

She was angry with Korey for the way he had treated his stepmother, but she was also hurt by how Tyler had avoided her all evening. He had barely spoken to her — except for a strained hello when she arrived — and he had looked at her only once during supper. She missed his friendship, she missed their talks, she missed *him.*

"Michelle?"

"Huh?" She turned to where Crystal and Charity watched her, both with worried expressions. "I'm sorry. Did you say something?"

Crystal gave her a warm smile. "I asked if you were okay."

Michelle fingered the wet dishcloth. No, she wasn't okay, but she didn't want to share all of her feelings with them. After all, how could she tell her best friend that she had feelings for her boyfriend?

"Michelle?" Charity's pretty face filled with concern.

"Crystal," Michelle began, "is Korey always that rude to you?"

Crystal hesitated and then gave a half shrug. "Like I've told you before, he's still adjusting to having me in his life, and he's still struggling with the idea that his *dat* has a new *fraa*. So, I just let it go and keep praying that the Lord will warm his heart toward me."

"He's twenty-four," Michelle said. "He needs to start acting like it."

Charity gasped.

Michelle put down the dishcloth. "It's true. I understand that he's still grieving his *mamm* and always will, but he has no right to be rude to Crystal." She gestured widely. "I still remember the first day I met you when I brought over that cheesecake, and he was so nasty to you. I had hoped and prayed that he had already softened his heart toward you, and I've even spoken to him about it and told him to grow up. However, I saw here tonight that he's still behaving badly. It upsets me more than I can say."

"It's okay," Crystal said. "Duane and I have talked about it, and I know I need to give Korey some grace and more time."

Michelle huffed a breath. Her disappointment with Korey ran deep, and she would share how she felt later when they were alone.

Crystal smiled brightly. "Why don't we finish this up and then make some hot cocoa to take outside?"

"I love that idea," Charity said.

307

Michelle nodded and returned to the task of wiping down the table.

Once the kitchen was clean and the cocoa was ready, Michelle and Charity each carried out a tray with mugs of hot cocoa topped with whipped cream toward the back porch, where the men were sitting and talking in the cool November afternoon.

Crystal held open the door, and Jayden and Tyler popped up from their chairs.

"Let me take that from you," Jayden said, reaching for Charity's tray.

Charity handed it to him. *"Danki."*

"I'll carry that." Tyler took Michelle's tray, and when their fingers brushed, she felt that familiar sizzle.

She nodded and then distributed mugs to Korey and Duane before setting the last two on a table next to the porch swing.

Duane and Korey were engrossed in a conversation regarding work while Crystal and Charity sat beside each other in rocking chairs and started discussing their plans for Thanksgiving and when they hoped to start on their Christmas cards.

"I'll take this tray inside," Tyler muttered before slipping through the back door.

Michelle picked up the second empty tray from where Jayden had set it on another small table and followed Tyler, carefully closing the storm door and back door behind her.

When she stepped into the kitchen, she found him leaning forward on the sink, his chin dipped down while taking deep breaths.

"Are you okay, Tyler?" She rushed over to him and touched his arm.

He jumped back as if her fingers had burned him, holding up his hands. "You need to go back outside."

"What's going on, Tyler?" Her voice was thin and reedy. "Why are you pushing me away and avoiding me?"

"Haven't you figured it out, Michelle? I can't be near you."

She blinked. "I-I don't —"

"It's because of Korey," he said, whispering and peeking toward the doorway. "If you won't leave, then I will." He stalked toward the mudroom and then out the back door.

Michelle leaned against a kitchen chair and then squared her shoulders. Deep in her heart she knew Tyler was right. Her relationship with Tyler would hurt Korey and possibly Charity, and she refused to hurt either of them.

If only she could be Tyler's friend without allowing her feelings for him to get in the way, but that wasn't possible.

She grabbed a container of sugar cookies and then returned to the porch. "I brought sugar *kichlin* for everyone." She handed the container to Jayden and then took a seat beside Korey on the porch swing.

As Michelle pushed the swing into motion, she picked up her mug of hot cocoa and looked out toward the brown patchwork of pastures while trying to convince her heart that someday she'd accept having lost Tyler's precious friendship.

"*Danki* for bringing lunch over today," Korey told Michelle late that afternoon while they walked toward her farm.

She nodded, while Tyler and Charity walked ahead of them, holding hands. "*Gern gschehne.*"

"You've been awfully quiet all afternoon, Michelle."

She stuck her hands in her pockets and kept her eyes focused on her shoes, avoiding both Korey's gaze and the sight of Tyler and Charity walking together in the distance.

Korey stopped walking and swiveled toward her. "Have I done something to upset you?"

She looked up at him, surprised he'd noticed her reticence. She folded her arms over her chest and tilted her head. "*Ya,* you have, Korey."

"What did I do?" He gave a little laugh, and then his smile faltered. "Wait. You're serious?"

"*Ya,* I am."

"Why?"

"I'm appalled by how disrespectful you were to Crystal."

His face contorted into a scowl. "I don't know what you're talking about," he mumbled.

"*Ya,* you do." She held her hand up to stop him from interrupting. "I know you're grieving your *mamm,* and you always will. But it's time that you stopped taking that grief out on Crystal. Your *dat* has been married to her for more than a year now. I'm sure that it's difficult for you to see your *dat* with her, but you need to stop being so hostile."

"You have no idea what my life is like." He took a step away from her, his eyes sparking.

"Korey, stop," she said, and he stilled. "I'm not discounting what you feel, and you're entitled to your feelings." She took a deep breath. "But Crystal is a wonderful person, and she's entitled to your respect. She's your stepmother, and you're no longer a child. You need to start acting like a grown man. Your *bruders* have accepted her, and you should also."

His jaw tightened. "I know you mean well, but you really need to mind your own business, Michelle. You have no idea how it feels to have your *mamm* ripped from your life and then have your *dat* remarry less than two years later."

"Korey, please just listen to me, okay?" Michelle took his hands in hers. "I know you miss her, but she'll always live in your heart. God chose to take her, and I know it hurts. I miss her too."

"She wasn't your *mamm*." He ground out the words as he yanked his hands from her grasp.

"I know that, and I'm not saying she was. But you know it's not unusual for widows and widowers to remarry in our community."

"So soon?" He scoffed. "I don't think so." He took a few more steps back from her. "Look, I'll see you later."

She grabbed his arm and pulled him back. "No! You're not going to head home without working this out with me. You need to tell me that you're going to treat Crystal better. I want to hear you say you're going to make an effort."

312

Korey sneered as he looked out toward the pasture behind her and then met her gaze. "Fine. I'll try." His indignation rolled off him in waves.

"*Danki,*" she said.

They ambled up to her back porch in silence, and the tension between them was palpable.

"Have a *gut* week," she told him when they reached her back door.

"You too," he said before loping down the porch steps toward the driveway.

Michelle hung her coat on a peg by the back door and then walked into the kitchen and blew out a deep sigh.

"What's that sigh for?" *Mamm* asked as she stepped through the doorway from the family room.

Michelle dropped into a nearby kitchen chair. "Korey." She rested her elbow on the table and her chin on her palm while she explained how rude Korey had been to Crystal during supper.

"Oh my." *Mamm* shook her head. "You had mentioned that Korey struggled with Duane marrying Crystal, but I thought he'd gotten beyond that."

"I did too." Michelle stared down at the wood grain on the tabletop.

"Penny for your thoughts?"

She looked up at her mother. "It upsets me so much, *Mamm.* Crystal is so thoughtful and loving, and she deserves to be treated with respect. Tyler and Jayden are kind to her. Why can't he behave like his *bruders*?"

"Because he's not his *bruders.*" *Mamm* smiled. "Isn't that why you love Korey? Because of who he is?"

Michelle examined her fingernails as her mother's question floated through her mind.

"Is there something else on your mind?"

She met *Mamm*'s concerned expression. "It's not just that. He's been so distant lately. We seem to run out of things to talk about, and he's not supportive of my painting. I feel like . . ."

"You feel like what, Michelle? You know you can say anything to me."

"This is so difficult to say." Michelle hugged her arms to her middle. "I feel like I'm pulling away from him, and I don't know what to do about it. I care for him, but I'm not sure if he's the one I'm supposed to spend my life with. In fact, he doesn't know when he'll be ready to get married." She paused. "And I've already been praying about all of this, so you don't need to tell me to talk to God about it."

Mamm gave her a sympathetic expression.

"And what do you think God is trying to tell you?"

"I-I'm not sure, but I'm starting to question my feelings for Korey."

"Sometimes couples outgrow each other. Maybe you and Korey are headed on different paths, and that's okay."

Michelle sniffed. "But I can't imagine not having him in my life, and I don't want to hurt him."

"God might have someone else in mind for you. You just have to be sure to keep your heart open to that possibility. And if you and Korey do break up, it will hurt for a little while, but I promise you'll both be okay."

Michelle nodded as more confusion taunted her. Could God be leading her to someone else? And if so, then how would her heart ever heal if she lost Korey forever? And what would that mean for her broken relationship with Tyler?

CHAPTER 23

Tyler took a seat in the last row of the unmarried men's section of the congregation on a Thursday morning two weeks later. He picked up his hymnal and hung his head, keeping his eyes focused down. The chilly early-December air crept into the barn and brought with it the aroma of a wood-burning stove.

"There you are," Jonah said as he sat beside him. "I was looking all over for you, but you slipped away so quickly."

"I wanted to find a seat and get settled before the wedding started." Tyler covered his mouth to shield a yawn.

His best friend studied him. "You look wrung out. You okay?"

"*Ya,* it's been a long couple of weeks." Tyler rubbed at a tight muscle in his shoulder and contemplated the past two weeks.

He had tried to focus on work and Charity, but nothing had changed. He still couldn't see himself spending the rest of his life with her, and no matter how hard he prayed, he still couldn't get Michelle out of his mind. She lingered in the back of his thoughts during the day and appeared in his dreams at night.

Tyler turned toward Jonah. "How are you doing?"

Jonah shrugged. "Fine."

Just then the unmarried women entered the barn and began taking their seats across from the unmarried men. While Tyler tried to pull his gaze away from the young women, his eyes immediately found Michelle's beautiful face, and it jolted his heart. If only he could stop his overwhelming feelings for her, but no matter how he tried, he felt caught by her eyes and drawn to her as if an invisible force was pulling him to her.

Tyler forced his eyes downward toward the hymnal. He was grateful when the song leader, a young man sitting a couple of rows in front of him, began the first syllable of each line, and then the rest of the congregation joined in to finish the verse.

Soon the attendants, Kendra's younger sister, Lisa, and Dwight's older brother, Arlan, walked down the aisle between the rows of benches to the four matching cane chairs that sat at the front of the barn. They stood facing each other, waiting for the bride and groom.

Several minutes later, Kendra and Dwight made their way down the aisle. While Kendra and Lisa wore matching green dresses, Dwight and Arlan were dressed in their Sunday black-and-white suits. Once the bride and groom joined their attendants, the four of them sat down in unison, and the wedding service began.

Tyler did his best to focus on the ceremony, but he couldn't stop his mind from wandering as the bishop, Wilmer Flaud, spoke. He peered at the bride and groom and found them gazing lovingly at each other. While he normally didn't contemplate his future as a husband, he suddenly wondered if he would get a chance to marry the love of his life.

Tyler turned his attention back to the bishop as he lectured concerning the apostle Paul's instructions for marriage included in 1 Corinthians and Ephesians. He did his best to concentrate on the bishop's words, but Tyler's thoughts began to churn once again.

He looked over toward the unmarried women's section, where he found Charity studying her lap. She was lovely in her pink dress, but his heart didn't warm for her the way it should for a girlfriend or a future wife. And he couldn't fabricate those feelings. He'd proven that during the past two weeks, but he felt stuck and had no idea how to get out of the situation without hurting her.

Tyler's eyes defied him once again, and they moved to the left, where they locked with Michelle's intense blue eyes. His heart began to beat triple time, and he feared Jonah might hear it. Heat crept up his neck, and his breath froze in his lungs while they stared at each other.

Finally, Tyler broke the gaze and looked down at his hands as the bishop instructed Kendra and Dwight on how to run a godly household before moving on to a sermon on the story of Sarah and Tobias from the intertestamental book of Tobit.

The sermon took forty-five minutes, and when it was over, the bishop looked back and forth between Kendra and Dwight. "Now here are two in one faith — Kendra Marie Beiler and Dwight Joseph Smoker."

The bishop turned to the congregation. "Do any of you know any scriptural reason for the couple to not be married?" he asked. He waited a beat before looking at the couple again. "If it is your desire to be married, you may in the name of the Lord come forth."

Dwight took Kendra's hand in his, and they stood before the bishop to take their vows.

The bishop addressed Dwight first. "Can you confess, brother, that you accept this, our sister, as your wife, and that you will not leave her until death separates you? And do you believe that this is from the Lord and that you have come thus far by your faith and prayers?"

"Ya," Dwight said.

Then the bishop looked at Kendra. "Can you confess, sister, that you accept this, our brother, as your husband, and that you will not leave him until death separates you? And do you believe that this is from the Lord and that you have come thus far by your faith and prayers?"

"Ya," Kendra said.

Tyler looked down at his shoes but felt someone watching him. He tilted his head up and expected to find Charity studying him, but she was wiping her eyes and looking at Kendra.

Instead, he found Michelle still studying him, which sent his senses whirling. Was she thinking of Tyler and a possible future together? No, she couldn't be. After all, they were dating other people, and there was no way Tyler would betray his brother this way. But the intensity between them was tangible. Surely she could feel it too. But there was nothing that they could do about these feelings. They were both trapped.

Tyler once again tore his eyes away from her and focused on the bride and groom.

Then the bishop looked at Dwight again. "Because you have confessed, brother, that you want to take this, our sister, for your wife, do you promise to be loyal to her and care for her if she may have adversity, affliction, sickness, weakness, or faintheartedness — which are many infirmities that are among poor mankind — as is appropriate for a Christian, God-fearing husband?"

"Ya," Dwight said.

The bishop asked the same of Kendra, and she responded with a strong, *"Ya."*

While Dwight and Kendra joined hands, the bishop read "A Prayer for Those about to Be Married" from an Amish prayer book called the *Christenpflict.* Then he announced, "Go forth in the name of the Lord. You are now man and wife."

Tyler's eyes stung as he took in the bride and groom. He suddenly understood why his father married Crystal. He could feel that longing deep in his heart for Michelle, and he knew to the depth of his bones that he truly loved her, even though he could never have her as his girlfriend or his wife. Staying away from her was agony, but he knew it was the only way to keep his brother in his life.

He closed his eyes as the truth seeped under his skin — he couldn't lead Charity on anymore. He had to be honest with her as soon as possible, even though it would hurt her. He couldn't keep her hanging on any longer, and he had to tell her the truth *today.* It wasn't fair of him to allow her to keep believing they had a chance at a future. Since he could never have Michelle, he would rather be alone than risk hurting someone else.

Kendra and Dwight sat down for another sermon and another prayer, and Tyler forced himself not to look at Charity or Michelle and instead listen to the bishop.

After the bishop recited the Lord's Prayer, the congregation stood, and the three-hour service ended with the singing of another hymn.

And then it was official — Kendra and Dwight were married.

Keeping with tradition, younger members of the congregation filed out of the barn first, followed by the wedding party.

Tyler shivered as he walked out into the early-December air. He lingered by the barn door, standing back until he spotted Charity and Michelle striding out into the cold.

"Charity," he said.

His girlfriend spun and smiled at him. Michelle glanced over and then quickened her steps, hurrying toward the kitchen.

"Tyler," Charity said, walking over to meet him. "What are you doing over here? Shouldn't you help with the benches?"

"Actually, I was hoping we could talk for a minute."

"Oh." Her smile faded. "Okay."

Tyler nodded toward the pasture. "I know it's cold, but I'd like to talk in private."

They headed toward the fence.

"Wasn't the wedding wonderful?" she gushed. "It was just so romantic. Maybe that will be us next year."

He closed his eyes for a moment and took a deep breath. This was going to be more difficult than he imagined. When they reached the fence, he looked out toward the rolling patchwork of brown fields.

Lord, give me strength. Help me choose the right words to be honest with Charity but somehow not break her heart.

"Tyler, what's on your mind?" Her voice held the hint of worry.

He turned toward her and sighed. He could see his breath in the cold air. "Charity, I need to be honest with you."

"I thought you were always honest." She gave him a nervous smile.

"Well, I haven't been, and I'm sorry for that."

Her brow puckered. "What do you mean?"

"You're a lovely *maedel.*" He took her hands in his. "You're *schee,* sweet, kind, thoughtful, intelligent, and sincere. I like you a lot, but I'm not in love with you."

"Well, that's okay. You want to take things slow, right?"

"That's not what I mean, Charity."

"Wait." She pulled her hands out of his grasp, her eyes flashing with panic. "Are you breaking up with me?"

"Look, you deserve someone who loves you completely, and that's not me. I've tried, but I —"

"You've *tried* to love me?" She winced. "Are you saying I'm not lovable or I'm not *gut* enough for you?"

"I never said that. You're a really *gut freind,* but I can't see myself planning a future with you. I wanted to tell you the truth so that you can find the right man."

She studied him. "Is there someone else?"

He hesitated, not wanting to lie to her but

also doing his best not to hurt her any further. "Charity, I never meant to hurt you. I'm so sorry I'm not the one for you, but I don't want to lead you on anymore. I have to be honest with you because I respect you."

"You respect me?" She sniffed and shook her head.

"I'm so sorry."

She took a step back. "I should have known you'd break my heart." Then she spun on her heel and raced toward the house.

Tyler leaned back on the fence and tried to stop his guilt from swallowing him whole.

Michelle shivered as she carried a coffee carafe from the Beilers' kitchen toward the barn. She looked out toward the pasture, and when she spotted Tyler and Charity talking, jealousy curdled in her belly. Her heart ached when she imagined what Tyler could possibly be saying to Charity. Perhaps he was telling her he loved her. Or maybe he had already asked her father's permission, and he was proposing to her.

Stop it, Michelle! You're with Korey!

Her heart thudded against her rib cage as she recalled the intense looks she and Tyler had shared during the wedding. But he cared for Charity. If only she could convince her stubborn heart to let go of him!

Michelle made her rounds in the barn, filling cups and nodding hellos to members of the congregation. Then she hurried back through the cold into the kitchen.

When she set the carafe on the counter, she felt someone tug her arm. Turning, she found Charity beside her, her eyes red and puffy as if she'd been crying.

"*Ach* no, Charity! What happened?"

"I need to talk to you, Michelle."

"Let's go upstairs."

They climbed the stairs and walked into Kendra's room, where the women had deposited their shawls and winter bonnets before the wedding began.

"Tell me what's wrong," Michelle said, taking her best friend's hands in hers.

Charity sniffed and pulled a tissue from her pocket. "He broke up with me." She blotted her eyes and nose and looked crestfallen. "It's over."

"What?" Michelle's stomach dipped. "Tyler broke up with you?"

Charity sank down on the corner of the bed. "*Ya.* He said he doesn't love me, doesn't see a future with me, and isn't the man for me. I'm shocked. I can't believe it. I knew he wanted to take it slow, but I thought maybe someday we'd get married."

"*Ach* no. I'm so sorry." Michelle rubbed Charity's shoulder.

"I'm-I'm devastated! When he said he wanted to talk to me alone, I thought maybe he was finally going to tell me he loved me and kiss me."

"He hasn't kissed you?" The question sprang from Michelle's lips without warning, and she immediately regretted it.

Charity shook her head. "No. Tyler would only shake my hand at night. He hasn't even hugged me."

Michelle stared at her as an unfamiliar mixture of emotions writhed within her — relief, jealousy, confusion, and hope. Then guilt smacked her in the face. Michelle was silently celebrating that Tyler was single while her friend was submerged in sadness.

Lord, please remove this sin from my heart! Make me a better friend to Charity.

"I'm so sorry, Charity. I know you cared for Tyler, and I had hoped it would work out with you two."

"I don't just care for him. I love him, Michelle. What am I going to do?" Charity buried her face in Michelle's neck and began to sob.

Michelle rubbed her back. "It will be okay, Charity. I promise you that you'll meet someone who loves you the way you should be loved."

While Michelle tried to focus on her friend's broken heart, she couldn't help wondering if Tyler had broken up with Charity because he loved someone else. And if so, could that someone possibly be her?

CHAPTER 24

Tyler glanced around the wedding reception while the aroma of baked chicken and bread mixed with a faint whiff of animals permeated the area around him. He felt as if the barn were closing in on him as remorse and heartache threatened to drag him under and suffocate him. He had to get out of there — *fast!*

He spotted his father and Crystal and waded through a sea of young folks laughing and talking and then past a table full of cookies and cakes until he reached them.

"*Dat,*" Tyler said, working to keep his voice low. "I'm going to head home."

His father's brows drew together. "Why?"

"I'm not feeling well." It wasn't a lie.

"*Ach* no!" Crystal said. "*Was iss letz?*"

Tyler swallowed. "I have a headache and I'm queasy."

"Feel better soon, *sohn.*" *Dat* patted his arm.

Crystal gave him a sympathetic smile. "Go home and have some toast."

"*Danki.*" Tyler lowered his gaze and excused himself while he plodded past the knot of people filling their plates with food while chatting.

He was grateful when he stepped outside the barn and allowed his lungs to fill with the crisp December air. His shoes crunched along the cold ground as he moved toward the barn to retrieve his horse.

"Tyler! Tyler Bontrager!"

He inhaled through his nose and turned as Jonah jogged to catch up with him. So much for slipping out unnoticed. "*Ya?*"

"Where are you going?" Jonah asked.

"Home."

"Why?"

"Because I have a headache." And a dull throb had started behind his eyes.

Jonah folded his arms across his wide chest and studied him.

Oh no. Here come the questions I don't want to answer!

"You've been acting strange lately," Jonah said. "What's going on with you, Ty?"

Tyler shrugged. "Nothing. I just have a headache and really want to take a nap."

"No, it's not that." Jonah shook a finger at

him. "I'm your best *freind.* So, I want the truth."

Tyler looked up at the clear sky.

"Please tell me what's going on with you."

"I can't." Tyler met his best friend's worried gaze.

"I've been concerned for a while." Jonah paused. "You can trust me."

Something inside of Tyler cracked open, and he felt a confession bubble up inside him. "Fine. I'll tell you. The truth is I'm in love with *mei bruder*'s girlfriend, and it's tearing me apart. The best thing I can do is stay away from her, but it's not as easy as it sounds."

Jonah's mouth fell open as his eyes widened. "You're in love with Michelle?"

"You can't say a word about this to anyone. Understand?"

"I won't tell anyone. I'm just shocked to hear this." Jonah shook his head. "Wow. What about Charity?"

"I broke up with her earlier. She's upset. I feel guilty for hurting her, but I can't live a lie anymore. It wasn't fair of me to keep seeing her when she believed we might have a future." Tyler rubbed the back of his neck. "I didn't plan this. I've been trying to get over Michelle, but it's just not possible. I've begged God to help me get over her, but I can't."

Tyler shoved his hands in the pockets of his coat and then kicked a stone with the toe of his shoe. "You know how fragile my relationship is with Korey. If he knew how I felt about Michelle, we'd never recover, and I don't want to lose him. Losing *mei mamm* was difficult enough. I plan to cherish the family I have left."

"What are you going to do?"

"The only thing I can do is just pour myself into work and try to forget Michelle. I'm better off alone until I can find a way to move on."

Jonah shook his head. "I'm sorry."

"I am too." Tyler shook his hand. "I need to go. Remember, Jonah, you need to keep this between us."

"I know."

Tyler continued on to the barn, hoping he could somehow get Michelle out of his mind for good.

"I saw Charity wiping her eyes and talking to you during the reception. Why was she so upset?" Korey asked Michelle as he guided his horse toward her farm later that evening.

Michelle turned toward him. "Tyler broke

332

up with her."

"He did?"

"Ya." She turned her attention back to the side window and watched the traffic rumble by while a rush of emotions overtook her — shock, hope, grief, longing, and confusion.

A weighted pause stretched between them like an ocean, and she continued to keep her eyes trained on the passing traffic while she pondered why Tyler had broken up with Charity.

"I'm sorry for being such a lousy boyfriend to you."

Michelle sat up straight and swiveled toward him. "What do you mean?"

"I told you that I would do better, but I haven't made enough of an effort. I'll try harder." He gave her a sheepish expression. "I mean it."

She smiled. *"Danki."* She scooted closer to him and then leaned down, resting her head on his shoulder.

Closing her eyes, she sent a prayer up to God:

Lord, please put love in my heart for Korey and stop my mind from concentrating on Tyler.

The following morning, Tyler pulled his stocking cap around his ears and then knelt down on the roof of the apartment complex and began hammering.

He tried his best to concentrate on the job, but his thoughts kept swirling with images of Charity and how upset she'd been when he told her how he felt. And to make matters worse, he kept seeing Michelle in his mind's eye and recalling the stares they'd shared during the wedding ceremony.

"Ty? Tyler!"

"Huh?" Tyler sat back on his heels and shielded his eyes from the sun as he peered up at Korey, who was looking down at him and grinning.

"I've been calling you, but you're in your own world." Korey pushed his mirrored sunglasses up on his nose and crouched down beside him. His smile faded. "You okay?"

"Is this a trick question?"

"No." Korey rubbed his hands together. "Michelle told me that you and Charity broke up yesterday. I wanted to make sure you were doing all right."

Tyler blinked.

"Look, I know I've been really hard on you, and I'm sorry. I can tell that you've been respecting my relationship with Michelle, and I appreciate it. So, I'm trying to be a better *bruder* to you. I really do care about how you're doing." Korey's expression was full of concern. "Are you doing okay?"

"*Ya,* I'm fine, but I don't think Charity is. Unfortunately, it was necessary. We just aren't right for each other."

"I understand." Korey looked out toward the traffic rushing by on the road. "How do you know if your girlfriend is the one?"

Tyler stilled for a moment as his brother's question rolled through his mind. "What do you mean?"

"Nothing." Korey stood. "I'll go check on Dennis and Roger."

"No. Wait." Tyler jumped up. "Are you having doubts about Michelle?"

Korey shrugged. "I don't know how to explain it. Our families were close, and I always felt like she was the right one to date and maybe have a future with since *Mamm* was so close to her *mamm.* It's as if *Mamm* is blessing my relationship with her. Plus, I can't imagine not having her in my life since everything else has changed so quickly." He played with the hem of his black coat. "But sometimes I wonder if we should feel more connected. Sometimes it seems like we don't know what to say to each other."

"Wow." Tyler tried to hide his shock.

"Am I overthinking this?"

Tyler cleared his throat. "I'm not an

expert. I would ask *Dat* for relationship advice."

"Thanks, Ty." Korey smiled and patted Tyler's shoulder. "I'm glad we can talk like this. Now, get back to work," he teased before heading across the roof to Dennis.

Tyler knelt down and shook his head as Korey's words rang through his mind. Korey had doubts about Michelle. Tyler pondered if that meant they might break up. But even if they did, it wouldn't improve Tyler's situation. His brother would still think him a traitor if he considered dating his ex-girlfriend.

Forget Michelle! Concentrate on work!
As Tyler resumed hammering, he hoped to find relief for his battered and bruised heart.

Lisa Beiler rushed over to where Michelle and Charity stood outside the King family's barn on Sunday before the service.

"Hi, Lisa. The wedding was lovely," Michelle told Kendra's sister.

"Oh *ya*. Wasn't Kendra gorgeous?" Lisa touched Charity's arm. "I heard you and Tyler broke up at the wedding. Are you okay?"

Charity nodded as her lips formed a thin line. "I feel so immature and *gegisch* for believing he actually loved me. I just made it all up in my head like a schoolgirl."

Michelle glanced behind Charity as Korey and Tyler sauntered past with a group of friends. When her eyes locked with Tyler's, her stomach dropped, and her heart flopped around. When she turned her focus on Korey, his gaze slid between her and Tyler.

Oh no.

She forced her lips into a smile and gave Korey a little wave before he moved on.

"What do you think, Michelle?"

She turned toward Lisa and Charity. "I'm sorry. What did you say?"

"I asked if you thought I was wrong for believing in Tyler," Charity said.

Michelle shook her head. "No, you weren't wrong. And God will lead you to your perfect mate. Just keep praying."

"*Danki,* Michelle." Charity wrapped her arms around Michelle. "I don't know what I'd do without your encouragement."

As she hugged her best friend, Michelle felt like a liar and a sinner. If only she could erase Tyler from her heart.

Tyler stepped outside the barn after lunch and spotted Charity talking to Michelle and a few of their friends. He stepped over toward them and nodded. "Charity. *Wie geht's*?"

She nodded at him and then turned and started walking toward the King family's large farmhouse.

Tyler met Michelle's gaze, and she hastened after Charity.

With his shoulders sagging, Tyler continued toward the barn.

"Tyler," *Dat* called as he caught up to him. "Have fun at the youth gathering."

"I'm not going. I'll see you at home."

"Why aren't you going with your *freinden*?"

"I'd rather be home."

Dat held out his arm and stopped Tyler from moving forward. "What's going on, *sohn*?"

"I'd rather not discuss it. I just want to be home today. That's all."

"Okay." *Dat* nodded. "But when you're ready to talk, I'm here."

"Thanks." Tyler fetched his horse and then hitched up the buggy. He opened the driver's side door just as Jayden jogged over.

"Hey. I'll see you at the gathering."

Tyler shook his head. "No, I'm heading home."

"Why?"

"It's obvious Charity doesn't want me around."

Jayden shrugged. "So what? You can just avoid her."

"No, I'm going home. I'll see you later, okay?"

His youngest brother frowned and then said, "All right."

Tyler climbed into his buggy and began guiding his horse toward home, in search of some solace. If only he could escape his thoughts.

"I heard Jayden tell you that Tyler wasn't going to the youth gathering. Do you know why?" Michelle asked Korey as they rode to the Blank family's farm to meet their friends.

Korey gave her a sideways glance. "Why do you care about what *mei bruder* does?"

"Oh." She blanched. "I-I don't care. I was just being nosy. That's all."

"Do you care about *mei bruder*?"

"I've known you and your *bruders* my whole life. Why wouldn't I care about your *bruders*?" she asked.

Korey led the horse to the side of the road and halted it. Then he turned toward her, his expression seeming to be a mixture of frustration and resignation. "Tell me the truth, Michelle. Do you have feelings for my older *bruder*?"

She felt a strange stitch in her chest. She didn't want to lie to him, but the truth was stuck in her throat. "Korey, I want to build a future with you."

He stared at her for a long moment and then turned back toward the horse. Silence filled the empty space between them as Korey led the horse back onto the road and continued toward their destination.

Michelle fought back the guilt and embarrassment that squirmed in her chest. She knew deep in her heart that she needed to come clean with Korey, but she just didn't know how to do it without breaking his heart.

Later that afternoon, Tyler stared at the plain, white ceiling in his bedroom while his anxiety ran rampant. If only he could sleep and turn off his thoughts!

A soft knock sounded on his door.

"Who is it?" Tyler called.

"It's me," *Dat* said. "May I come in?"

"Ya."

The door opened with a squeak, and his father's tall frame filled the doorway. "I know I said I'd wait for you to want to talk to me, but I'm concerned about you, Ty. What's going on?"

Tyler heaved a deep breath. "I need some

time away from Charity, so I didn't feel like going to the youth gathering."

"You two broke up?"

"*Ya,* at Kendra and Dwight's wedding."

"I'm sorry to hear that. I had a feeling something was wrong when you said you had a headache." *Dat* moved to the foot of his bed. "Is that the only issue that's bothering you?"

Tyler rested his forearm on his forehead. "I'm too embarrassed to tell you the truth."

"You can tell me anything, and I'll listen without judgment." His face was full of empathy, and it gave Tyler the confidence to keep talking.

Tyler sat up. "I now understand why you married Crystal."

"What do you mean?"

"I care about a *maedel,* and I can't stop thinking about her. I've asked God to remove my love for her from my heart, but it gets stronger every time I see her. I can't stay away from her, so I'm forcing myself to."

"Who is it?"

"I can't tell you."

"Tyler, you can trust me. Please tell me."

"Fine. It's Michelle." Tyler held up his hands. "I know what you're going to say. And I don't want to hurt Korey this way,

341

which is why I'm staying away from her as much as I can."

Dat grimaced. "That's a complicated one."

"Korey and I already have a rocky relationship, and I can't let this come between us."

Dat nodded.

Tyler groaned and flopped back onto the bed. "You think I'm terrible."

"No, I don't. I've wondered for a long time if Michelle is the right woman for Korey."

"Why?"

"Because he's had cold feet about her ever since they started dating. I remember how he hemmed and hawed about asking her out last year. He's always seemed to have doubts about her, but you know Korey would be upset if you pursued her."

"Dating Michelle would be the ultimate betrayal, and I don't want to lose *mei bruder.* He's always acted like we were in competition, but I never wanted our relationship to be like that. So I'm going to keep praying that I get over Michelle, but it's so much more difficult than I thought it'd be."

Dat nodded slowly. "Well, if I were you, I'd keep praying about it and let God lead you. You never know what God has in mind. And you already know that with God, all things are possible."

"Danki," Tyler whispered as a tiny glimmer of hope took root in his heart.

CHAPTER 25

Tyler added cinnamon and sugar to his oatmeal the following morning. He looked across the table at *Dat.* "How is your project going over in Ronks?"

"*Gut.* We're on schedule to finish tomorrow," *Dat* said. Then he smiled up at Crystal as she set a mug of steaming coffee in front of him. *"Danki, mei liewe."*

His stepmother gave his father a sweet smile before placing a mug in front of Tyler.

"Danki," Tyler said. He reached for the creamer and sugar and added some of each to his cup.

Jayden rushed into the kitchen and retrieved a bowl from the cabinet and began filling it with oatmeal from the pot on the stove. *"Gude mariye,"* he said.

"I'll get your *kaffi,*" Crystal offered as she filled a mug for him.

Then Jayden and Crystal joined Tyler and *Dat* at the table. They all began eating their oatmeal and drinking their coffee.

After a few moments, Korey appeared, and the family greeted him.

Tyler took a sip of coffee as Korey slipped into the chair beside him.

"So, tell me the truth, Ty," Korey began with a sardonic smile, as Tyler took another gulp of the warm liquid. "Are you in love with my girlfriend?"

Tyler started to sputter and then choke. He covered his mouth with his hand as he coughed and coughed, trying to recover.

"You okay?" *Dat* leaned over and patted his back.

Tyler took deep breaths, and finally, the coughing ceased. He wiped his eyes with a napkin and faced Korey, who continued to eye him with a mixture of suspicion and disdain.

"Did I catch you off guard, big brother?" Korey asked in a snippy voice.

Tyler worked to keep his expression blank. "Why would you say that?"

"I thought that your feelings for Michelle were platonic because you seemed so sincere when you gave me advice. But then yesterday I saw the look that passed between you and Michelle at church, and let's just say, it couldn't have been more obvious if her name was written across your forehead."

345

Korey gave him a mocking smile.

Tyler held his breath and debated how to respond for a moment. "Korey, I would never do anything to deliberately hurt you, your relationship with Michelle, or our relationship. You're *mei bruder,* and I care about you."

"So, it's true then." Korey ground out the words as his face turned as red as a ripe tomato and fire danced in his eyes.

"Korey," *Dat* began slowly, "just calm down, *sohn.*"

Jayden sighed, pushing back his chair. He crossed to the counter and refilled his mug of coffee.

Tyler clutched his mug as his thoughts spun. If only he could tell Korey the truth without losing his trust, but it seemed it was too late for that.

Korey turned his scowl toward their father. "I want to work on your crew, *Dat.* Jay can work with Ty. I can't even look at him." He pushed his chair back and stood.

"Please don't leave, Korey," Crystal said. "Work this out with your *bruder.* You're family, and family members are the most important people in your life."

Korey glared at her. "This is between Tyler and me." His voice was charged with fury.

"You need to be respectful, Korey," *Dat*

warned.

Korey picked up his bowl of oatmeal and his mug of coffee as he sneered at Tyler. "You always have to outdo me. You have to be the boss on the site. You have to run the business. You always have to be better than me because you're eighteen months older than I am. And now you have to meddle in my relationship with Michelle. You just can't stand the idea that I'm dating when you can't manage to have a relationship. Well, I'm over it, Tyler, and I'm over *you.*"

"Please, Korey. Please, forgive me. I didn't mean to hurt you. You're *mei bruder,* and I can't lose you. I would never hurt you, which is why I'm staying away from Michelle. I'll never get between you two. Just give me a minute to explain. I didn't plan any of this. It just sort of happened." Tyler's voice trembled.

"I'm *done,* Tyler." Korey looked at *Dat* once again. "Call me when it's time to leave. I can't ride with him." Carrying his breakfast, Korey banged up the stairs.

Tyler covered his face with his hands as his world began to collapse around him. Everything he had feared had just come to fruition. He'd lost his brother over his foolish heart.

Why, God? Why did I have to fall in love

*with the woman who belongs to my brother?
Why would my heart choose to betray Korey
instead of loving Charity, the woman who
would fit into my life perfectly?*

"It's all going to be okay, Tyler." *Dat*'s
voice was soft and full of sympathy.

Tyler placed his hands on the table and
shook his head. "Actually, it's not." He
pointed toward the upstairs. "Korey is furi-
ous with me and won't even work with me."
He looked over at Jayden, who had returned
to the table and kept his focus on his
oatmeal. "Will you work with me, Jay?"

Jayden lifted his mug. "You know I will."

"I'll go talk to him," *Dat* said before heading toward the staircase.

Tyler's insides knotted up as his hands
began to tremble. "I'm not a cheater. I
would never do anything to deliberately
interfere with Korey and Michelle's relationship. I never planned to fall for her, and I've
never even told her how I feel. You have to
believe I never wanted any of this to happen."

"We believe you, Tyler," Crystal said, her
voice warm and encouraging.

Jayden nodded. "I know you're not a
cheater, and I can tell you've been trying to
be a *gut bruder* to Korey."

"I've also been trying to stay away from

348

Michelle. I've been channeling all of my energy into work, but I guess he just figured it out since I broke up with Charity. Still, I didn't want to lead Charity on. I knew in my heart that she and I weren't meant to be together." Tyler rubbed his eyes with his fingers. "Everything is a mess. I've been begging God to remove my feelings for Michelle from my heart, but nothing has helped."

"You can't help who you love," Crystal said softly. "Your *dat* and I never expected to fall in love, and I had given up on finding a husband and having a family. But now I'm here, and I'm grateful to call you all my family. God leads us to the people we're meant to love."

Tyler let his hands drop to the table and shook his head. "But why would he lead my heart to Michelle when she's with *mei bruder*?"

"I don't know." Crystal shrugged.

Jayden's smile was encouraging. "It's going to be okay. You and Korey always bicker, but you always have each other's backs. Korey will forgive you."

"I hope so," Tyler said.

"Just have faith."

Thursday evening Michelle set another

349

finished milk can on the drying rack and then turned toward the shelf, where her dry milk cans sat waiting to be packaged up and delivered to the store to be sold.

Her gaze moved to the milk can on the bottom right of the shelf — the can that she and Tyler had painted together, and her heart turned over in her chest. She had set the can aside each time she packaged up cans to take to Lola's store since she couldn't bring herself to sell that one.

Michelle picked up the can and turned it over in her hands, recalling the evening she and Tyler had spent in the studio, talking, laughing, and enjoying each other's company. She closed her eyes and tried to imagine what it would be like to have Tyler in her life — sharing their secrets while sitting on the porch together, sharing meals, sharing birthdays and holidays, sharing kisses . . .

Somehow Tyler had become the focus of her thoughts when her thoughts used to always center around Korey. There had been a time when she had been certain Korey was the love of her life. She recalled when his hugs provided all of the comfort and affection she needed, but eventually those hugs became fewer and farther between and more and more platonic. If only she knew what had gone wrong between them.

Groaning, she carried the milk can over to her worktable and sat on a stool. It was time she admitted to herself that she loved Tyler. But how would she ever tell Korey the truth?

"Lord," she whispered. "I know in my heart that I love Tyler, and I think Korey and I have grown apart. I'm so confused and also embarrassed, but I can't live a lie. I don't want to hurt Korey, but I'm already hurting him by not telling him the truth about how I feel. It's time for me to let him go so we both can move on." Her voice quivered and she sniffed. "Please help me figure out how to tell him that I've fallen out of love with him. Please guide me toward the right words and also help us both heal from our broken hearts."

She turned the milk can over and inscribed a Scripture verse on the bottom and then blew on the paint to help it dry.

Mamm burst into the studio, excitement etched on her pretty face. "Michelle! Lainey had her baby! It's a boy. They named him Noah Junior. And they're both doing well. Noah just called, and *Dat* answered and called me outside to hear the news."

Michelle gasped. "Oh my goodness! That's so wonderful. Praise God!"

"Oh, I know." *Mamm* took Michelle's hand in hers. "I'm so *froh.* I can't wait to meet him."

Michelle nodded as tears stung her eyes. Then, without warning, she began sobbing as all of her emotions for Tyler and Korey spilled out of her. She covered her face with her hands as her tears flowed.

Her mother pulled her into her arms and rubbed her back. *"Ach, mei liewe. Was iss letz?"*

Michelle rested her cheek on her mother's shoulder and worked to stop her tears.

"Whatever it is, I promise it will be okay."

"I'm not so sure," Michelle managed to say. She pulled a handful of tissues from a nearby box and mopped up her eyes and nose.

Mamm pulled over the extra stool and sat beside her. "I've noticed that you've been quiet all week. I've been concerned, but I wanted to give you space. Please tell me what's going on."

"I've been praying about Korey and me." Michelle fingered the edge of the worktable. "I've been examining my feelings for a while, and I've finally accepted that I don't love him anymore. I've realized it's time for us to break up, and it's a difficult decision."

She sniffed and took a tremulous breath.

"We've just grown apart, but we've been together for more than a year now, and it's going to hurt both of us. And to be honest, I don't know how to let go of him. He's been the man I thought I would marry for so long."

Mamm rubbed her shoulder. "I'm so sorry. I know it's difficult. I dated a young man for more than a year before I started dating your *dat.*"

"That's right." Michelle sniffed. "I remember you mentioned him once."

"*Ya.* He was handsome and sweet. He trained horses with his *dat.* He lived over in New Holland. We met at a combined youth gathering."

"What was his name?"

"Ben." *Mamm* had a faraway look in her eyes. "We were *froh* at first. I thought I was so in love with him, but I realized I was in love with the idea of being with him. I didn't really want to marry him. I just wanted to get married and have a family. When we broke up, I was devastated."

"Remind me what happened."

Mamm smiled and touched Michelle's cheek. "We decided it was time to move on, and then your *dat* and I started talking at a youth gathering one evening. He asked me to ride home with him, and we sat on my parents' porch until after midnight. Being with him was so natural. It was as if we were meant to be together."

Michelle nodded as she recalled all of her conversations with Tyler. They were just so easy, and they never ran out of words. They could discuss anything and laugh.

But being with Tyler would be such a betrayal of Korey!

"What's on your mind, Michelle?"

She shook her head. "Nothing." She cleared her throat. "Did *Dat* ask you out after that?"

"*Ya,* he did. And we were engaged six months later because, like I said, everything just felt so natural and right with us."

Michelle picked up a paintbrush as she stared at the milk can she and Tyler had worked on together. "So, you're saying that it will hurt when Korey and I break up, but God will lead me to the man he has in mind for me."

"*Ya.* I know it will be difficult to say goodbye to Korey, but you need to do what feels right."

"I know." Michelle sighed. "I've prayed about it, and I keep coming back to the same answer — I need to move on. I just don't know how to take the first step." She set down the brush as a block of ice formed in her chest. "I hate the idea of hurting him."

Mamm frowned. "When Ben and I broke up, I found out that he was having the same doubts as I was. Korey might feel the same way, but he's afraid of hurting you too."

"I-I hadn't thought of that." A strange wave of relief overtook her. "He has admitted that he's not ready to get married, and he doesn't know when he will be. He told me that he wasn't even ready to talk about it."

Mamm touched her arm. "That could be an indication that the relationship isn't working for him. If he can't imagine being married to you, then you might not be the one God has in mind for him."

"Right." Michelle folded her arms over her waist as an idea formed in her mind. "I'll give him a call and see when he can come visit so that we can have a *gut,* long talk and figure it all out together."

Mamm stood and patted Michelle's shoulder. *"Gut."*

"Danki for talking with me, *Mamm."*

"I'll listen anytime." She started toward the door. "I'm heading inside. You should come in soon too. It's cold out here. We need to work on our Christmas cards and discuss our Christmas baking too."

"Oh, I had forgotten about that." Michelle stood. "I'll be in after I clean up." She stowed the special milk can in the corner of the shelf and then cleaned up her paints and brushes.

When she walked out of the studio, she stopped by the phone in the corner of the barn and dialed the number for the Bontrager family's phone.

After listening to the greeting and waiting for the beep, Michelle began to speak. "Hi, this is Michelle. This message is for Korey. I was wondering if you could come by to visit me Sunday. Let me know if that works for you. Bye."

When she hung up, her hands trembled as her heart threatened to beat out of her chest.

She closed her eyes and prayed once more: *Please, Lord, grant me the right words to tell Korey how I feel and not shatter him.*

Then she zipped through the chilly December evening toward the house.

CHAPTER 26

A knock sounded on Tyler's bedroom door midmorning on Sunday. He looked up from the book he'd been reading while sitting on his bed. "Come in."

The door creaked open, and Jayden leaned on the doorframe. "Hey. Want to ride together to the youth gathering?"

"*Danki,* but I'm not going."

Jayden's pleasant expression dimmed. "Oh. Because of Kore?"

"*Ya.* I think it's best if I just stay away from him, especially when he's with Michelle."

Tyler frowned as he recalled the events of last week. Korey hadn't spoken to him since their encounter at breakfast on Monday, and the silence was slowly killing his spirit. While he appreciated having Jayden join his crew, he also missed working with Korey.

Jayden sank down onto the chair in front

of Tyler's desk. "Have you tried talking to him?"

"Several times."

"Keep trying," his youngest brother suggested. "You know how stubborn he is."

Tyler snorted. "That is the understatement of the year."

"I never enjoyed being the peacekeeper between you two, but to be totally honest, I actually miss the bickering. At least you two were talking to each other." Jayden rested his elbow on the desk. "Why don't you try starting a fight with him?"

"I don't think that would work too well."

"No, probably not."

They were silent for a moment, and Tyler contemplated how to get through to his middle brother.

Finally, he moved to the edge of his bed and shoved his feet into his shoes. "I suppose I'll just try apologizing again."

"Good plan." Jayden walked through the doorway ahead of him. "I'll be downstairs if you change your mind and want to ride together."

Tyler smiled, grateful for Jayden. "*Danki,* but I'll stay home."

"Your choice. See you later." Jayden headed for the stairs, and his footfalls echoed as he jogged down them.

Tyler stood in front of Korey's door and took a deep breath. Then he knocked.

The door opened, and Korey scowled as he started to push the door closed.

"Wait." Tyler shoved his foot out, blocking the door before it clicked shut. "Just listen. I never wanted to hurt you. I just want you to know that I'm going to stay away from you and Michelle. I won't go to youth group. I won't go near Michelle. I'll do everything in my power to prove to you that I won't interfere in your relationship." He held up his hands. "I want to work this out with you."

"As far as I'm concerned, you're no longer *mei bruder.*"

"But you're mine."

Korey opened the door and pushed past him. "Just stay away from me," he mumbled on his way to the stairs.

Tyler padded back to his bedroom and slumped in his desk chair as more despondency made him feel heavy and hollowed out.

If only he hadn't worn his heart on his sleeve. If only he'd managed to keep his emotions trapped inside, then he wouldn't have lost his brother.

"Lord," he whispered, "help me find a way to earn back Korey's trust."

Then he yanked off his shoes and climbed onto his bed, hoping to nap away his heartache.

"I made this crumb cake yesterday," Michelle told Korey as she set it down in front of him. Then she poured two mugs of coffee and brought them to the table.

As soon as Korey had walked into her kitchen, she'd noticed his lips were clamped shut, the muscles bunched in his jaw. He seemed to be in one of his bad moods, and her attempts at making conversation had failed to pull him out of his funk, which caused her to dread this conversation even more than she already had.

He cut two pieces of crumb cake, set them on plates, and pushed one toward her. After a silent prayer, he forked a piece of cake into his mouth.

"How was your week?" she asked while stirring cream and sugar into her mug.

Korey swallowed the cake. "Fine."

Silence hovered over the kitchen. She glanced toward the doorway leading to the family room where her parents sat reading, and a murmur of conversation drifted in.

"Mine was *gut* too," she continued. "I brought more milk cans to the store yesterday since Lola had sold out again."

360

"Gut." He sipped his coffee.

She studied his dark eyes, the ones that had once comforted her, the eyes that used to fill her dreams, and the eyes that held a promise of her future, but today she felt nothing except friendship for him. And if she were honest, his eyes also filled her with annoyance since he wasn't looking at her or talking to her. He was ignoring her now, which was what he did too often lately.

Michelle squared her shoulders. "Are you angry with me, Korey?"

"What?" He blinked.

"Are you angry with me?" She said the words slowly.

He shook his head. "No."

"Then why are you so quiet?"

He sat back in his chair. "It's been a rough week."

"Why? What happened?"

"I really don't want to talk about it."

That was possibly the key to all of their issues — they didn't talk anymore. They didn't share their secrets or dreams. They had somehow gotten off track and never found their way back — like a ship adrift at sea without a lighthouse to lead it back to shore.

He sipped his coffee and then took another bite of cake. After swallowing it, he looked over at her. "It's *gut.*"

"Glad you like it." She folded her hands on the table and licked her lips. It was time to be honest with Korey, no matter how much it hurt them both. "Do you see a future with me?"

Korey stopped chewing and stared at her.

"Go ahead," she said, her heart pounding. "Be honest with me."

He swallowed. "I thought we had already agreed to take it slow."

"We did, but there's something I need to get off my chest. I've been doing a lot of thinking, and I've realized that it's time we have a heart-to-heart. You said you're not ready to get married, but surely you know whether or not you could ever see yourself marrying me."

Korey cupped his hand to the back of his neck. "I-I don't know." His words faltered.

Michelle hesitated and tried to breathe past the lump swelling in her throat. "Do you love me, Korey?"

Still holding the back of his neck, he shifted his eyes down toward his lap.

"Korey?" When he didn't look up, she leaned forward. "Korey, I'm asking you for honesty. You at least owe me that."

His eyes snapped to hers, sparking in the afternoon sunlight pouring in through the nearby windows. "Owe you?"

"Yes, owe me. For months now, you've refused to talk about where we're headed with this relationship. I've noticed lately that we've run out of things to say to each other." She paused as the lump in her throat swelled, and her eyes stung. "I feel as if we're growing apart, but I don't know if it's all in my mind. I don't know if I'm over-thinking everything, but you never even tell me that you love me anymore. So, I need to know the truth." She tapped the table with her finger.

"Michelle, I love you as a *freind*." His voice was soft.

She nodded as the truth smacked her in the face — he didn't love her the way a boyfriend should love his girlfriend or the way a husband should love a wife. They *had* grown apart.

"What about you?" he asked. "Do you love me?"

"I feel the same way. And I think that we should stop spinning our wheels."

His eyes became hard again. "What do you mean by that?"

"Korey, I care about you. I always have. Some of my best memories are of our child-hood, playing and laughing while our *mamms* drank tea and reminisced about

363

their school days together."

He swallowed, and his eyes glittered.

"Korey, please listen to me." She reached across the table for his hands and threaded her fingers with his. "You'll always be a part of my life. You were my first love and my first kiss. I've cherished your friendship since I was a little girl, and I always will."

He released his hands and rubbed his chin. "Is this about *mei bruder*?"

"What do you mean?"

"Tyler," he said. "Is this about Tyler?"

"No. This is about honesty. I always believed that I wanted to marry you, but I've realized that I just wanted to get married. I've been doing a lot of thinking and praying lately, and I feel that we need to talk honestly about whether we have a future together, and I don't think we do anymore. I think we've grown apart."

His stare was hard and accusing, making her feel itchy in her own skin. Then he pushed back his chair and popped up to his feet. "So you're dumping me? You invited me over here just to *dump* me?"

"No, I invited you over to talk to me. I want you to tell me how you feel about me and our future," she said, standing.

He started toward the door, and she grabbed his arm and spun him toward her.

"Korey, talk to me. Tell me how you feel. If I'm wrong, then tell me I'm wrong. If you believe you'll want to marry me someday, then tell me that. Don't accuse me of breaking up with you if you're feeling the same way I am," she pleaded with him.

He dropped back into a kitchen chair and stared at the tabletop.

"Korey, you never tell me how you feel. You never respond when I talk about the future." She could hear the quaver in her words. "Do you see a future with me?"

"I don't know," he mumbled while studying the table as if it held all of the answers he craved.

"I thought if you wanted to marry me, you would know." She worked to keep the strain out of her voice.

He sighed, and when he finally looked up at her, he appeared to be wading through something in his mind. "You've always been important to me because you helped me stay connected to *mei mamm.*"

"What do you mean?"

"I cherish our childhood memories of playing together while our mothers visited, and being with you helps me feel closer to *mei mamm.* Sometimes I imagine her telling me that she would approve of our relationship."

Michelle sniffed as memories of his mother twirled through her mind.

"But honestly, I've felt like we were always *freinden.*"

"That's how I've felt lately. I used to believe I loved you, but it's changed."

He pursed his lips and relaxed back in the chair. "I think we should just be *freinden.*"

"I do too." She nodded and sniffed. "But it breaks my heart to admit it. We've been together for so long, and I'll miss you."

He folded his arms over his wide chest. "Are you sure this isn't about Tyler?"

"It's not." She wiped her eyes with a tissue. "Why do you keep asking me that?"

Korey stood. "Just wondering." He pointed to the cake and coffee. "*Danki* for the snack. Tell your parents I said goodbye."

Then he stalked out the back door, and she hugged her middle, certain he had just marched out of her life. She took deep breaths as she felt her heart crumbling.

"Michelle?"

She shifted toward the doorway, where *Mamm* stood watching her. *"Ya?"*

"How did it go?"

Michelle shrugged as *Mamm* joined her at the table. "It was pretty awful, but he admitted that he doesn't see a future with me. In fact, he only loves me like a *freind.* He has seen us as *freinden* for a long time."

"How does that make you feel?"

"Like a *dummkopp*." She cradled her mug. "I thought he loved me and wanted to marry me."

Mamm gave her a warm smile. "You're not a moron, Michelle. You're just young, and you're growing up and figuring out what you hope to find in a husband. You're starting to see the plan the Lord has for you."

"What do you mean?"

"You believed that Korey was the one the Lord had chosen for you, but now you see that he isn't. I know it hurts, but you'll be okay." *Mamm* looped her arm across Michelle's shoulders and gave her a side hug.

Michelle rested her cheek on *Mamm*'s shoulder. "*Danki.*"

Closing her eyes, she asked God to heal both her heart and Korey's.

Tyler stood with the owner of the Horse and Buggy Motel in Bird-in-Hand Monday morning. "We should have this done by the end of the week, Chad."

"Perfect." Chad Wilson shook his hand. "I appreciate it, Tyler." He jammed his thumb toward the motel office. "I'll be inside if you need me."

"Thank you." Tyler glanced up at the

cloudy sky and breathed in the chilly mid-December air. He was actually grateful for the cold weather. At times it was a wonderful relief to work in the cold instead of sweating all day on a hot roof in the middle of summer.

He turned toward Dennis and Roger, who were chatting by the pile of shingles. "We're all set. Let's get to work."

Dennis and Roger waved before Dennis grabbed the tallest ladder and carried it toward the one-story motel.

"Hey, Ty," Jayden said as he sidled up to him. "Do you have a minute?"

"Sure. What's up?"

Jayden motioned for Tyler to follow him to the corner of the building. "I need to tell you something, but I wanted to share it in private."

"Okay. So, what is it?"

Jayden frowned. "Now, you know that I don't like to get between you and Korey, right?"

"*Ya,* I know."

"And you know I can't stand when you two argue. It's been agonizing witnessing the rift between you two, and I'm not trying to play sides or anything." Jayden held up his hands.

Tyler leaned against the corner of the

building. "Jay, just get to the point, okay? We need to get this job done by Friday afternoon. What happened with Korey? Is he okay?"

"He went over to Michelle's yesterday afternoon. She had invited him to visit."

"That's nice." Tyler tried not to imagine Korey and Michelle together — holding hands, whispering, kissing . . .

Stop it! Korey is her boyfriend. You have no hold over her.

Jayden hesitated. "He told me in confidence, but I feel you should know."

"What *is it,* Jay?" Tyler demanded.

"They broke up."

Tyler blinked. "What did you say?"

"You heard me, Ty. They broke up."

Tyler was dumbfounded for a moment. "Why did they break up?"

"All he would tell me is that it was mutual. They both decided that they were better off as *freinden* since neither of them saw a future together."

Flabbergasted, Tyler just stared at him.

"You okay, Ty?"

"Ya."

Jayden tilted his head. "What are you going to do?"

"About what?"

"About Michelle, of course."

369

"Nothing." Tyler started walking away, his entire body vibrating with the news that Michelle and Korey were no longer together. "We need to get to work."

Jayden appeared beside him. "Hold on! We need to talk about this."

"There's nothing to discuss. I told you that I won't pursue Michelle, and I meant it. Even though they broke up, I wouldn't risk having Korey blame me for their breakup. My goal is to get him back into my life." Tyler swallowed. "I love Michelle, but I know that I can't ever be with her since she dated Korey."

Jayden's expression brightened. "But what if God found a way for you to have Michelle and get Korey back too?"

"It would be a miracle."

"Don't ever doubt God."

Tyler nodded. "I'm glad that you told me, Jayden, but it doesn't change anything. Now, we have work to do."

As Tyler and Jayden walked over to the ladder, Tyler tried to stop himself from imagining a life with Michelle. It just wouldn't ever be possible.

But he would keep praying anyway.

CHAPTER 27

"I'm so glad you all came today," Lainey said Wednesday afternoon while Michelle, Jorie, and *Mamm* sat in her kitchen.

Mamm gazed down at her new grandchild and smiled. "I'm so *froh* to meet my handsome new grandson."

"He is handsome," Jorie said as she leaned over and looked down at him. "Hello, Junior. We're so excited to meet you."

"*Danki* for bringing the groceries, diapers, and poinsettia. I can't believe Christmas is less than two weeks away. I need to get back to working on my cards. I'm going to include birth announcements in them," Lainey said.

Michelle smiled over at the baby and then turned back to Lainey. "How are you feeling?"

"Tired and sore." Lainey smiled. "And so grateful and blessed." She glanced toward the family room, where Jana Beth played with a doll and a few books. "She loves Junior so far. She tries to help me feed him."

Jorie picked up one of the chocolate chip cookies she and Michelle had baked yesterday. "We're here to help, so please put us to work, Lainey."

"I would love to take a shower." Lainey gave a sheepish smile.

Mamm lifted Junior up to her shoulder and rubbed his back. "Go and take your time."

Michelle stood and gathered up their mugs from the tea they had enjoyed with the cookies. "What else can we do besides clean this up?"

"Well, Noah's *mamm* and *schweschder* came yesterday and his *mamm* handled the laundry," Lainey said. "His *schweschder* also cleaned the bathrooms for me."

"I can mop the kitchen," Michelle offered.

Jorie stood. "Would you like me to dust and sweep downstairs?"

"That would be fantastic," Lainey said. "I'll be back soon." Then she disappeared down the hallway that led to the downstairs bedroom and bathroom.

While *Mamm* took Junior into the family room with Jana Beth, Michelle washed and put away the dishes before wiping down the table and counters and mopping the floor.

Jorie dusted the family room and then swept.

When Michelle and Jorie were done with their chores, they joined their mother in the family room. Michelle sat on the floor and played with Jana Beth until she started whining and rubbing her eyes.

"I'll take her upstairs and put her down for a nap," Michelle offered. She carried her niece upstairs and changed her diaper before placing her in her crib and reading her a story.

Once she was tucked in bed, Michelle said, "Now take a little nap, and we'll play when you're awake."

"Okay," Jana Beth said.

Michelle bent down and kissed her niece's cheek and then tiptoed out into the hallway and softly closed the door. When she turned, she found Lainey waiting for her at the top of the stairs, and she gasped with a start.

"I'm sorry. I didn't mean to startle you." Her older sister looked refreshed from her shower as she smiled. "I just wanted to see how you're doing."

"I'm fine. Why?"

Lainey shrugged. "No reason."

"Let me guess," Michelle began, "*Mamm* told you about Korey and me."

"*Ya*. Let's talk in the nursery."

Michelle followed Lainey into the nearby bedroom, where Lainey took a seat in a rocking chair, and Michelle sat on a padded footstool.

"So, how are you really, Shell?" Lainey pushed the chair into motion.

Michelle brushed her hands over her black apron. "I feel guilty for hurting him, but I had to. Neither of us saw a future together." She closed her eyes. "But I can still see the hurt etched on his face before he left."

"Don't feel guilty."

Michelle's eyes opened. "Why?"

"I've had a feeling for a while that it wouldn't work out with Korey."

"What do you mean?"

Lainey shook her head. "I couldn't ever put my finger on it, but he just never seemed like he was as committed to you as you were to him. I always got the impression that you were ready to spend your life with him, but he was more standoffish."

"That was precisely the problem, and then I realized one day that I didn't want to spend my life with him anymore. I was more interested in just getting married and having this." Michelle gestured around the nursery. "I was so immature that I was focused on having a husband, a home, and a family, and I didn't realize that I wanted to be married and he didn't. I think he was trying to tell me, but I was just blinded by my own dreams for my future."

Lainey gave her a sad smile. "Don't beat yourself up, Shell. I think many young women go through that."

Michelle nodded as thoughts of Tyler hijacked her mind. Oh, how she missed him! She swallowed as the truth bubbled up in her throat. "I'm in love with Tyler."

"Tyler Bontrager?" Her older sister looked confused.

"*Ya.*" She sighed. "I didn't plan it. It just sort of happened." She explained how she and Tyler had bonded over her milk can paintings the night Korey forgot she had planned to bring him supper. "Ever since then, conversations with him have been easy and natural. I feel as if I could say anything to him." Michelle folded her hands in her lap. "He was dating Charity for a while, but then they broke up. And after that he stopped talking to me."

"Do you know why?"

"I would imagine because he doesn't want to hurt Korey. I didn't want to hurt Korey either. And when Korey and I spoke and decided to end our relationship, he asked me twice if it was because of Tyler."

"So he figured out that you two have feelings for each other."

"I guess so." Michelle frowned as sadness whipped over her. "I don't know what to do. I don't want to betray Korey, but I can't get Tyler out of my mind. I feel this strong connection to him. It's something I've never felt before."

Lainey smiled. "That's how I felt about Noah. It was as if nothing could keep us apart. I knew in my heart that God wanted us to be together."

"I had hoped to feel that, but God wouldn't want us to hurt Korey. And that's if Tyler feels that way about me."

Lainey nodded. "You know that if God wants you and Tyler to be together, he will provide a way."

"And if he doesn't, then I just need to pray for him to repair my battered heart." Michelle sighed.

"Don't give up hope," Lainey said.

Michelle pinned a smile on her face. "I'll try not to."

Sunday morning Michelle shivered as she walked with her sister and parents down the road toward the Bontragers' house for church. The mid-December sky was covered with clouds, and the air was chilly.

"It looks like it might snow," *Dat* said.

Mamm nodded. "*Ya,* I was just thinking that too."

Michelle hugged her cloak closer to her body as anxiety threaded through her. It had been a week since she and Korey had broken up, and it would be the first time she would face Korey, Tyler, and their friends. While she had nothing to be embarrassed about, she still dreaded all of the questions and accusations that would spread throughout the community like wildfire.

They reached the Bontrager family's house, which was surrounded by a sea of buggies. The men gathered by the barn. Michelle's mother headed toward the kitchen while carrying the pie she had baked yesterday, Jorie dashed off to join a group of her friends near the fence, and *Dat* walked toward the barn.

Michelle turned just as Charity strode over, her expression sad or possibly even hurt.

Charity took Michelle's arm and pulled her over toward a tree. "Is it true? Did you and Korey break up?"

"*Ya,* we did. Who told you?"

"Everyone knows." Charity gestured around the field. "Lisa and Willa were talking about it. I'm not sure who told them."

Michelle groaned. Her suspicions were

right — the news had already spread throughout the community.

"Why didn't you tell me that you and Korey broke up?"

"I'm sorry. It's just been an emotional week."

"But I'm supposed to be your best *freind.* I could have helped you through this like you helped me when Tyler broke up with me. You could have cried on my shoulder." Charity searched Michelle's eyes. "Did I do something to make you not trust me?"

Guilt nipped at Michelle as she touched Charity's arm. "No, no, no. You did nothing wrong, and I'm sorry if I hurt you. I just needed to work through it myself."

"What happened?"

"We finally had an honest conversation about what we saw in our futures, and we decided we were better off as *freinden.*"

Charity nodded slowly, her brow wrinkling. "That's truly how you feel?"

"*Ya.* Why?"

"Because you always said you wanted to marry Korey. When did you suddenly change your mind?"

"It wasn't really sudden. I realized that I was just focused on getting married more so than on my relationship with Korey, and we grew apart. We really haven't talked in a long time."

Charity frowned. "Why didn't you ever tell me that you felt that way?"

"I had a tough time accepting it myself. It wasn't easy admitting to myself that my relationship with Korey was falling apart after more than a year as a couple. I truly believed we would get married. I wasn't keeping it from you, Charity. Instead, I was lying to myself."

"I'm so sorry, Michelle." Charity hugged her. "I should have been there for you."

"You always have been, Charity. I'm sorry I didn't visit you and tell you this during the week, but I was just trying to get through each day while asking the Lord to heal my broken heart."

Charity smiled at her. "I promise you that everything will be okay. We'll both meet and fall in love with the men the Lord has chosen for us. Then we'll both get married and raise our *kinner* together, right?"

"That would be such a blessing."

Looping her arm around Michelle's shoulders, Charity led Michelle toward where the young women stood talking near the porch. "Let's go see our *freinden.*"

They climbed the porch steps, and the muscles in Michelle's shoulders knotted as their group of friends turned and focused their curious eyes on her.

"Michelle! Michelle!" Lisa exclaimed. "Is it true that you and Korey broke up?"

Mary frowned at her. "Was he seeing someone else?"

"Are you okay?" Willa asked.

"*Ach,* you must be so heartbroken," Lisa cooed. "You were so sure he was going to ask you to marry him."

Suzanna shook her head. "We all thought he'd propose, for sure."

Michelle pushed past them. "Excuse me. I need to use the restroom."

As she scooted into the house, memories of the times she'd spent with the Bontrager family overwhelmed her — birthdays, Sunday suppers, holidays, and late-night talks on the porch while holding Korey's hand.

But now she was just another member of the congregation here for church, and her heart fractured at that realization.

She slipped into the bathroom and leaned on the sink, closing her eyes as she tried to convince her embarrassed cheeks to cool down. She was strong. With God's help, she'd find the courage to face the gossip and the snide comments. She could get through this.

Help me, Lord.

She washed her hands and walked out of

the bathroom. The buzz of conversations from the kitchen spilled out into the hallway where she lingered, leaning against the wall.

When heavy footfalls echoed in the nearby stairwell that led up to the Bontrager sons' rooms, she stood up straight and brushed her hands down her cloak. A moment later, Tyler sauntered out from the stairwell, and she sucked in a breath.

He froze, and an unreadable expression flickered across his face. He looked handsomer than usual, clad in a green shirt that complemented his hazel eyes.

"Hi," he said.

"Hi," she managed to say, her body quivering as her throat dried. "How are you?"

He shrugged. "Okay. You?"

"The same." Her thoughts were a jumbled mess as everything she yearned to tell him swirled through her mind. She longed to tell him she missed their talks, she missed their friendship, she needed him in her life, and she *loved* him . . .

But humiliation trapped the truth in her throat.

Tyler peered down the hallway and then back at her. "I should go."

"Ya," she said. *"Gut* to see you."

"You too," he said before starting for the kitchen.

She took a step toward him. "Tyler, wait."

He stopped and faced her.

"I miss you. I miss our talks. I miss our friendship."

He swallowed, and his Adam's apple bobbed. "I'm sorry, but we can't be *freinden.*"

"Why?" she asked, her voice croaking and her heart breaking.

"We just can't." He heaved a deep breath before disappearing into the kitchen.

Michelle remained in the hallway, where a fresh crush of sadness immersed her. When she heard the clock in the kitchen begin to chime, announcing it was nine o'clock, she hugged her arms to her chest. It was time to head to the barn for church.

The sounds of the married women filing out the back door toward the barn filled the hallway. Michelle closed her eyes and considered sneaking out the back door and going home. But her family would worry about her.

"Michelle?"

Charity stood in the doorway that led to the kitchen. Worry filled her best friend's face. "Are you *krank*?"

Yes! "I was just . . ." What was she doing? Hiding? "I needed a minute."

"I'm sorry our *freinden* were so nosy."

382

Michelle tilted her head and wondered if they were really her friends, but she kept the question to herself.

Charity smiled and held out her hand to Michelle. "Come on. I'll walk with you to church, and we'll ignore their rude questions."

"Danki." Michelle allowed Charity to tow her toward the barn for the service. She smiled, grateful for her best friend.

But then another thought hit her — how would Charity feel when she found out Michelle had fallen in love with Tyler? Surely Charity would feel betrayed, and Michelle would run the risk of losing her best friend.

Michelle swallowed back her new worry as she sat beside Charity in the unmarried women's section of the congregation and turned her thoughts toward worshipping the Lord.

After church Michelle followed the women to the kitchen to help serve the noon meal. She had done her best to concentrate on the bishop's holy words during the service, but her mind had defied her and wandered back to her worries about losing Charity when she told her the truth about her feelings for Tyler.

She had also caught herself peeking over at Tyler, and a few times she found he had also been watching her. The intensity in his expression had sent a zing of heat through her, and she tried in vain to dismiss it.

Michelle nodded greetings to the other women in the kitchen and gathered up bowls of peanut butter spread and set them on a tray. Then she lifted the tray and started toward the door.

When she felt a hand on her shoulder, she turned and saw Crystal. *"Wie geht's?"*

"Do you have a moment to talk?" Crystal asked.

"Ya." Michelle set the serving tray on the kitchen table and then followed Crystal into the family room. *"Wie geht's?"*

Crystal gave her a sad smile. "I wanted to see how you're doing."

"I'm doing all right." Michelle hesitated. "How's Korey?"

"He's okay." She grimaced.

Worry filled Michelle. "What is it?"

"Well, he and Tyler still aren't talking, and it's been tough on everyone." Crystal explained how Korey refused to work with Tyler anymore. "Duane has spoken to him many times, reminding him that family is important, but you know how stubborn Korey is. Jayden told me that Tyler has tried to apologize to him on numerous occasions, but Korey won't forgive him."

Michelle held up her hand. "Wait. I'm confused. Why is Korey upset with Tyler?"

"You don't know?" Crystal looked bewildered.

"No, I don't."

"It's because of you."

"Because of me?" Michelle pointed to her chest. "What did I do to drive a wedge between them?"

Crystal pursed her lips. "It's not really my place to get in the middle of it."

"Please, Crystal, I need to know what's going on. Tyler refuses to talk to me now too."

"Korey is angry with Tyler because he cares for you."

Michelle's mouth fell open as excitement and confusion filled her. "That doesn't make any sense. Tyler told me before the service that we can't be *freinden.*"

"He said that because he's trying to save his relationship with his *bruder,* but he cares for you deeply."

Michelle nodded as understanding flooded her. "I see." She took a step toward the kitchen. "I should go help serve the meal."

As Michelle walked into the kitchen, the

truth hit her, along with a deep, soul-crushing grief. She had lost *both* Korey and Tyler.

Now she had to find a way to move on without having either of them in her life, and she had no idea how she would cope without them.

CHAPTER 28

Michelle sat on the porch swing a week later and looked out toward her father's pasture, covered in snow. She snuggled into the quilt wrapped around her shoulders as flurries shimmered in the cold, late-December evening air and drifted down onto the ground. The scent of a wood-burning fireplace in the distance filled her nostrils, and she enjoyed the silence while thoughts of Tyler rolled through her mind.

It had been a week since Tyler had declared that they couldn't be friends — a week since Crystal had shared that Tyler cared deeply for her — a week since her heart had been completely shattered by the realization that she'd lost both Tyler and Korey and that she would lose Charity if she shared the truth that she'd hidden from her.

And now it was Christmas Day, and she was too focused on her worries to enjoy this

387

special, holy day.

The back door opened with a squeak, and Jorie stepped outside dressed in her heavy winter coat. "There you are. Why are you out here alone on Christmas?" She sat beside Michelle.

"I was just thinking." Michelle smiled over at her sister. "*Frehlicher Grischtdaag, schweschder.* I love the basket of lotions and shower gels you gave me. *Danki.*"

Jorie bumped her shoulder. "You already thanked me. And I love the books and journal you gave me."

"*Gut.*" Michelle sighed, and her breath came out in a puff of steam as she gazed in the direction of the Bontrager family's home, wondering what they were doing right now. Was Tyler thinking of her?

Stop torturing yourself!

"*Mamm* and *Dat* love the painting you created of our farm, and *Mammi* and *Daadi* loved their painting too."

Michelle nodded.

"I'm worried about you," Jorie said. "Why are you so *bedauerlich* on Christmas, Shell?"

Michelle pulled the quilt tighter over her body. "I have a gift for Tyler. I was hoping he would come to see me today so I could give it to him."

"You have a gift for Tyler?"

"Ya."

Jorie was silent for a moment. "You love Tyler?" she whispered.

"Ya." She held her breath, waiting for her sister's questions, but none came. She turned toward Jorie. "Aren't you going to chastise me and tell me how awful I am for betraying Korey and falling in love with his *bruder*?"

"No, but I do want to know what you were going to give him for Christmas."

Michelle laughed.

"There's *mei schweschder*'s smile."

Michelle bumped her shoulder against Jorie's. "Do you remember the night he came by and talked to me in my studio?"

"Of course." Jorie nodded.

"He helped paint one of the milk cans. Well, we sort of painted it together, and I saved it. I added a special Scripture verse to the bottom of it and decided to give it to him, hoping I'd see him today."

"Why don't you bring it to him?"

"If only it were that easy . . ." Michelle explained her conversations with both Tyler and Crystal. "I don't understand why God put love for him in my heart if we can't be together without hurting Korey. I also don't want to hurt Charity."

Jorie scrunched her nose. "How would being with Tyler hurt Charity?"

"I think she'd feel betrayed if she found out I had feelings for her ex-boyfriend. She might wonder if I interfered in their relationship."

"Did you?"

"No." Michelle scoffed. "But Charity loved him, and he broke up with her, which crushed her heart. I don't want her to blame me and say that I'm the reason their relationship didn't work out."

"So, you haven't told Charity how you feel about him?"

"No, I haven't, and I feel so guilty for not telling her." Michelle pushed the swing into motion. "Keeping a secret from her feels like another betrayal." She gazed over at her sister. "What would you do?"

Jorie laughed. "You're asking me for relationship advice? I've never had a boyfriend, Shell."

"But you're super *schmaert.*"

"Now you're just flattering me." Jorie grinned, and then her smile faded. "Honestly, I'd keep praying about it, but I wouldn't give up hope. I had a feeling you and Tyler had feelings for each other the night he was here in your studio."

Michelle stopped the swing with her toe and angled her body toward her younger sister. "You did?" she asked, and Jorie nodded. "Why?"

"It was the way you looked at each other. I hadn't seen you and Korey ever look at each other that way. Your connection was almost tactile."

Michelle's heart came to life. "Really?"

"*Ya*. I would just wait and see what happens. If he loves you, he won't be able to stay away from you for long."

"But he wants to save his relationship with Korey."

"Honestly, Michelle, I think Tyler will find a way to make Korey realize that true love isn't really a betrayal."

Michelle grinned. "See? I told you, you were *schmaert*!"

They both laughed.

The back door opened, and *Dat* stood in the doorway. "Would you look at this? It's snowing again. Isn't it *schee*?"

"*Ya*," Michelle said, her heart feeling light for the first time in a week.

"Christmas snow is the best kind of snow," Jorie declared.

Mamm appeared behind *Dat*. "Oh, it's cold out here! Why don't you all come in and have some hot cocoa and Christmas *kichlin*?"

"That sounds perfect." Michelle stood and

smiled at her sister. "Let's go inside."

"Okay."

As Michelle walked into the house, she breathed out a happy sigh. She was so grateful for her family members, who always seemed to brighten her day.

"I can't believe how big Junior is," Michelle told Lainey as she and Jorie sat in Lainey's family room on a Thursday, two and a half weeks later. "He's grown so much since we saw you on Christmas Eve."

Jorie nodded while rocking him. "He has."

"*Kinner* grow too fast." Lainey yawned.

Michelle touched her older sister's arm. "Are you getting any more sleep?"

"A little, but it's okay. Noah helps, which is a blessing. We take turns at night. He's a *gut dat*."

Michelle's heart turned over in her chest as her thoughts once again turned to Tyler for what felt like the thousandth time since she'd last talked to him.

While they had nodded to each other at church, they hadn't spoken since he'd told her that they couldn't be friends a month ago, and she still missed him and wondered what could've been in store for them if they found a way to date without hurting those closest to them.

"*Danki* for your help with chores," Lainey said. "You two are a blessing, and it's so *gut* to spend time with you."

Jorie rubbed Junior's back. "We enjoy coming to see you and the *kinner,* right, Shell?"

"Of course. *Mamm* wanted to come today, but she had promised *Aenti* Raesha that she'd go to her quilting bee. The driver took her to Auntie Raesha's *haus,* and she told us we could take *Dat*'s horse and buggy to come see you and the *kinner.* She said she'd come with us to see you next week." Michelle stood. "We need to get home and start cooking for *Mamm.* We can help you with your supper before we go."

Lainey shook her head. "Oh, no, no. I don't expect you to do that. You've already done so much. I can handle it. I'll put Junior in his bassinet, and Jana Beth will play in her play yard when she wakes up."

"Okay." Michelle gathered up her coat. "I'll go leave *Dat* a message and let him know that we're on our way."

Jorie stood. "No, I will. You can hold Junior until I get back." She handed Michelle the baby and then picked up her coat and disappeared out the back door.

"Hello, *mei liewe,*" Michelle whispered to the baby as he wiggled in her arms.

"Have you spoken to Tyler?"

Michelle shook her head and summarized the conversations she'd had with Tyler and Crystal a month ago. "We nod in passing at church. He doesn't attend youth group anymore."

"I'm sorry to hear that."

"*Danki.* I'm trying to accept it, but my feelings for him haven't changed." Michelle kissed her nephew's head and breathed in the smell of baby lotion. "I hope someday I'll get over him, but he's carved out a piece of my heart."

"Don't give up hope, Shell."

Michelle smiled despite her grief for the loss of his friendship. "I won't." She needed to change the subject. "How's Noah's furniture store?"

"*Gut.* He's grateful that the Christmas rush is over." Lainey talked on about her husband's work until Jorie returned to the family room, her teeth chattering.

Michelle stood. "You okay, Jorie?"

"It's sleeting out. I already hitched up the horse and buggy. We should get going before the roads get any worse."

"*Ach* no. Be careful," Lainey said as she stood and took Junior from Michelle. "I'm going to worry about you two out on the road in this bad weather. Please call and leave a message when you get home."

"We will," Michelle promised.

After they said goodbye and kissed Junior, Michelle and Jorie headed out into the cold, carefully walking down the slippery porch steps to the waiting horse and buggy.

Michelle climbed into the driver's side, and Jorie hopped in beside her before draping a quilt across their laps.

Soon they were on their way, and Michelle guided the horse down the road.

"I can't believe how big Junior is," Jorie said. "I think he's gotten a few pounds heavier since we saw him at Christmas. And Jana Beth is taller."

Michelle peeked in her mirrors as she continued to lead the horse. "She is taller."

"*Ya,* before you know it, she'll be helping us bake, and she'll be quilting with *Mamm* and me."

"You're right." Michelle halted the horse at a stoplight.

"What do you think we should make for supper, Shell? I was thinking of maybe pulling together a quick casserole. Or we could make fried chicken since we defrosted some chicken the other night."

Michelle shrugged. "Whatever you want to do is fine with me. *Mamm* will just be *froh* that we cooked for her."

395

"We could also make pork chops."

"Okay," Michelle said.

The light turned green, and Michelle started to lead the horse through the intersection. She glanced to her left and spotted a red pickup truck rumbling to the stoplight.

"Or we could have breakfast for supper. Maybe pancakes," Jorie continued. "I could make bacon too."

When Michelle heard the squeal of tires, she looked to her left again as the truck began skidding and sliding toward them, heading straight for the passenger side of the buggy, since Michelle, the driver, sat on the right by the shoulder of the road.

"Jorie!" she screamed just as the truck roared into the intersection and slammed into the passenger side of the buggy.

The sound of metal smashing filled the air. Michelle felt the impact and then heard screams as the buggy rolled over onto its side, sending her and her sister twisting and turning through the air.

And then everything went black . . .

CHAPTER 29

Tyler climbed out of his driver's pickup truck and walked around to the tailgate to begin unloading supplies. His back and shoulders ached, and he was grateful that their day had been cut short by the sleet. While it slowed down their production, it also gave him an excuse to rest since he hadn't gotten much after losing both Korey and Michelle. Regret and grief were his constant companions.

"Are you expecting company?" Jayden asked, pointing behind him as Michelle's parents hurried up the driveway.

"No."

"Tyler! Jayden!" Elaine Lantz called, her voice frantic. "Have you seen Michelle and Jorie?"

Simon held on to his wife's arm. "Are they here?"

The panic etched on Michelle's parents' faces sent adrenaline roaring through Tyler's veins. He rushed over to them. *"Was iss letz?"*

"They went to visit Lainey, and they left us a message before they left her *haus,"* Elaine began, her voice cracking.

Simon rubbed her shoulder. "They should have been home nearly forty-five minutes ago, but they're still not here. Lainey called, worried that they hadn't checked in to let her know that they had arrived safely."

"We just got home from work," Jayden said. "I'll go see if Crystal has seen them." He took off toward the house, slipping and sliding his way up the icy path.

Tyler closed the tailgate on the truck as worry punched him in the gut. "I'll see if Jack has time to take us out to look for them."

"Oh, *danki,* Tyler!" Elaine said as she wiped her face.

Tyler came around the driver's side of the truck, and Jack rolled down his window. "Two of my friends are missing, and their parents are worried. Could you possibly take us on a ride toward Ronks to check their route and see if they need help?"

"Sure," Jack said. "Hop in."

"They're not here!" Jayden called from the porch.

"Elaine and Simon," Tyler called. "Climb

in the truck." Then he looked toward the house. "Tell Crystal we're going to search for them."

Jayden gave him a thumbs-up. "We'll be here. I'll watch the house and call your cell phone if they come home."

"Danki," Tyler said before climbing into the passenger seat.

Once Elaine and Simon were settled in the back seat of the four-door truck, Jack backed down the driveway and started toward the main road.

The diesel engine chattered, and the wipers hummed as sleet pelted the windshield.

"The roads are so slippery," Elaine said, her voice thick with anguish. "What if Michelle and Jorie were in an accident?"

"It will be all right. I'm sure they're okay," Simon said, but angst reverberated in his tone as well.

Tyler hugged his arms to his chest and silently prayed. *Please, Lord. Deliver Michelle and Jorie home safely.*

Jack steered onto Old Philadelphia Pike and continued toward Ronks.

Tyler drummed his fingers on his thighs and took deep breaths. His pulse was racing and feverish as Jack slowed the truck to a stop at a red light.

If only all of the other vehicles on the road

would disappear! Then they could get to Michelle and Jorie faster!

Behind him, Simon murmured to Elaine as she softly sniffled.

Soon the light turned green, and Jack motored through the intersection.

Tyler scanned the road for any horses and buggies that were stopped. Perhaps the horse was injured. Or they had trouble with a wheel. Or maybe they stopped at a store.

But Jorie had left a message saying that they were on their way, which meant that they most likely never intended to make a detour on the way home.

Jack steered onto North Ronks Road. As they continued driving, Tyler spotted flashing lights, and his insides turned and dropped. Two police officers had traffic stopped while two ambulances and a fire truck were nearby.

Oh no. Lord, protect whoever is involved in this accident.

When Jack stopped the truck, Tyler pushed the heavy door open, jumped out, and sprinted toward the scene despite the icy pavement. He felt the blood drain out of his face when he spotted a smashed buggy on its side and EMTs loading two young Amish women onto stretchers. Dread pooled in his gut.

An *Englisher* stood by a red pickup truck with a damaged bumper and broken headlight while a police officer and an EMT spoke to him.

"Sir," a police officer told Tyler. "I need you to stand back."

Tyler's body quavered with fear, worry, and anxiety. "I think I know those young women." He turned as Simon and Elaine caught up. "These are their parents."

"Jorie! Michelle!" Simon hollered.

The police officer shook his head. "Sir, I'm sorry, but —"

"Those are my daughters!" Simon exclaimed as he moved past him and towed Elaine over to the stretchers. Both of them had tears streaming down their faces.

The officer turned to Tyler. "Are you family too?"

"I'm a close family friend here to help the parents," Tyler said, determined to make sure Michelle and Jorie were all right.

The officer made a sweeping gesture. "Go on," he said.

Tyler's eyes pricked with tears as Elaine leaned over Jorie and Simon stood by Michelle.

"Ma'am. Sir," a female EMT told Elaine and Simon. "Please give us some space."

Simon and Elaine nodded, wiping their

tears. Simon looped his arm around his wife's shoulders and whispered to her.

"Mamm? Dat!" Michelle called from the stretcher. *"Dat!* Where's Jorie? Is she okay?"

Simon took Michelle's hand in his.

Tyler took a step toward her, and his breath caught when he spotted a large bruise already beginning to purple on her beautiful face. He longed to rush over to her, pull her into his arms, and tell her he would take care of her. But he had to try to remain calm and stay out of the way to allow the EMTs to do their job.

"Where is my sister?" Michelle asked again, her voice hitching.

"Shhh," the female EMT cooed. "Sweetie, I need you to calm down, okay? We're going to take you to the hospital and let the doctors check you out."

Tears poured down Michelle's face. "Please tell me where my sister is. Please!"

"She's over there, okay?" The EMT pointed toward the other stretcher. "I'm sure she'll be fine."

Tyler wiped at his eyes and turned toward where the EMTs stood by Jorie. She looked limp on the stretcher, her eyes closed. Elaine moved over toward her and started to sob. One of the EMTs approached Elaine and touched her arm before murmuring to her.

Another EMT walked over to Simon. "Do you and your wife want to ride in the ambulance with us?"

"*Ya,* of course," Simon said, and then he turned to Tyler. "Would you please get my horse home?"

Tyler nodded. He had forgotten about the horse! "Yes, I'll handle the horse and the buggy. Would you let me know how Michelle and Jorie are?"

"I will," Simon said, apprehension etched on his face. "*Danki,* Tyler."

Tyler nodded and then hugged his arms to his chest while the EMTs loaded each sister into an ambulance.

Simon climbed in with Michelle while a male EMT helped Elaine into the second ambulance with Jorie. After they were loaded up and the doors were closed, the ambulances took off down the road, their sirens wailing and lights flashing. Tyler's throat swelled as more anxiety and worry clobbered him.

Please, Lord, place your healing hand on Michelle and Jorie.

Then he jogged across the street to where the horse stood.

"Hey, Bucky." He rubbed the horse's neck

and checked for injuries. "Everything is going to be all right. I'm going to get you home." His hands trembled, and he willed himself not to get emotional. He had to be strong for Michelle.

"Tyler!" Jack called as he sprinted over to him. "Do you need help?"

"Do you know anyone who has a horse trailer?"

Jack nodded. "I do. I'll make a call. I can get a car trailer to take the buggy too."

"Thank you," Tyler said.

"When can I see Jorie?" Michelle asked while she sat on the bed in the emergency room.

Her entire body hurt — especially her head and her wrist — but all she cared about was Jorie. Her mind kept replaying the moment when she realized the pickup truck was headed toward their buggy — no, *toward Jorie,* since the passenger side of the buggy was the side that faced the oncoming traffic.

Tears filled Michelle's eyes and then sprinkled down her hot cheeks.

"It's okay, honey," said the nice nurse with the hair that looked too yellowish blond to be natural. "I promise you can see your sister soon, okay?"

Michelle sniffed. "Okay." Her voice sounded too small, like a child's voice instead of her own.

"Here you go, darlin'." The nurse handed her a tissue. "How's that wrist feeling now that we got it wrapped up for you?"

"It hurts." Michelle looked down at her left wrist, which was covered in an Ace bandage. She had bandages all over her body — on her face and her legs — but she was grateful nothing was broken.

Jorie was the one who had taken the brunt of the accident. *Mamm* had said she had a broken leg and possibly a concussion.

More tears poured down Michelle's face.

"Would you like me to get your folks?" the nurse asked.

Michelle shook her head. "No. My sister needs them more than I do."

"You're too sweet. I'll get your mama for you." The nurse headed toward the curtain. "I'll be right back, darlin'."

Michelle wiped her eyes once again as the accident replayed in her head. She could still hear the squealing tires, the crash of the impact, the screams. Were they her screams or Jorie's? Or maybe both?

If only she hadn't insisted they go to see Lainey today, but sleet wasn't predicted in the forecast she'd seen in the newspaper that morning.

The curtain slid open, and *Mamm* stepped into the examination room. "I'm so sorry, Michelle. We were talking with the doctor."

"How is she?" Michelle asked, her voice sounding like she had a frog in her throat.

Mamm sat on the edge of the bed. "She's going to be okay. She's sore like you are, and she has a lot of bumps and bruises."

"And a broken leg."

"*Ya,* but she will be fine." *Mamm* touched Michelle's cheek. "Oh, you two gave us such a scare."

Michelle's lip trembled. "I'm so sorry."

"Shhh. It wasn't your fault."

Michelle sniffed and wiped her eyes again. "How did you find us?"

"Tyler's driver took us."

Michelle blinked. "Why did Tyler's driver bring you to the scene?"

Mamm explained how she and *Dat* had gone looking for Michelle and Jorie and stopped by the Bontrager family's house to see if they were there. "We had checked Charity's *haus* first, but no one was home there. When Jayden confirmed you weren't there, either, Tyler asked his driver to take us out to find you."

Her heart swelled at the news. Tyler had

helped her parents! He was her family's hero!

"Your *dat* asked Tyler to take his horse home, too, and Tyler told *Dat* to let him know how you and Jorie are. He was really worried about you both."

Michelle sniffed.

Mamm covered Michelle's hand with hers. "It's obvious he cares for you, Michelle."

Michelle shook her head. "He said we can't be *freinden.*"

"We don't choose who we love."

"But it doesn't always work out. He and Korey are no longer speaking because Korey figured out Tyler cares for me. He's focused on trying to make things right with Korey, and that means he can't be with me."

"Do you love him?"

Michelle nodded. "*Ya,* I do."

"Never give up on love."

The curtain slid open and *Dat* walked in.

"*Dat,* how's Jorie?" Michelle asked, her voice thick.

"She's asking about you." *Dat* came around the bed and gently kissed Michelle's forehead. "We were so terrified that something had happened to you two."

"I'm so sorry. It's all my fault. I never should have taken Jorie to see Lainey. If we had stayed home, this never would have happened." She sniffed as more tears spilled from her eyes.

Dat rubbed her arm. "It's not your fault. I spoke to a police officer, and she said it was no one's fault. The man driving the truck couldn't stop because of the icy roads."

"Is he okay?" Michelle asked.

"*Ya, mei liewe.* He's worried about you and Jorie," *Dat* said. "He said he did everything he could to stop, and he even tried to steer away from the buggy, but it all happened too fast."

"Thank the Lord everyone is okay," *Mamm* said.

Michelle nodded. "When can we go home?"

"The doctor said he would release you and Jorie in a little while." *Dat* stood. "They're still working on her cast and need to run a few more tests."

Michelle bit her lower lip. She couldn't wait to get home.

Tyler thanked and paid Jack and his friend and then climbed the porch steps and walked into the house, grateful for the warmth. After kicking off his boots and hanging up his stocking cap and coat, he walked into the kitchen, where his family was gathered around the table eating supper.

Korey looked up from his bowl of stew. "How's Michelle?"

Tyler blinked. It was the first time his brother had asked him a direct question in more than a month. "I don't know yet. I just got Bucky and the buggy to the barn. Jack called his buddy who has a horse trailer, and he took the horse. Jack hooked up his car trailer, and we loaded the buggy onto it."

"Do you think the buggy can be fixed?" Jayden asked.

Tyler grimaced. "Probably not. I think it's too far gone." He shuddered, imagining the force of the blow Michelle and Jorie had endured.

Please, God, let them be okay!

"I'm so glad you took Elaine and Simon to look for Michelle and Jorie," *Dat* said.

Tyler washed his hands at the sink. "I'm grateful Jack had the time to take us. I'm just praying that they're both okay. They both looked banged up, and Jorie wasn't talking."

"She wasn't talking?" Crystal asked with a gasp.

Tyler took his usual spot at the table. "Not that I saw."

"We all need to keep praying for them, their parents, and the driver that hit them," *Dat* said.

Tyler bowed his head in silent prayer and once again begged God to heal both Michelle and Jorie. Then he filled his bowl with stew. He tried to keep his thoughts focused on his family's discussions of news about Crystal's brother's family, the roofing business, and the cold weather, but he couldn't stop worrying about Michelle and Jorie.

He moved his stew around in the bowl, only managing to eat a few pieces of beef. His insides were tied up in knots of worry for Michelle and Jorie, and his appetite had dissolved the moment he'd seen the smashed buggy and the bruise on Michelle's face.

When Tyler lifted his glass of water to his lips, he noticed Korey watching him, and he waited for Korey to glare at him, but instead, Korey licked his lips as if he were pondering something important or complicated.

"Tyler," Korey finally said. "I know that you care about Michelle, and I think she cares about you. I'm okay if you want to see her."

"Are you saying you'll give me your blessing?" Tyler's pulse picked up speed.

410

Frowning, Korey sighed. "*Ya,* I suppose I am."

"*Danki,*" Tyler managed to say as shock rocked him.

After supper, Tyler carried his bowl and glass to the counter.

"How are you holding up?" Crystal asked as she took the bowl and glass from him.

Tyler shook his head. "I'm so worried that I can't think of anything else." He nodded toward his bowl. "The stew was *appeditlich,* but I don't have an appetite."

"I understand." She gave him a warm smile. "Are you going to go see her?"

He nodded. "I need to know she's okay."

"Please tell us how she is."

"I will." Tyler retreated to his room, pushed his chair in front of the window, and stared out toward the Lantz family's farm. Then he opened a book and tried to read while he waited for headlights to shine on the house, indicating that they were home from the hospital.

A knock sounded at Tyler's door.

"Come in," he called.

The door opened with a squeak, and Jayden leaned in the doorway. "Would you like some company while you wait for Michelle to get home?"

Tyler closed his book. "That would be fantastic. Come in."

CHAPTER 30

"I'm so grateful to be home," Michelle said as she stepped into the kitchen later that evening. Her entire body was sore, but she was still happy she and Jorie were finally there.

Mamm began opening cabinets. "What can I make you to eat?"

"It's Jorie's choice." Michelle moved to the doorway leading to the family room and looked to where *Dat* had deposited her sister on the sofa. "What do you want to eat, Jorie?"

"How about soup?" Jorie asked, still groggy from her pain medication.

Michelle turned to *Mamm.* "Let's make her favorite — cream of potato."

"I'll make it. You go sit, Michelle," *Mamm* ordered.

"But I want to help."

Mamm pinned her with a stern look, and Michelle retreated into the family room.

Dat walked toward the kitchen. "I'm going to call Lainey and let her know you're both home. She's been worried sick," he said before heading toward the back door.

Michelle picked up a sofa pillow with her good hand and walked over to her sister. "What can I do to make you comfortable?"

Michelle put a pillow behind Jorie's back and then retrieved another one and placed it under her injured leg. Then she retrieved a glass of water for her.

Soon the delicious smell of cream of potato soup floated out from the kitchen. Michelle ignored her mother's disapproving look and helped pour four bowls. She added a handful of oyster crackers to each bowl and then carried one out to her sister while her mother loaded the other three on a tray, along with four spoons, and brought them into the family room.

Michelle took a bowl and set it on the coffee table and then sat down on a chair by her sister.

Mamm's blue eyes misted over as she sat across from them. "I can't tell you how distraught I was about you two. When we arrived at the scene, I was so upset. I just kept praying and praying, begging God not to take two of my precious *dochdern* from me." She sniffed and shook her head. "I'm

414

so very grateful you're both here with us."

"I was so worried about you, Jorie." Michelle touched Jorie's shoulder as her own emotions welled up in her chest. "I don't know what I would have done if . . ." Her voice trailed off.

Jorie looked up at her. "I know, Shell."

They all bowed their heads in silent prayer and then began eating their soup.

"I wonder what's taking your *dat* so long," *Mamm* said. "His supper is getting cold."

They continued to eat their soup, and soon their bowls were empty.

"Do you want more?" Michelle asked as she picked up Jorie's bowl.

Her sister shook her head and then covered her mouth to shield a yawn. "No. I really want to go to bed, but *Dat* needs to carry me upstairs. I can't use those crutches to get up the stairs, and I'm too tired to hop."

"I'll check on him," Michelle said.

Just then the sounds of the back door opening and two male voices talking floated out from the kitchen.

Michelle's heart beat triple as she immediately recognized the second voice — it was Tyler's. But it couldn't be him. Perhaps she was imagining it since she had hit her head in the accident.

Dat stepped into the doorway. "Michelle. You have a visitor."

She stood frozen as disbelief and anxiety warred inside of her.

"Michelle?" *Dat*'s salt and pepper eyebrows lifted. "Are you okay?"

She nodded. *"Ya."* Her voice sounded raspy.

"Are you not prepared for company?" *Dat* asked.

"No. I mean, yes. Yes, I am." She brushed her hands down her wrinkled dress and apron and then touched the bandage on her face. Maybe she should have changed and freshened up, but she hadn't expected to have company tonight — especially not Tyler.

"*Dat,* would you please carry me up to my room?" Jorie asked. "I really want to go to bed."

Their father crossed to the family room. "*Ya,* of course." He gathered Jorie in his arms and lifted her as if she were weightless.

"I'll come with you and help you get ready for bed," *Mamm* said. Then she turned to Michelle and whispered, "Go! Visit in the kitchen."

Michelle pointed to their empty soup bowls. "But the dishes —"

"Go, *mei liewe,*" *Mamm* insisted as she gave her a gentle nudge. "He came to see *you.*"

Michelle took a deep breath, moved to the doorway, and peered over to where Tyler stood by the table, his hands fidgeting with his dark-blue stocking cap. She felt as if she were dreaming as she took in his handsome face. His gaze locked with hers, and her eyes stung with fresh tears.

Tyler was here! He had come for her! But maybe he just wanted to make sure she was okay before he walked out of her life forever.

"Michelle," he breathed her name. "Do you want me to leave?"

She shook her head. "No." She crossed the threshold and stepped into the kitchen.

"When I saw the buggy and you on that stretcher, I felt like . . ." His face contorted. "I-I felt like my world was coming to an end. I can't imagine losing you forever."

She sucked in a breath as he dropped his stocking cap onto the table and closed the distance between them.

Tyler cupped his hand to her cheek, his eyes racing over her, checking her features. "I saw the bruise on your face, and I felt as if the ground had dropped out from under my feet." His voice caught and then recovered. "I was so, so worried about you. In

417

fact, I've been worried sick and begging God to protect you and Jorie."

She looked up at him and blinked. Yes, she was definitely dreaming. How hard had she hit her head?

"Are you okay?" He touched her injured wrist. "Your wrist. Is it broken?"

"No, it's sprained, and I have a lot of bumps and bruises."

"Your *dat* said that Jorie's leg is broken."

"*Ya,* that's right." Michelle nodded. "She has some cuts and bruises, too, but all in all, the Lord protected us."

"I'm so grateful. I was trying not to imagine the worst, but the idea of losing you had me tied up in knots." His concern was etched on his attractive face.

"*Danki* for helping my parents find us," she said. "I can't thank you enough."

"I'm just so grateful that the Lord led them to *mei haus* and I was home."

She nodded. "Me too."

"I didn't come here only to check on Jorie and you. I came here to tell you something."

She braced herself for another rejection. *Oh no. I can't take any more stress today!*

He took a deep, shuddering breath. He looked as if he had the words in his mouth and was trying to fit them together like a complicated puzzle.

"Michelle, I'm so sorry I told you that we couldn't be *freinden.* I was trying to avoid you because of Korey. He's been so angry with me since he found out I'm in love with you that he stopped talking to me." He moved his fingers over her cheek with a featherlight touch that warmed her from the inside out.

She leaned into his touch, closed her eyes, and enjoyed the sound of his voice.

"I told him I would stay away from you as a way to try to get him to forgive me, but I can't do it anymore," he continued. "Being away from you is slowly killing me. I need you in my life. I miss you. I haven't gotten a full night's sleep since I told you that —"

She held her hand up to stop him speaking. "Tyler. Wait. Did you say you . . . you love me?"

He nodded. "*Ya.* I have for a long time. That's why I had to break up with Charity. I knew in my heart that I could never love her the way I love you."

Michelle covered her mouth with her hand as butterflies swept through her stomach.

"Do you care for me?" His hazel eyes searched hers.

She nodded and sniffed. "*Ya,* I do."

"Michelle, I can't stay away from you anymore." He took her hands in his. "I want to date you, and if the Lord sees fit, I want to have a future with you. You're my best *freind.* I see things and think of things during the day that I want to share with you — things I think you might find interesting or that would make you laugh. I miss your smile, your beautiful eyes, your voice, and your laugh."

He touched her cheek again. "I miss everything about you. You're the smartest, most beautiful, most talented *maedel* I've ever known, and today I realized that I can't stay away from you. I feel as if the Lord has been leading me to you all along. I tried to ignore it, but I can't anymore. My heart craves you, and I need you in my life."

Her lips started to tremble.

"You're not answering me." Tyler's hand dropped to his side, and his expression fell. "You don't feel the same way."

She reached for his hand, threaded her fingers with his, and pulled him to her. "*Ya,* I do. I've loved you for a long time, but I thought you would never give us a chance. I'm just so stunned to hear you say the words that I've dreamed of hearing you say for so long."

"I'm so relieved." Tyler smiled. "You've taught me so much. Because of you, I understand why *mei dat* felt led to marry

420

Crystal. I understand what it means to truly fall in love and need someone in my life, and I want to start dating you as soon as possible — with your *dat*'s permission, of course."

She sniffed. "I would like that very much. *Mei dat* should be downstairs soon."

"Okay," he said. He touched her face again. "I love you, Michelle."

"I love you too." She released her hand from his and touched his chin, running her fingers over the stubble. "I've missed you so much."

He leaned down and kissed her cheek, and her toes curled in her stockings.

When heavy footsteps sounded on the stairs, she took his hand and led him to the family room. "You wait here for *mei dat*. I need to go get something from my room."

Michelle padded toward the stairs, her footsteps feeling light, as if she were walking on a cloud despite her injuries from the accident.

"Is Tyler still here?" *Dat* asked when he met her at the bottom of the stairs.

"*Ya*, he wants to talk to you, and I need to get something from my room."

Dat looked confused. "Okay."

Michelle climbed the stairs slowly and peeked into Jorie's room, where *Mamm* sat

421

on the edge of Jorie's bed. "Are you okay, Jorie?"

"Ya," her sister said. "We were just talking."

Mamm turned toward her. "Did Tyler leave?"

"No, he's talking to *Dat,*" Michelle said. "He just told me that he loves me and wants to date me."

"That's great!" Jorie said.

Mamm smiled. "I had a feeling."

"I'm going to get the gift I have for him, and then I'm going back downstairs."

"I want to hear everything tomorrow," Jorie said.

Michelle nodded. "I promise you will. Get some rest."

She entered her bedroom next to Jorie's, picked up the shopping bag with the milk can in it, and then walked slowly back down the stairs, where she found her father and Tyler discussing the weather.

Dat stood. "Well, I'll let you two visit." He shook Tyler's hand. *"Danki* again for helping us tonight."

"I'm glad I could, Simon."

"Gut nacht," *Dat* said before heading down the hallway toward his bedroom.

Tyler smiled over at her and then patted the sofa cushion beside him. "Would you please sit with me?"

"*Ya.*" Her knees wobbled as she set the bag on the coffee table and sank down beside him.

Tyler touched her hand. "Michelle, I would be honored if you would be my girl-friend."

"I'd love to."

He lifted her chin with the tip of his finger and then kissed her. She looped her arm around his neck as euphoria surged through her body at the sensation of his lips brush-ing against hers. The feeling was so intense and so unlike anything she'd ever experi-enced before.

When he broke the kiss, he leaned his forehead against hers. "*Ich liebe dich,* Mi-chelle."

"I love you too." She touched his chest. "I have a gift for you. I had planned to give it to you for Christmas if you came to see me."

He looked pained. "I'm so sorry for not visiting you."

"It's okay." She pointed to the bag. "Please open it."

Tyler lifted the bag and placed it on his lap. Then he opened it and pulled out the milk can. "Michelle, this is gorgeous." He turned it over and then chuckled. "Is this the one I helped you paint?"

"*Ya.* It was so special to me that I couldn't bring myself to sell it. I decided to give it to you."

"I'm honored." He turned it over. "First Corinthians thirteen, verse thirteen." He swallowed and touched her hand. " 'And now these three remain: faith, hope and love. But the greatest of these is love,' " he recited from memory with his eyes sparkling. "That was my mother's favorite verse."

She gasped. "It was?"

"*Ya.*" He looked down at the milk can again. "I will cherish this always, Michelle." He set it on the coffee table.

She leaned her head on his shoulder. "What are we going to do about Korey?"

"He actually gave me his blessing when I got home tonight after taking care of your *dat*'s horse and buggy."

Michelle gasped. "He did?"

"*Ya.*" He looped his arm around her shoulder. "But even if he hadn't, we won't let other people dictate our relationship. *Mei dat* found a way with Crystal, and I believe the Lord will help us find our way too."

Michelle closed her eyes and breathed in his familiar scent. "I'm so glad to hear you say that."

"You've had a really tough day, and I think

I should let you rest."

She nodded. "I agree, but I don't want you to go."

"I promise I'll be back to check on you and Jorie tomorrow."

Michelle walked him to the back door, and he leaned over. When his lips brushed hers, she closed her eyes, savoring the feeling and losing track of everything. She felt as if she were floating as she kissed the love of her life.

"Gut nacht, mie liewe," he whispered in her ear, sending goose bumps chasing one another up her arms.

"Gut nacht." She stood by the back door as Tyler walked outside and flipped on his flashlight, her heart swelling with love for her boyfriend.

Tyler couldn't stop his smile as he walked through the cold back to his house. He spotted a lantern glowing in the kitchen window and assumed Jayden had waited for him.

When he walked into the kitchen, he was surprised to find his family sitting at the table. "What's going on?" Tyler asked.

"We wanted to hear how Michelle and Jorie are," *Dat* said.

Crystal looked concerned. "Are they home from the hospital?"

"Ya." Tyler sat down in his usual seat. "Jorie has a broken leg and cuts and bruises. Michelle has a sprained wrist and cuts and bruises. Thankfully, the Lord protected them."

"I'm so relieved," Jayden said.

Korey nodded. "I am too." He pushed his chair back and stood. "I'm going to bed. *Gut nacht.*"

Tyler breathed a sigh of relief as Korey headed upstairs.

"Did you talk to her?" Jayden asked Tyler after Korey had disappeared.

Tyler's heart lifted as he smiled. "*Ya,* Simon said yes, and so did Michelle."

"You're dating Michelle?" Crystal grinned as Tyler nodded.

Jayden patted Tyler's shoulder. "That's fantastic."

"I told you God could find a way for you two," Jayden said.

Tyler's heart lifted. "*Ya,* and he did." *Thank you, God!* He was already counting down the hours till he could see her again and feel her soft hands intertwined with his as their lips brushed.

CHAPTER 31

Michelle opened the back door midmorning the following day and found Charity standing on her porch holding a covered dish. *"Gude mariye."*

"I just found out that you and Jorie were in a terrible accident yesterday. I got here as soon as I could to check on you."

"Come in." Michelle opened the door.

Charity stepped inside and gasped as she looked at Michelle's hand. "Your wrist! And your face! Oh, Michelle. Are you okay? How's Jorie?"

"I'm very sore, but I'm okay. Jorie broke her leg, so she's hobbling around with crutches, but we're blessed." She explained how the road was icy and the truck couldn't stop. "We're just so grateful that the Lord protected us."

Charity set the dish on the counter. "Oh my goodness. *Mei mamm* and I made you a hamburger casserole. You just have to stick

427

it in the oven."

"*Danki.*"

Charity pointed to the family room. "Is Jorie around?"

"*Mei mamm* is helping her get cleaned up, but she'll be down soon." Michelle pointed to the table. "Sit, and I'll make you some *kaffi* and pull out some *kichlin.*"

"No, you sit. You're injured. I know where everything is, and I'll bring it to the table."

Michelle smiled. "Yes, ma'am."

Charity got the percolator going and then retrieved a container full of lemon bars and carried them to the table. Soon the heavenly fragrance of coffee filled the kitchen, and Michelle and Charity were sipping coffee and eating lemon bars.

"I'm so sorry about the accident," Charity said. "You must have been so terrified."

Michelle shivered as she recalled the seconds before the impact. "*Ya,* I was. And then I woke up, and there were people trying to help us. It was awful, and I was so worried about Jorie. I was so grateful when my parents arrived."

"How did they find you?"

Michelle explained how her parents went looking for her and Jorie at Charity's house and then at Tyler's.

"Oh, I'm so sorry I wasn't home to help."

428

Charity shook her head. "We had gone to see my grandparents for *mei mammi*'s birthday."

Michelle reached across the table and touched her hands. "Don't apologize. No one knew this would happen. It's not your fault. It all worked out since Tyler asked his driver to take my parents to look for us."

"I'm so glad he did that."

Michelle nodded and turned her attention to her mug of coffee. She needed to tell Charity about her and Tyler, but she was afraid Charity might be upset. Still, she had to tell Charity the truth, and the sooner the better.

"Are you all right?"

Michelle looked over at Charity and hesitated. "I need to tell you something, but you might be upset."

"I'm sure I won't be." Charity smiled, and then her smile faded. "What is it?"

"Charity, I've kept something from you because I was afraid it might hurt you, and now I need to tell you." She took a deep breath. "I've had feelings for Tyler for quite a while, but I was afraid to tell you."

Her best friend studied her. "Is that all you needed to tell me?"

"No, there's more. Tyler has cared for me for a while, too, and last night he told me that he loved me." Michelle held her breath, praying Charity wouldn't be angry with her.

Charity's mouth fell open. "How long has this been going on?"

"What do you mean?"

"How long have you cared for him?"

Michelle remained silent.

"Did you care for him when I was dating him?"

"That doesn't matter, Charity."

"*Ya*, it does." Charity's voice rose. "So you did?" She pushed back her chair.

"Wait. Please. I'm telling you the truth, and I need you to listen to me, okay?"

Charity stilled. "I'm listening."

"I've cared for him for a long time, but I never acted on it because I didn't want to hurt you or Korey. I never did anything to sabotage your relationship with Tyler. We never even told each other that we cared for each other until last night."

Charity's frown dissipated.

"You know me, Charity." Michelle's voice wobbled. "You know that I would never betray you or our friendship. The last thing I wanted to do was hurt you or Korey."

"Why didn't you tell me sooner?"

"I wanted to, but I was afraid you'd think I was trying to break you and Tyler up. He never knew how I felt."

Charity nodded slowly. "So, you're dating him now?"

"*Ya.*"

Charity looked down at her napkin.

"Talk to me, please. I can't stand the idea that you're angry with me."

Her best friend looked up at her. "Does Korey know?"

"*Ya.* Korey gave Tyler his blessing before Tyler came to see us last night. But please understand that this wasn't planned, Charity. We believe God led us to each other."

Charity nodded.

"How do you feel about it?" Michelle touched Charity's hand. "Please be honest."

"It will be strange at first, but I'll try to accept it. After all, Tyler and I didn't belong together."

"*Danki,*" Michelle said with a deep sigh. "I can't lose you."

"You won't," Charity said.

Michelle and Tyler sat together at her kitchen table on a Sunday afternoon five weeks later.

"I'm so glad you wanted to visit instead of going to youth group today," Michelle said as she threaded her fingers with his.

Tyler's smile was coy. "Well, I've already

431

found *mei maedel,* and you clearly have the man of your dreams, so why would we bother mingling?"

She laughed and bumped her shoulder with his.

"How's your wrist feeling?" he asked.

"Much better."

He ran his fingers down her cheek. "Your bruise is all healed."

She smiled and enjoyed the feel of his touch.

"Is Jorie's leg healing well?"

"*Ya,* she's tired of the crutches, but she's getting around much better and she's staying positive about it. We're both so grateful that the Lord was with us that day."

"*Ya,* I am too."

"How are things with Korey?" Michelle asked.

Tyler ran a fingertip along the rim of his coffee mug. "He's been quiet around me, but he hasn't been argumentative or nasty. I think someday we'll work things out. I just keep praying and leaving it to the Lord."

"That's *gut.*" She rested her head on his shoulder. "I'm praying too. I'm glad that Charity seems to have adjusted to the idea of us."

"I know a secret," he teased.

"You know I love secrets!"

Tyler grinned. "I know someone who is planning to ask Charity out."

"Who? Tell me!"

"Guess." He touched her nose.

"Ugh. I can't stand when you won't tell me!"

He laughed. "Go ahead. Guess, Michelle."

"Hmm . . ." She tapped her chin. "Roger?"

He shook his head.

"Dennis?"

"You're close . . ."

She gasped. "Jonah?"

"Yup." He nodded. "He told me that he's been talking to her at youth group, and he's going to ask her father for permission."

"That's wonderful. They'll make a nice couple."

"I thought so too." Tyler took a long drink of coffee and then picked up a snicker-doodle.

"Would you like to stay for supper?"

"*Ya,* I would."

She smiled. "Perfect."

After supper, dessert, and playing board games with Michelle and her family, Tyler kissed Michelle good night and then bundled up in his heaviest coat, gloves, and stocking cap before heading out into the bitter cold February night. He flipped on his flashlight and started his walk home.

His heart felt light as he considered how much closer he and Michelle had become in such a short time. Life would be just about perfect — if only he could get his middle brother to forgive him completely.

As he strode through the crisp, dark night, his shoes crunched on pebbles on the road, and he pondered ways to try to convince his brother to be part of his life again. But every idea that filled his mind was something he had already tried. The only thing he could do was pray and wait for God to soften his brother's heart toward him.

Tyler was still contemplating his broken relationship with his brother when he hung up his coat and hat in the mudroom and slipped off his shoes. He breathed in the warm air and rubbed his arms as he walked into the family room. He stopped in his tracks when he found Korey sitting on the sofa.

"Hi," Tyler said with surprise.

Korey nodded toward the chair across from him. "Would you please sit for a moment?"

"Sure." Hope filled Tyler. Perhaps they were finally going to repair things and look to the future as brothers once again!

Korey rested his right ankle on his left

knee. "I've been doing a lot of thinking lately. And I've realized that I wasn't the best fit for Michelle. Our relationship wasn't going anywhere."

Tyler was silent, afraid to say the wrong thing and risk sending Korey stomping off to his room in one of his temper tantrums.

"You *might* be the right man for Michelle, but I still can't help feeling betrayed by you both. It was obvious that you had feelings for each other while I was dating her. You say that you weren't doing anything behind my back, but I still have a really hard time watching *mei bruder* with my ex-girlfriend."

Tyler swallowed. This wasn't going the way he'd hoped at all. "Korey," he began slowly, "is there any possibility that you might forgive us?"

His brother sighed. "I believe I've found the best way to do that."

"How?" Tyler asked as hope filled him. "What can I do to make things right between us?"

"I've been talking to one of *Mamm*'s cousins in Sugarcreek. He said I can come stay with him and work in the RV factory with him for a while. They're hiring, and he's already put in a *gut* word for me. I had an interview over the phone with the manager, and the job is mine if I want it."

"Wait a minute. You're going to Ohio?" Tyler exclaimed as he stood.

"*Ya.*"

"Does *Dat* know?"

"*Ya.*" Korey nodded. "I've already bought my bus ticket. I leave Tuesday."

"When are you coming back?"

Korey shrugged. "I'm going to let the Lord lead me."

"Look, Korey, you don't have to leave, okay? I want you in my life. You're part of this family, and you belong here." Tyler pointed to the floor.

"No, Tyler. I can't stay here. The idea of living here and watching you and Michelle possibly plan a future is like torture. It's better if I just go away for a while." Korey stood. "*Dat* is going to hire someone to replace me on his crew. I'll stay in touch."

"But you will come back, right?"

Korey nodded. "*Ya.* Eventually." Then he ambled toward the staircase, and his footsteps echoed as he made his way up toward the second floor.

Tyler sank back on the armchair as emotions spun inside of him. While he was grateful the Lord had blessed him with the love of his life, he was grief-stricken that he was about to lose his brother.

Lord, please bring Korey back to our family

someday soon and help repair our broken relationship.

Michelle and Tyler held hands as they walked around the pond on her father's farm on a Sunday afternoon. The warm mid-May sun kissed their cheeks, and the azure sky sparkled, as happy birds sang in the trees and flowers smiled over at them.

"It's the perfect day," she said as she gave his hand a gentle squeeze.

He nodded. "It is."

"Have you heard from Korey?"

"*Ya.* He talked to *Dat* and said he's doing well."

"Has he mentioned coming home?"

Tyler frowned. "No." He sighed.

"I'm sorry." She touched his arm. "I know you all miss him."

"We do."

Michelle looked out over the pond, where a family of ducks played in the glittering water. "I love the spring."

Tyler stopped walking and untangled his hand from hers. "I wanted to talk to you about something."

"Oh." She swiveled to face him, and the ties of her prayer covering flittered over her shoulders as a warm breeze brought with it

437

the fragrance of flowers.

He looked down at the lush, green grass and then up at her once again. "I've been doing a lot of thinking, and these past four months have been the happiest of my life. You've shown me what love can be like, and I'm so grateful God brought us together."

She smiled up at him. "I thank God every day for having you in my life, Tyler."

"Michelle, I know we've only been together for four months, but I know in my heart that I want a future with you. I believe God brought us together, and I can't wait to start our life together." He reached into his pocket. "I made you something to try to show you how much you mean to me." He handed her a small wooden, heart-shaped box. "This is my heart, and it's yours."

Joyful tears filled her eyes as she picked up the little box and ran her fingers over the smooth side. She lifted the lid and peeked inside. "Tyler, this is magnificent."

"Michelle," he continued, his voice tremulous, "I've already asked your father's permission, and he said yes." He took a shaky breath, and her heart began to beat wildly in her chest. "What I'm trying to say is, Michelle, would you please do me the honor of being *mei fraa*?"

"Yes, yes, Tyler! Yes!" she exclaimed. She

slipped the heart-shaped box into her apron pocket and then wrapped her arms around his neck and kissed his cheek.

Then she stepped back and took his hands in hers. "Tyler, I should be the one who is honored. You've shown me what true love is. When I was with Korey, I thought he was my future. The truth is that I was just focused on getting married. I was immature, but you've helped me grow. You've shown me what it means to truly find my life partner and the man I want to share my life with. When I look into your eyes, I see our future together — a home, and if God sees fit, a family. I know in my heart that you're the one God chose for me."

Cupping his hands to her cheeks, he leaned down and gently kissed her. A quiver of desire danced up her spine, and she closed her eyes and enjoyed the feel of his lips against hers.

"*Mei dat* said he'll make me a partner in the business and help me build a *haus* on his property. We can start building it right away and get married in a couple of months if you'd like."

She smiled. "The sooner the better." Then she touched his cheek. "*Ich liebe dich,* Tyler. *Danki* for showing me what true love is."

"I can't wait to start building my future

with you," he said before he kissed her again.

Closing her eyes, Michelle smiled against his lips. Her heart felt like a flower opening its bloom toward the sun. She couldn't wait to see what their future would hold.

ACKNOWLEDGMENTS

As always, I'm thankful for my loving family, including my mother, Lola Goebelbecker; my husband, Joe; and my sons, Zac and Matt. I'm blessed to have such an awesome and amazing family that puts up with me when I'm stressed out over a book deadline.

Thank you to my mother and my dear friend Susie Koenig, who graciously read the draft of this book to check for typos. I'm also grateful to my special Amish friend, who patiently answers my endless stream of questions.

Thank you to my wonderful church family at Morning Star Lutheran in Matthews, North Carolina, for your encouragement, prayers, love, and friendship. You all mean so much to my family and me.

Thank you to Zac Weikal and the fabulous members of my Bookworm Bunch. I'm so grateful for your friendship and your excitement about my books. You all are amazing!

To my agent, Natasha Kern — I can't thank you enough for your guidance, advice, and friendship. You are a tremendous blessing in my life.

Thank you to my wonderful editor, Laura Wheeler, for your friendship and guidance. Thank you for all you've done to help me improve this book. I'm excited to work with you, and I look forward to our future projects together.

Special thanks to editor Becky Philpott for polishing the story and connecting the dots. I'm grateful that we are working together again!

I'm grateful to each and every person at HarperCollins Christian Publishing who helped make this book a reality.

To my readers — thank you for choosing my novels. My books are a blessing in my life for many reasons, including the special friendships I've formed with my readers. Thank you for your email messages, Facebook notes, and letters.

Thank you most of all to God — for giving me the inspiration and the words to glorify you. I'm grateful and humbled that you've chosen this path for me.

DISCUSSION QUESTIONS

1. Michelle likes to paint farm scenes on milk cans. Do you have a special or unique hobby that you use as your personal ministry?
2. When Korey realizes that Michelle and Tyler have feelings for each other, he's upset. What are your feelings about his reaction?
3. Because Charity believed Tyler loved her and they had a future together, she is distraught when Tyler breaks up with her. Think of a time when you felt lost and alone. Where did you find your strength? Which Bible verses helped?
4. Tyler tries to banish his feelings for Michelle and avoid her in order to save his friendship with Korey. Do you agree with how he handled this predicament?
5. When Michelle realizes that she has feelings for Tyler, she still feels obligated to stay with Korey to avoid hurting him. Do

you think this was a good decision? Why or why not?

6. Korey decides to go to Ohio to get away from Tyler and Michelle. Do you think this is the best way for him to move on from his relationship with Michelle?

7. Jayden acts as the peacekeeper of the Bontrager family, always trying to encourage his brothers to get along. Did you ever have that role in your family? If so, how did you handle it?

8. Michelle realizes throughout the book that she was more focused on getting married than on finding the right person. Can you relate to those feelings? Have you ever found yourself in that same situation?

9. Korey feels that Tyler has always tried to be the center of attention and overshadow him in the family. Have you ever felt that way about a family member? If so, how did you overcome it?

10. Crystal endures Korey's disrespectful attitude toward her and patiently continues to pray for his heart to warm toward her. Do you think this is a good way for her to manage her stepson's behavior? Why or why not?

ABOUT THE AUTHOR

Amy Clipston is the award-winning and bestselling author of the Kauffman Amish Bakery, Hearts of Lancaster Grand Hotel, Amish Heirloom, Amish Homestead, and Amish Marketplace series. Her novels have hit multiple bestseller lists including CBD, CBA, and ECPA. Amy holds a degree in communication from Virginia Wesleyan University and works full-time for the City of Charlotte, North Carolina. Amy lives in North Carolina with her husband, two sons, and six spoiled rotten cats.

Visit her online at AmyClipston.com
Facebook: @AmyClipstonBooks
Twitter: @AmyClipston
Instagram: @amy_clipston
BookBub: @AmyClipston

The employees of Thorndike Press hope you have enjoyed this Large Print book. All our Thorndike, Wheeler, and Kennebec Large Print titles are designed for easy reading, and all our books are made to last. Other Thorndike Press Large Print books are available at your library, through selected bookstores, or directly from us.

For information about titles, please call:
(800) 223-1244

or visit our website at:
gale.com/thorndike

To share your comments, please write:
Publisher
Thorndike Press
10 Water St., Suite 310
Waterville, ME 04901